SEVEN DAYS TO TELL YOU

RUBY SOAMES

www.bloodhoundbooks.com

Print ISBN: 978-1-916978-23-2

PRAISE FOR RUBY SOAMES

The ChickLit Club, September 2011

Ruby Soames writes with an eloquence and lyricism that belies the
fact that this is her first novel, and absolutely nails the
characterisation.

France Magazine

This debut novel by Ruby Soames is fast-paced and finely crafted,
examining in great detail the impact of grief and the minutiae of love.
And it's a real page-turner; as the story progresses, the reader can't
help but be drawn into the plot - it really is an irresistible read.

The Riviera Reporter: Bookshelf

Soames offers a McEwanish sophistication of style and structure.

Jerwood Uncovered Fiction Prize 2013 - Sara Veale

Ruby Soames manages to marry tender subject matter with a
remarkably compelling plot in *Seven Days to Tell You*. Its restrictive
time frame ensures it remains gripping throughout – revelations are
divulged reliably up until the last page, and we are permitted little
respite from Kate's quandary: "I need to pull the plug one way or
another. You stay or you go, either way, I can start living." Our
reprieve is ultimately reserved for the last page, when the truth
accompanying Marc's desertion is uncovered and Kate discloses her
long-awaited decision.

Claire McAlpine Word by Word

This book has a way of hooking you in and stirring your curiosity in an unputdownable kind of way. It shifts and changes in time and point of view, keeping you wondering and guessing through its many twists and turns.

For Mimi and Xan

Thursday Night

I don't hear the key in the door when the intruder enters my home. There's no light when he steps in from the hall and no click when he releases the door handle behind him. He waits inside my flat, sucking the air into his lungs as the winter wind escapes from his clothes.

His pupils widen as he scans the room. Shapes in shades from black to grey, claim his focus. The cushion on the sofa has retained a half-moon compression from where I'd been lying in front of the TV. There is a damp towel twisted around a chair leg with a near-empty bottle of wine next to it. I'd been too tired to put the wine away. It ferments next to a left-open box of chocolates with a card depicting a teddy bear holding up a sign saying, *Thank you*!

His eyes take in the remains of my last few hours.

The intruder treads into the room as cars project silver balloons of light over the ceiling. He touches my coat collapsed over a chair. He moves back a little, wary of my iPhone earphones dangling out of my pocket, they sway to the silent jig of an underground train. The darkness around him is losing. A plate of half-eaten lasagne is now hard and congealed in its microwaveable carton. The streetlamp illuminates the faces smiling out from my photographs. The man looks at each picture without moving from where he stands: my face, tanned and smiling from holiday destinations or miscellaneous landmarks in my life: graduation, weddings, parties; the shelf below is devoted to photographs of my nieces and nephews.

To his left is the kitchen, separated from the main room by what the estate agent called a 'breakfast bar'. Not that I've ever had breakfast there, I just use the surface of the low dividing wall to dump keys and post, though sometimes, if I have time or people over, I'll put fruit in a large hand-painted salad bowl, a wedding present. He sees a bunch of flowers still wrapped in cellophane in the sink half-filled with water, the petals pushed uncomfortably against the frosted windows.

He holds his breath as if the air will make him lighter as he walks across the living room. He stops outside my bedroom. Since I was a little girl, I've always slept with the door open the width of my mother's foot.

The tips of his fingers push just enough so he can creep through.

The blinds in my bedroom almost shut out the streetlights so he feels the way to my bed. I still don't hear anything, even the thud of his shoes dropping to the floor, the muffled fall of his jumper, T-shirt. He unbuttons his jeans, lets them slide down to his knees, tugs them from his feet. Even a few inches away, he must feel the heat from my body on his thighs. He bends down near to my face to tug and peel off his socks, lower his boxer shorts.

My sleep isn't disturbed by the movement of someone undressing so close to me. Even when he sits on the edge of the bed, lifts the duvet and curls onto the mattress. And not when he slides over and touches my skin.

Not once do I wake up with the knowledge that someone is in my home and in my bed, placing a hand on my heart and holding it there.

Our heads lie on the same pillow. I turn and breathe in what you exhale.

Somewhere, deep in my unconscious, the person I was begins to reassemble, your hand on my thigh and I flow into you, I know that you are back, that it is you touching my hair and stroking my face, laying your mouth into my deadened hand, folding my palm around your kisses.

The coolness of your skin chases my blood under the skin's

surface. You draw me into you, the capillary action of desire – I can't resist moving into you although I fight reaching out for you – there have been too many times, too many disappointments. There was that dream once, almost as real as this, when I found you in the hospital car park curled up in the back of my granddad's Morris Minor, I said, 'Marc, we've been looking everywhere for you! We thought you were dead...' and you said, 'Katherine, I was just sleeping,' and I replied, 'Sleeping? For three years?' and you said, 'I was really tired.' We laughed, and I told you everything we had done to find you and all the ways we had tried to understand. And it seemed so funny... then the dream started to break up, vanish, and I couldn't get it back. I woke up. I still don't know how I got through that day. To lose you, to find you, and lose you again.

Your leg hooks me in its grip and pulls me further into you. You kiss my neck, and I open my fingers to feel the ends of your hair. You nuzzle into the hollow under my collarbone, nip around my ear. You have returned.

That's what I keep saying in my head, *He's back, he's back...* And you feel the same to me as you always did – though bristlier – perhaps your hands are rougher. Have you put on weight or are you more muscular? But it is you. I've had these dreams before, and this is real. I don't want to notice the differences, don't want to open my eyes or speak. I don't even try to find out whether you are still wearing your wedding ring. Hold me close and don't let the light in.

Your hands knead my stomach, mould and squeeze me into a foetus which only you can bring to life. You drown out the world with your heartbeat; it's all that's ever made sense to me. You. I drive my face into your solar plexus: opening my mouth for more, for all of you, for something you.

You have come back, just as you left: no warning; no words.

Winter sun edges through the blinds as the soundtrack of London life begins its overture of sirens, buses braking, rushed steps and kids calling out to one another. The bankers upstairs move around. You never met them, the American couple who arrived a year after you left, we often pass on the stairs and they laugh when I tell them they work longer hours than junior doctors. But later, later. This is our time. There is that sweet smell behind your ears which takes me back to our first summer. I fill up on the smell of you. It's never enough. You tighten your hands around my hips, I press the soles of my feet on top of yours and you kiss the hollow curves around my eyes. The world can wait.

I know about waiting. That first year after you left, I'd reach out in the night to touch you and when my fingers padded the cold sheet next to me and there was an empty space where you had once been, I'd press the pillow to my mouth and scream until morning. In the beginning, of course, I didn't even go to bed at all. I slept on a line of cushions in front of the door, next to the phones and laptop. Usually with the television on. All night. All those nights.

After the first year, I accepted that I'd be waking up alone. I had to. I kept a pillow close, clung to it as people do a faith. And I talked to you. From that first night when you didn't return and I started calling your work, your friends, I was talking to you. Defending myself against you when you'd return and be cross that I'd worried unnecessarily. Then, when I had reason to worry, I begged you to come home, bargained, pleaded. And all the time I spoke to you in my head, and now you are here and I am still talking to you.

And you are really here. I keep my eyes closed as once again I let my hand go out on its own accord until it touches someone whose skin is more familiar to me than my own. Together again.

My alarm goes off. Your hand reaches out before mine and you press the button. Silence. It's almost as if the last three years hadn't happened. As if we'll wake together, maybe make love before charging into the bathroom, shouting out the evening's plans from the shower, treading on each other's clothes, drinking each other's coffee by mistake and saying, 'Love you! See you tonight'.

Most mornings I wake before the alarm. For nearly three years, I haven't slept, not slept like people do, abandoned, untroubled. Since the day you left, there's been no release, neither peace nor cure; even in my sleep, I've still been looking for you. One thing about dreams is that you don't get to dream in them.

We turn together, your front against my back, you weave your arm through mine, holding the middle of me to the middle of you. The recovery position. I hesitate at first, then I bring my fingers up to trace the tattoo on your upper arm with my index finger. I touch the K, the T, the I, N, E. Whenever I see my name printed, I wonder about those letters on your skin. Who is reading the Braille of your commitment to me? I was asked, over and over, to describe your 'distinguishing features', and I told them, he has the name Katherine written on his upper left bicep. 'Hard to lose, eh, tatts like that,' said one policeman looking at a photo of us on holiday. 'Course there's always laser surgery but that can leave a right messy scar, some people tattoo over, but...' So here it is. Your mark. The letters that make up my name, engraved, embedded into your epidermis. Some things don't go away.

You lift yourself over me, your elbows taking the weight of

5

your torso. I feel the current of air from your nose on my face. You hold me down like a collapsed building and close my lips with your mouth. We stay like that as the minutes go by. I don't want you to move. I do not want to go back to my life. You kiss my eyes and I have to open them now to see you. To see you again. The glare of the sky shuts them closed but your silhouette is imprinted on my lids. When I look again, I see your blue eyes, Alpine eyes. Holiday eyes. You have more creases in the corners when you smile now. You drop your elbows, lift me and make yourself into a blanket, covering me with your skin. And we laugh. At first it sounds canned – like a director has asked two actors to laugh. And laugh. And cut. And laugh. And then it becomes real and we laugh because we are so happy right there and then. The day is starting and all I want is my husband home and he is home: here, covering every part of me.

You are back.

We stop laughing, I draw my knuckles up to my mouth and bite hard to stop myself from crying – I learnt this trick the first year you left when I needed to stop the tears in supermarkets or driving the car, sometimes in mid-conversation with someone I didn't know. I'd just start melting and nothing could mop me up. I hold my breath, teeth cutting into the back of my hand. You pull my hand away, kiss where the skin's been broken and kiss my mouth again. I lick your shoulders. I can't leave you but I must.

June 6th, 2007: you left.

You didn't need to get up that morning just because I had to be at work for eight, but it was one of the rules you made for yourself when we first married, that you would always have breakfast with me if you could. You said a big love is made up of all the little things, the little acts of appreciation, and that once they stopped, people started taking each other for granted and then, what was the point?

I didn't always do that for you, Marc, and I was sorry for that later.

You made me coffee, brought me a couple of painkillers. I didn't have time to drink it but swallowed down the pills.

We'd been to dinner with an old school friend of mine whom I'd not seen since sixth form and never liked anyway. She'd arranged the supper so I could meet a friend of hers who had returned from medical training in the US. It had been a mistake to drag you out there. That night you'd said you wanted to stay in, you had something to tell me. I said if it was important, couldn't we wait till the weekend? I hadn't caught up on my sleep after a long shift, I was working the next day, a Wednesday, and we'd barely seen each other the week before. I was snappy. We were running late. You know I hate to be late and I was resentful about having to go out, having to wake up early the following day, having to galvanise you into doing something neither of us wanted to.

I hadn't eaten that day and the wine on an empty stomach knocked me out. I drank too much and couldn't stop apologising to you while we waited for a taxi. We'd quarrelled on the way home, something about Gina's friend flirting with me and her trying to set me up with him. I said things that hurt you; hurt you because they were true.

I've run over those last twelve hours so many times, always hoping that in the autopsy of your words, your gestures, what was unsaid, I might uncover a detail that would lead to a different ending.

And now I could ask you, was it that night? My friend and her shrill excitement, the conversations about children's schools, house prices and the fridge covered with animal-shaped certificates announcing Gold Star! for Grace's enthusiastic rabbit-hutch cleaning. Months later, that's what I thought. It was that boring dinner party that drove you out. Their indifferent questions to you, their educational holiday plans and tucked-up eco-friendly children. You saw a glimpse into our future, and it wasn't for you. I wasn't for you. So after I apologised again, dressed and kissed you goodbye, I left our flat.

When I returned, you were gone.

It's policy in hospitals to let relatives have time alone with the deceased. In some hospices families can video a relative's last hours. I've always encouraged wives and husbands to stay as long as they need to say goodbye. Since you disappeared, I've envied the grieving the chance to see those they've lost one last time.

I've witnessed how loved ones cry over a corpse. How they bury their faces into a cold, hardened frame. How they try to warm the bodies, shake the arms out of their torpor, bringing lifeless hands up to their faces. Sometimes they'll shout at the cadaver; other times, pat the torso, gingerly, as if afraid of waking them up. How they wait for a smile to appear on lips that can't speak. Junior house doctors have asked me to help remove a family member who's fallen asleep with a dead body in their arms. Mothers sometimes believe that if a dead baby will breast feed, it'll come back to life. Some talk – saying all that was never said while the person was alive. Sometimes there's wailing or a low guttural croak. Often, nothing at all. A father might stand in silence for just a few seconds before leaving his child to the morgue.

And then there are the ungrieved, the unclaimed. Before I specialised in paediatric cardiology, I worked in Accident &

Emergency – well, you know that. Remember sitting on those wonky chairs trying to hold a melting plastic cup of scorching coffee, waiting for me to be free long enough to have a quick chat or a snog in the utility room? I frequently saw cases of the homeless or people who'd lived on their own, who'd died with no one but the doctor on duty to record their last breath. After you left, I couldn't leave those bodies without fretting that someone needed to be notified: someone who couldn't sleep, who checked the missing persons websites, whose life was devoid of meaning because that person had never come home.

You close your hand over the back of my neck then release it like a mother cat does her kitten. You turn, look at the ceiling. I reach my hand over your chest. It rises and falls. Your heartbeat is regular. I have my body.

We line up our profiles on the pillow, and I see half of you. I have only ever seen half of you.

You touch my face, everyone has their touch, like a fingerprint or a snowflake, and yours is the touch I have been searching for. In all those men, I found no one who came anywhere close to touching me like you do.

FRIDAY

Friday Morning

'I'm going to move into radiology,' says Mona, making incisions into her cheese and tomato sandwich. 'I've decided. I can't take the nights anymore, just can't.'

She squints over her plate while carefully extracting the tomato slices with two plastic spoons. She looks up at me. 'Want it?'

'Why d'you have tomatoes in your sandwich if you don't like them?'

'Well, I thought I did, but then I remembered I didn't. It's the nights and,' she looks around the room before divulging, 'we're trying for a baby... don't tell anybody, will you? Y'know what they're like around here.'

'Sure.'

'And with Johnny being made a consultant we can afford to have one of us at home... I'm not saying I want to be like some "stay-at-home mom" or something, but with kids and that, you can't be rushing out the house with a weekend bag three nights a week, and I don't want to give up absolutely so, if I make a change now... what do you think?'

'I think it'd be a good move. Marc and I always said that if we had a family I'd have to stop being on-call, at least for the first few years.'

Mona grimaces at the khaki-coloured lettuce leaves and slides them across her plate. She wonders if she'd been insensitive talking about families when I don't have a husband, or I have a husband, he just disappeared.

Disappeared that is, until last night.

Mona's one of the few friends who still asks about you. Most feel they've put in their time supporting me over the worst bits and are now looking forward to my new life. 'Focus on the future, Kate,' they say, looking ahead with their eyes. They believe that part of encouraging me in the getting-on-with-it process is not to remind me of you – if they remind me, I'll remember, get upset and then they'll be the cause of my distress. But Mona isn't like that. She attributes her talent as a doctor to not shying away from the questions that others dare not ask. And she's fascinated by my extra-curricular life of private detectives, morgues, clairvoyants, being a minor celebrity in the missing persons world.

'Any news... of *him*?'

'Funnily enough, he came back last night.'

Mona stops chewing. I look at her with a straight, no-messing expression. She knows I'm not joking. Not the type.

'What?'

I bite my bottom lip.

'Kate? Kate! You saying he came back? Last night?'

'Yes.'

'What do you mean?'

'I mean, when I was sleeping he got into bed with me.'

'He got into *bed*? With you? Last night? You being funny?'

I nod.

'How did he get in?'

'With his key.'

Mona draws up her lower jaw.

'What did he say?'

Her sandwich balances limp in her hands.

'Nothing.'

'Nothing?'

I nod again.

'How do you know it was him? Maybe it was a burglar?'

'Well, he didn't take anything and he looked very like the Marc I was married to.' My jaunty tone sinks into a whisper. 'It was him. It was Marc.'

'It was him? Him? Marc?'

'Mona, you're repeating everything I say.'

'But I can't believe it! What, he really came back? You didn't just imagine it, did you, Kate?'

'No, he was there.'

'He must have said something?'

'He didn't need to.'

'Kate, he what? He didn't need to?'

'You're doing it again.'

'Babe, he walks in after nearly three years and not so much as a "sorry I'm late, love, the traffic was murder"?'

Devinder from Paediatrics brings his tray over and sits down with us. He smiles while taking out an extremely red apple from his pocket and polishes it on his white coat. He checks the shine.

'All right, ladies?'

'Kate's husband came back last night after three years.'

'Oh.'

'Can you believe that?' Mona asks, holding on to his sleeve to keep reality in check.

'Oh,' he says, sinking his teeth down into his apple.

'Is that all you can say?'

Mona's head swivels from Devinder to me, from me back to Devinder.

'So he just got into bed with you. Fine. That's it. Fine. He just got into bed with her after disappearing in 2007. I mean, is he back? Is he not? Is he... what? And Kate, what the hell are you doing here sitting with us?'

People turn to look at us.

I continue eating, not really acknowledging the food or the questions.

'Oh, I don't know.' Mona sighs. 'I don't!' She slaps the table in frustration. 'What do you think, Devinder, huh? He just

13

turns up out of the blue after all these years wanting a cuddle and no one thinks that's odd?'

Devinder looks at me while he chews. 'My mum had a cat like that.'

I often asked myself, what would I do if I found you? Of all the scenarios I came up with, playing dead was never the role I'd cast for myself. Mona's right to react as she does, but I can't explain what it was like, to have you back, and just want that moment.

You turned, sat up and, after waiting a few seconds, walked to the bathroom. I heard you urinating. You returned after three years to take a piss, I thought, leaning over the side of the bed and touching your clothes. Different clothes. I picked up a T-shirt and sniffed it. I listened to see if you flushed the toilet – no, you never did. So you're still trying to conserve water.

You stood in the doorway like in a dream. You moved with a look of concentration over to my wardrobe, opened it, and took out a dark green suit. It is, in fact, my interview suit, which I'd only recently worn, but you wouldn't have known that. You bent down and picked out a pair of black boots. You opened my top drawer and touched my underwear gently, as though the tossed-in pants and bras were kittens gathering for warmth. You drew out a pair of black pants, stroked your cheek with them and then plucked out a bra. You lay the outfit on the bed, then, after consideration, added a pair of tights. The look was a little austere for me – but I let you dress me all the same, moving your hands over my breasts, drawing the skirt over my hips, turning me over in the bed as you closed me up for the day.

You walked me to the bathroom and while I peed, you squeezed the toothpaste on my toothbrush and held it up to me. I wanted you to insist I didn't go to work today but we both knew it was the right thing to do. I took the brush – held it up as if to say, *Enough, I'm not letting you do that* – and you smiled. You brushed my hair and then looked in my make-up bag. You pulled out a lipstick, Fuchsia Fun it was called.

You touched my lips with the colour and you were about to open the mascara but put it back. Why did you put it back, Marc, because I might cry today?

The mime continued with you sitting me down and returning with a coffee and my boots. You kissed my toes and slid them into the tights, after that my legs were shut up in the boots. Then you took me by the elbows, levelled your eyes with mine.

'When you come back, I'll be here,' you said. 'Katherine, I will be here. I have something I want to ask you.'

I slit open a KitKat for Mona and me. We sip our murky filtered coffee. The three of us look out the windows at the rain.

'So where was he then?' Devinder asks.

'I don't know. We didn't say anything, just slept.'

'I know the feeling,' he says, stretching.

'God, you two! This is so unreal! I don't get – really – just don't. You didn't say anything? I'd have... I'd have punched his bloody lights out! I'd have... I'd have... Have you told the police?'

'No. I've a lot on today... anyway, I don't know what to say.'

Mona shakes her head as she chops her chocolate into four equal pieces and lines them up.

'Well I don't know what to say either. This is weird – too weird for me. I can't believe you didn't even ask him where he'd been... I mean, there's a time for sleeping and a time for... sorting these things out. What the bloody hell did – that's my bleeper. Gotta go. You going to be okay?'

Mona stands up, shakes the crumbs from her coat over my

tray, shuffles over and hugs me, leaving slivers of wafer on my cheek.

'Uurgh.' Devinder winces. 'Do you mind not doing all that lesbo stuff while I'm eating, thank you very much.'

'It's called giving your friend support, freak. Kate, find me if you need – I don't know – need anything.'

Mona's bleeper goes off again. She squeezes my hand and drops her two strips of chocolate on my tray.

'This is really, really... too... too bloody weird.'

Katherine, I'll be here, you said. All this morning I've been about to run out of the hospital doors and go home to you, just to see you, to see if it really, really was true, but coming to work is what saved me over the last three years, it needs to save me now.

'There are tubes and wires and drips and bits of plastic stuck all over him and what's that going into his belly button?' asks baby Jamie's grandmother. 'It must hurt. Doesn't it hurt him?'

'The line going into his stomach was fed in today. I know it looks a little bulky but it's getting all the medication directly into him. Babies' veins can't keep taking perforations so this is the most effective way of giving Jamie what he needs. We're pleased with his progress so far.'

'But you don't think he'll make it, do you, Doctor?'

Red veins swim under her tears.

'Jamie's a fighter, so, for the moment, there's no indication that he won't. I know how–'

'But it looks so painful, all those–'

'Jamie's had extensive heart surgery, Mrs...'

'Harris.'

'Mrs Harris. Right now he appears comfortable.'

'Well, I'll tell my daughter he's "comfortable". He doesn't look very comfortable. He's her – our – first. And this is just so...'

It's Friday afternoon now, six hours after I left you in my flat. Our flat.

'Oh, and here she is now.' Mrs Harris says to her daughter, 'You were supposed to be resting, what are you doing back?'

'I couldn't sleep. Hello,' says Jamie's mother to me.

We all look at Jamie.

'The doctor says he's "comfortable". He's a "fighter".'

The granny nods to me, urging me to lay on the reassurance.

'It'll take a few days to see how the procedure has worked but he's as stable as can be for the moment.'

'See, "stable" the doctor said.'

I am just about to move on to my next patient when Mrs Harris grips my arm. 'It's just she can't touch him. She says she can't touch him, with all those tubes...'

With the help of two nurses, we manoeuvre the equipment around so that Jamie's mother can prise her fingers through a hole at the top of the clear plastic cot.

'Here, you can put your fingers through here and rub his ears. Babies like that.'

'See!' Mrs Harris rubs her daughter's back. 'He hasn't got anything going into his little ears at least.'

'Thank you, Doctor,' whispers the new mother.

'If he remains stable, you might be able to feed him some of your expressed milk through this drip here later tonight. So try and get some sleep – Jamie needs you to be well and rested, the nurses are here all the time. He's in very good hands. Goodbye. Goodbye. Bye, Jamie.'

'Mummy, I won't be able to make this Sunday.'

'Oh, Kate, how disappointing. You sound terrible. Ghastly week?'

'I'm sorry, but...' A consultant striding by frowns at me for making a personal call.

'I do wish you could be here. Daddy's got his Johns Hopkins' brigade over, such bores those Americans, and such fussy eaters! And so I won't be seeing the lovely Anthony either?'

'No, no...'

'You haven't had a tiff have you? You sound a bit like you have.'

'No, it's not that.'

'Well, what? Is everything all right?'

'Marc's back.'

There's a long silence, muffled sounds and a crack.

'Mum?'

'What do you mean, "Marc's back"?'

'Just that. He came back last night, actually very early this morning.'

'What? How, I mean, what happened?'

'I was asleep, I woke up, he was there and then I had to go to work.'

'Where is he now?'

'Home? I don't know. He said we'll see each other tonight. He has something he wants to ask me.'

'I bet he does! And I imagine you have a few things to ask him too!'

'I don't know.'

'Know what?'

'What difference it would make.'

'Kate, you off? asks Dr McKendrick while I drop my white coat into the laundry basket. 'So how did Monday go?'

'Monday? Oh, the interview. Yes. They asked a lot about budgets, databases, training hospitals, local authority funding and a little bit about whether or not I could tell the difference between a heart or a toe.'

'You did say that the heart was the one without nail varnish?'

'Now you tell me!'

I stand in front of him, lifting my winter coat over my shoulders, buttoning it up and then waiting like a child requiring permission to be dismissed.

'Have a good afternoon.' McKendrick nods.

I want to smile back, but I can't. After turning towards the door, I twist round to face him.

'You know, I minded you writing about my personal life in your report. You told them that I'd "had problems" and it wasn't necessary. I've never given you reason to doubt–'

'Hold on, hold on, Kate, I had to say something. I couldn't have recommended a thirty-one-year-old to take on a job of such responsibility without making sure they knew absolutely everything about you. So that's why I've been getting dirty looks from you all week. Look, I stressed emphatically that what you've been through has never affected your work.'

'So why mention it? Why? And you said I'd had counselling, didn't you? Made me look like a loony!'

'Don't be silly, Kate. It's all credit to you. The loonies are those who don't recognise they need help and I think we could both name a few in this department, hmm?'

I go to pull my hair out of my scarf before remembering I'd recently had it cut.

'Come on, if I hadn't said something, someone else would've, hmm? A lot of people want that post. You can read a copy of my letter if that'd make you feel better. It's embarrassingly effusive, sycophantic even. Anyway, you wouldn't be such a remarkable doctor if you weren't such a loony.'

'I just want to know, what did you say *exactly*?'

'I alluded to a "bereavement" of a personal nature, which you'd dealt with showing strength and maturity. I said you'd availed yourself of professional help and continued working as efficiently and competently as ever. It's nothing new, Kate, we all have problems – it's just a matter of how we deal with them. Look, I hope they give you the job, but you'll be sorely missed – I said that too if you want to know.'

I couldn't be cross at him anymore; McKendrick wasn't just my direct boss but an old friend of my father's. I lift my arms up as far as my coat will allow to give him a hug.

'Hurry up or I'll have to visit the counsellor myself.'

I follow the strip lights until I leave the building.

'Bereaved', so that's what they call it. I open the car door, sit. A bereavement: I had a bereavement. I repeat McKendrick's words to myself. Whenever I've had to describe my experience of losing you, that's what I've said, it's like a 'bereavement without the body'.

A better description would be 'deconstructed'. I've been completely deconstructed, slapped together in a rush job and dropped back into the world, looking normal but feeling nothing like it. As I insert my key in the ignition, I whisper, '*Dextrocardia with situs inversus*,' recalling the symptoms of an anomaly where one in ten thousand babies are formed with all their major organs arranged the wrong way around. The heart beats on the right side of the chest. I lean back in my car as it starts. My heart hurts with every beat, whichever side it's on.

Bereavement, I called it. A death without a body, a coffin, a note or a reason. But now what do I call it, what do I call it now that you've come back?

Friday Afternoon

I always knew you were coming back.

I put my gloved hand out of the window and press my security pass against the machine. The barrier lifts. I'm out.

Mona thinks I've dreamt you up. Perhaps delusion is better than nothing. Sometimes the force of wanting you knocked out all other instincts, my ability to reason and my desire to live. I even wonder myself if the person in my bed was really there, or that my mind delivered you just when I thought I was getting better.

You said you would still be there, but I should never have left. If I'd lost you once, were you mine to lose twice?

I look at myself in the rear-view mirror: I look strange, preternatural. My pupils take up most of my iris, my lips are red and dry from your kisses, my face is flushed. You did this to me, but I can't see your touches, can't see you now.

What did you see? Me, now, over thirty. A faint line in the middle of my forehead; a short, practical haircut like the one I had when we first met in France. I'm on my way to becoming a consultant now, and godmother to three children. My time is spent messing with the hearts of men, watching them cry with scientific fascination. I found my first grey hair about two years ago and I could probably identify a dozen now, but I let you dress me this morning, like I'd been lobotomised, drugged or limbless.

Windows down. The frosty breeze cauterises whatever's

clawing away in my chest. Someone beeps as I swing off Exhibition Road, drive parallel to the park. I wonder if we will go for walks together again, now that you are back.

This is my route home. A checklist of memories: Kensington High Street, shops where we bought things for the flat; cafés we sat in; *The Coronet* where you could smoke while watching films; the park where we'd often walk or picnic with friends; streets, restaurants, conversations – all landmarks in our story. There's no one else I can share my history with. So much time in my life that I keep to myself because when you left, our story was corrupted. All those memories were overwritten by irony, suspicion and hurt. Sometimes I tried to remind others of you or talk about something that happened to us, but I'd be met with silence, an embarrassed smile and sympathy. Sympathy that I felt all too much for myself.

Of course, Mona was right. I should have demanded something – everything – from you, but I didn't. It wasn't answers that I wanted this morning. Just you. I wanted to be there again, just us. Just like before.

I turn off Westbourne Grove for my street. There's a space just outside the block where I live. We lived. It's rare to be able to park just outside my building. I stop. Indicate. Reverse and the car stops, the engine cools.

He's either there, or he's not.

My phone shivers inside my bag. Another call. I've avoided looking at the messages all day, but it hasn't stopped them. I take out my mobile and see Frances' name on the screen. Frances picked up the phone and was there for me three years ago, and for that, I can never let her calls go unanswered.

'Kate? Kate? I can't hear you very well, I'm on the train. Can you hear me?'

'Yes.'

'Kate – I've got news.'

'I know.'

'Are you there?'

I'm surprisingly calm when I hear of the breakthrough.

'We got some info on him this morning. I think we found him, Kate. We found Marc. Kate, can you hear me?'

'Frances, can I call you back later?'

'Of course. You okay?'

'Yes.'

'Look, I'm here, if ever... and you've got my home number. Call. Whenever you feel ready. Or not or whenever.'

'Will do. And – thanks.'

'I'm going into a tunnel so...'

There must be times, and it would be understandable in her line of work, when she doesn't really want it all to end.

I lever myself out of the car as blood rushes down from my head. The bare trees prick into a filthy sky. I'm about to lean in and drag out my bag when I hear someone call my name.

You're sitting on the wall opposite our flat. You've been watching me all this time, smiling.

'Katherine.'

You swing your legs out and jump off, then walk over as if we're in a bar and you're about to test some chat-up lines. You slap your hand on the roof and say, 'I saved the place for you.'

You put your arm around me, or rather catch me, while picking up my bag with your other hand. You take my keys.

With your arm still around me we walk up the steps to the front door. You are so solid, strong. I stand back to let you push the key in. Your fingers are clean, like mine, a chef and surgeon must always have scrubbed hands. But unlike mine, yours show no sign of nerves or panic. You lean against the weight of the door and hold it open for me to pass through.

23

The hallway is in a half light and your shadow eclipses mine over the dusk-rose coloured carpet. I hear you behind me tugging the key out of the lock. I walk ahead so I don't notice if you see the poster of your face under the heading, *Missing*. I'll have to rip it down now. Call off the search.

I take each stair carefully as if it might give way, while thinking back to that bright Saturday morning when the estate agent bounced ahead of us for the first viewing of what became our flat. Do you remember? She'd been in the middle of yet another story about a dispute between her and a parking warden. We'd nicknamed her 'Hamster-Munster' for some reason – we should have been more grateful to her, one of the few agents who worked on a Saturday morning and didn't scoff at our budget. Still jabbering, she turned the key, pushed the door open and coughed at the dust.

We knew it was for us. It was the plane trees through the double windows, the light coming in from both sides, the nearby Central Line and the wooden floors. Two bedrooms. Original fireplace. Neither of us listened to Hamster-Munster as she listed all the problems of its dilapidated state. I didn't need to check with you when I said, 'We'll make an offer.'

That memory, you and I standing at the top of these stairs with the light coming in, the daffodils in the window boxes and the rubble on the floor, the space in front of us and Hamster-Munster saying we'd better hurry as she was double-parked: that's one of the moments I concentrate on so hard that I almost believe the force of my will can transport me back there.

But today it's dark, the stairs are worn and when you punch the timer switch, the light doesn't come on.

'Shh, shhhhh. It's okay, Katherine, it's okay now...'

Before

The policeman slid me the Missing Persons Report Form. I took out a pen, tugged off the lid and began writing the answers to questions about you. I thought I knew you so well: Name, address, date of birth, time last seen...

'Excuse me. Could you... ?' He gestured for me to move over for the next complainant.

'Sorry,' I said, taking the paper to one side and filling in the description of my husband.

My hands were shaking. Ethnic background? Colour of eyes? Height? I pressed down on the pen, wrote in capitals. That was not the time I wanted to be picked up on having a doctor's illegible handwriting. Distinguishing features? I filled out half the page until I arrived at, 'List previous convictions'.

'My husband has been missing for two days – no one's seen him. He could be in real danger. Every minute not searching for him is vital–'

'Is that you that's been on the phone?'

'Yes. Probably. I've telephoned every hospital, police station, the Foreign Office – nobody's doing anything. You said wait forty-eight hours and it's been forty-eight hours. I really need help. This... this...' I said, pressing my fingers into the Missing Persons Form, 'this is just a form. Isn't there anyone who can help? Please.'

'Madam.' He looked at the queue behind me.

'This is just wasting time. I need you to find my husband.'

'Madam, if someone is missing then we need their details before we can do anything – otherwise, how would we know who to look for? Excuse me,' he said, nodding at the woman behind me.

'It's just I've been through all this on the phone a hundred times and I don't see anything being done.'

'Madam, all you need to do is fill that in. Come back to me when it's completed.'

'But I'm asking–'

'Everything all right?' asked an older officer, stepping in from a side door and doing a quick mental count of the room. When I arrived there were only a few people, now there were some seated, some reading notices, others tutting behind me.

'Lady says she lost her husband, sir.'

His superior looked at me.

'Follow me, madam,' he said, before adding, 'with the form.'

I was still glaring at the young policeman who was taking down the details of a stolen bicycle. He pretended not to see me but as I was led off, he piped up cheerily, 'Thanks, Sergeant!'

Behind the counter there was a double door that opened into a grubby corridor. I followed him into the third room from the left. I looked around, noticing everything so I could tell you all about it later.

It was no larger than a changing-room cubicle. The sergeant landed on his chair, faced me, slapped the desk.

'Detective Sergeant Brian Wells.'

I saw too late that he had put out his hand. He pointed at the chair. 'Take a seat.'

And I did, facing a landscape of plastic coffee cups, folders, forms and files. There was a tray piled so high that it towered over a shrivelled African violet – was this a gift from a woman thanking him for retrieving her husband? Behind him there was an aluminium blind being slowly strangled by loops of knotted cord, the dust on the twisted slats looked like rats' fur hovering over rows of brown envelopes with sun-faded, peeling labels. That was what happened to the forms people filled in. There was a nest of wires trailing out from under his desk which housed two blackened, unplugged computer monitors.

'I have to ask some routine questions...' He glanced at my form. 'You're a doctor.'

'A specialist registrar. Cardiology. At University College Hospital.'

'Ah, cardiology, that's heart, isn't it? My wife's always going on about mine.' He patted his chest. 'Too many Indian takeaways. So, you still work all those long hours we read about, junior doctors... ?'

'Yes, unfortunately coronaries don't work nine to five.'

He laughed and my breathing relaxed into something more regular now that I'd found an ally.

'Same with this lark, eh? Criminals don't take the weekends off either, or Christmas, or... so sometimes you work maybe three days and nights in a row?'

'Frequently.'

'And so Mr Venelles – that's your husband, right? – he's quite used to being left on his own for a long weekend or a week even?'

So that was where it was going. I tried to stay calm. To find you, I had to keep these people on our side.

'Yes, but we talk, all the time. All the time. He's a chef at a restaurant. He works late too, but they haven't seen him either. No one has seen him. He's never done this before.'

'How long have you been married?'

'Two years.'

'So, when you say, he's never done this *before*, you mean in two years?'

I swallowed into a dry throat. I thought he was a friend, but he was tricking me, making me say things about you that weren't true.

'You haven't filled out this section, *State of mind when*

person was last seen? Did you have a row, disagreement, tension between you?'

'We are very much in love.'

'Good, good, nice to hear. Unusual these days. Has he had problems at work, debts, conflict with management, drinking a bit too much, anything like that?'

'His state of mind was normal. Yes, we've had the usual stress about money – we've just finished doing up our flat – but nothing serious. Please, I know you don't want to waste your time if he's just gone off in a huff or he's in bed with someone else.' The sergeant jolted at this. 'But I'm telling you something's really wrong. Something has happened and every minute we're just talking and filling in forms is losing us crucial time. He could be suffering – held captive – I don't know – can you go out and find him?'

Detective Sergeant Wells brought the heels of his hands together, the palms, and then the fingers, one by one, starting from the smallest. Finishing this exercise, he looked at me in a way that warned it would be the only time he was going to explain this to me.

'Dr Brenton, your husband has not come home for two days. He's a grown man. It doesn't appear that he is a danger to himself or others. There's been no sign of a break-in, no abduction. No one's reported anything suspicious, you've not heard from kidnappers or been threatened yourself. I have the details.'

'That's all?'

'For the moment.'

'But he's missing and–'

'He has a right to his privacy. Your husband's French–'

'So?'

'Maybe he had an urge to go home for a while, we have to be

realistic, he just might be with someone else. You're not there to keep an eye on things and–'

'What?'

'When husbands don't come home, I regret to say, infidelity is often the reason. Fast followed by credit card debt, but that's...'

'The last thing he said was, "A tout à l'heure" – see you later. And he never came back.'

'If you'd like to finish completing this, we can start the process of tracing him.'

Detective Sergeant Wells gave me some time to collect myself before handing me back the form. I opened my pen again, this time my writing was faint, jagged.

'About 250,000 people are reported missing every year; most of these turn up in the first seventy-two hours. I know all this admin may appear unnecessary to you but you have to trust we're experienced in this. That's your reference number.'

'So you're not going to do anything?'

'The thing is, Marc Venelles is probably not missing as far as he's concerned. He knows where he is.' Detective Wells couldn't resist a chuckle before concluding, 'All we can do is make the relevant authorities aware that you are looking for him should he turn up.'

'I don't believe this.'

'If I were to say to you that I thought I might have a heart condition but I had no symptoms or complaints, would you rush for your surgical knife and open me up?'

'No.'

'There you go.'

'But I'd give you more than just a form to fill out.'

'Good to know. But Mr Venelles is a consenting adult and if he wants to go walkabout, that's his privilege. After forty-eight hours we can only do as much as we are doing now.'

Detective Sergeant Wells pressed a leaflet into my hand, wrapping up the interview.

'I've got a hunch Mr Venelles will be back very soon and he'll have a lot of explaining to do. The next port of call for you, as it were, is the National Missing Persons Helpline. They'll assign you a liaison officer and get you onto the next level of enquiries. After seventy-two hours, mind. Here's a card for Frances White, she does a blinding job. But let's hope it doesn't come to that, eh?'

Friday Evening

'Katherine, look, I've made some food.'

And you have. I can smell your home-made lasagne. We used to joke that you, renowned for cooking the most elaborate, complex dishes, would come home and bake me a lasagne with white chocolate mousse to finish. And I can see the chocolaty glass bowl in the sink; you've replicated my favourite meal. I wonder if it could possibly taste the same.

The table is laid for two with a tablecloth I don't remember seeing before. The flowers I'd not bothered to put in a vase last night have been tended to. A bottle of wine uncorked and two glasses wait on either side like a shy couple. The dining area looks like an advert for an upmarket kitchen company. There's even a candle. You've really cornered all the clichés.

For months after you disappeared, I couldn't eat, but continued to shop for food, just in case you'd be hungry when you came home. The flat waited, ready for your return, full of food and wine, then, I can't remember when, but I got fed up throwing out rotten vegetables and fruit so just bought enough alcohol to knock me out at night.

'Drink?'

You pour two glasses of an expensive red.

I just don't know how to start this. I face you, mute because two questions are fighting in my throat and I don't want to let them out because they will destroy this gift of unreality you are putting on for me. Now we have to open our mouths and go public, and I have to ask you: why did you leave, and why did you come back?

And all the other questions in between.

Before

'Oh my God, you're baking cakes. What's up?' asked Anna, walking through the door and dropping shopping bags on the floor.

'I told you, Marc's not been home for three days.'

I crossed the living room, opened the window, and leant out of it fighting an urge to faint or be sick.

Anna perched next to me. 'I didn't know he did that too.'

'Did what?'

'Disappear. Nick does it all the time.'

'Nick's a travel writer. That's his job. Anyway, not all men are Nick.'

'Oh, I think you'll find, baby sister, they are.'

I closed the window. My hand left an imprint of flour on the pane. An arc of white petals should you look up.

'You know a quarter of his last book was about how he was taken in by a tribe of Tanzanians who believed he was a living god the girls had to satisfy in every way. This is while I was waiting by the phone every night, pregnant, with two screaming children and the electricity about to be cut off.'

I returned to the kitchen, stirred the mixture. Anna moved behind me, flicking through a pile of photographs of you that I'd taken out to show people.

'You know he wasn't even sorry. He said I should be proud of him!'

'Sounds like you are,' I said under my breath.

'Well! He's making it all up to me – treating me to a dirty weekend at Claridge's – so now I'll be satisfied in every way! We've packed the kids off to Mum and Dad's. I thought we'd go to the Tate Modern tomorrow afternoon. Do you know, I've still never been there? Oh, I had lunch with Elspeth – she's practically running that publishing house – I had to make an appointment weeks ahead to see her. Is she still in your book group?'

Anna's monologue wound down when she started to notice that most of the floor, chairs and tables were covered in papers, scribbled lists of names and timelines. There were clusters of half-drunk cups of coffee, phones dotted around and your clothes piled in a corner where I'd ransacked all the pockets looking for clues. Anna realised that she hadn't just popped in on an ordinary afternoon.

'Why don't you go to the police?'

'I have! I've been there, they've been here. I've filled out more forms than a Stasi officer. I've rung every hospital, police station, I've called the National Missing Persons Helpline, I'm thinking about private investigators – where is he? Where is he?'

'Okay, okay...' she said, tuning in to the wavelength of my disaster.

Anna made a space for herself on the sofa by putting aside my medical books and trying not to look at a picture of a boy with testicles the size of a football.

'Did you have a row?'

'We had dinner on Monday night with Gina Brightman. We got back late, exhausted. Tuesday morning we said that we'd both be home late that night. I went to work, when I got back about two in the morning, he wasn't home. The answer machine was already full of messages asking why he wasn't at work. I just waited, thinking any minute he'd come home. It's now Friday. All his stuff's here, everything! His wallet, credit cards, his phone... except his keys. I can't find his keys. The door was double locked so he must have locked it. I think he might have gone out and...'

I covered my face with my hands, tears turned the flour into pellets of dough.

'Oh, Kate.' Anna put her arms around me.

'I went through his address book – I've called every number – nobody's seen him. I've asked the neighbours, been to all the shops around here... even stopped people on the street. I just don't know what else to do...'

'It'll be all right.'

'Not till he comes home it won't.'

I slid down the wall and dropped to my knees.

'What're you making?'

'Sponge cake, just using what I've got here. I can't go out in case he comes back. I don't want to use the phone in case he's trying to call.'

She scoops up some mixture in her finger, puts it in her mouth.

'Yummy.'

'Anything to keep my mind off things. I'll take it to work. I'm back tomorrow morning unless I can swap the hours with someone. *Again.* God, Anna, where is he?'

'Have you any suspicion or reason to believe he was having an affair?'

Earlier she'd taken your disappearance as a tedious

interruption to her fun day out – now, she was looking into my face, squeezing my arms, and looking like me, desperate.

'Ow! You're hurting me.'

'Sorry but... was he? Was he seeing someone else?'

'No! You're worse than the police,' I said, moving back from her.

'Do they think that?'

'I don't know if they think about him at all. I'd have more support if he were a kitten.'

'He couldn't have been unfaithful, could he, Kate? Could he?'

'Anna, something has happened.'

'Have you tried Eddie?'

'Yes. He's talking to people in France – I told him not to tell Mum and Dad.'

'Good, good, on the ball as always...'

Anna put her hands on my shoulders and brought her pale grey eyes level with mine.

'I'm sure it's just a mix up or he's... I don't know... there'll be some explanation. Come and visit us at Claridge's – have a jacuzzi and a massage–'

'Until Marc comes back I just can't do anything, Anna. Don't you see?'

'Yeah, sure, well, when he gets back then.'

I stood by the window. That was where I'd been spending most of my time, waiting for you to cross the road and come home. Anna was downstairs, the door closing behind her. She stopped on the doorstep, moved her bags from hand to hand. I'd siphoned all the joy out of her big weekend and reminded her that London isn't just shopping and catching up with friends, it's a place where people disappear. A place where people go out of their minds for those they love who don't make it back.

The breeze shook the tough, glossy new leaves. You were going to return any minute. There'd be an explanation, a message, a note I'd overlooked. Or maybe a confession. I'd have been devastated, Marc, but then, to see you, I'd have forgiven anything. I understood then why Anna took Nick back time and time again.

Anna hesitated on the doorstep. A man crossed the road in front of her and caught her smile. Anna always looks as though she's smiling even if she isn't. He winked at her as if he knew that she was thinking naughty thoughts. Anna always looks like she's thinking naughty thoughts. And often is. This time it was probably of room service, champagne, hot baths and some TV before Nick returned from his publishers.

Only family can dish up that special brew of guilt, throwing in a handful of resentments, a spoonful of anger and a few pinches of shame covered with a light sauce of anxiety. And season with a taste of regret. Anna had her foot out – it was just about to land on the last stair out of the building – but it stayed there, stuck midway. She didn't know what to do.

I watched her. I didn't want it to be a test but I couldn't help thinking that if it were me, I would have stayed and helped. So would Mum. But Anna's not like either of us.

She didn't budge from my doorstep, just stared ahead of her, deciding what to do.

I won't come to the table. I will not sit down, eat and drink with you. You pull up a seat, drink the wine until your glass is empty. You refill it, drink again and bring out a packet of cigarettes from your inside pocket. You unwrap the cellophane, scrunch it up;

defiant, it springs open again on the work surface. You light a cigarette, draw in the smoke before releasing a long, grey gust between us.

I think about a woman somewhere – assuming there's just the one – who is waiting for you to return. At this point she will have rung your work, your friends. All those people who've never known you to be late or sick since you first appeared in their lives. She might have people out looking for you already, and she'll be walking from room to room strangling her phone. I could call her, talk to her. I've more in common with this person, my love, than I do with you.

'So, where were you?'

'Oh, Katherine.'

I'm disappointed too, that I can't come up with anything more original. You'd have thought I'd had enough preparation time. You look at me, weary, as if I'm returning to an argument you'd thought was long since over.

'Where were you all that time?'

'Why?'

'I want to hear you tell me.'

'Why?'

I look over at the shelves of reports, files, folders, Missing posters, letters to governments, banks, charitable trusts, photos pinned up of clothing found in forests or beaches – the only physical remains left from someone. There are quotes from private detectives, tracing agencies, letters from psychics, well-wishers – people all over the world. But not one word from you.

'I'm curious, Marc, curious to know which fucking square inch on this planet I didn't cover! I'm curious to know how you think you can walk back in and not have to answer for anything!'

I'm on the other side of the flat – the one devoted to your search. I pull out a folder named *Missing 2007* and throw it at your feet. Shouting, I throw another folder at you as well – *Missing 2008* – and another – you cover your head with your arms, ducking to avoid the onslaught.

'This wall chart is a timeline pinpointing where you might have been over the last three years – these lines and dates in green are for positive sightings, in orange for possible places and people you've been to. These lines in red are where I was taken completely down the wrong path – see! Hey, Marc, now you're back, you could check it for me, give me an overall grade!'

Swinging the board in your direction, the corner cuts down into your shoulder. You clasp the sudden wound but continue to move fast and low towards me.

'Did you ever think that I'd be out of my mind worrying about you? Can you imagine? Just a little bit? What I went through? And there you were, hiding! So tell me – was it West London? Eastern Europe? Was it America? It says here, "Mexico" in September 2008. Of course some men start up new families just down the road from where they were living – is that what you did? How far did you have to go to escape me?'

I turn the desk over, pick up a hole puncher and hurl it at your knee. A hit, you buckle.

'You know I even checked the lists of applicants for ESA space missions to Mars? Which galaxy, Marc? Which fucking rock have you been squirming under?'

You dart around the room until you're able to make a grab for my wrists. You don't even use half your strength and I'm immobilised.

When our breathing calms, you say, 'Boats.'

All the hours I spent searching through names of crew on boats. Marbella. George Town. Shanghai. Boats. Of course, boats. It's not easy to hide these days, but if you're not on land, it's one way.

'You must have been under a different name.'

'Of course.' You sit down. Light another cigarette. 'My father's.'

'Were you looking for him?'

'Who?'

'Your father?'

'No.' You half-laugh. 'Why would I look for someone I don't know?'

'I know, right?'

And then it's my turn to laugh, an in-joke. You'd have to be me to get it.

You move closer to me, cigarette hanging out the side of your mouth.

'You're upset.'

'Don't you think I have every right to be upset?'

'Of course, Katherine, of course.'

'You touch my cheek, gently. My throat.'

'I cut my hair.'

'Yes, I see. Very gamine.'

'You always liked it long. I cut my hair when I thought you would never come back.'

'Katherine, you always knew I would come back. But maybe you don't know if you want me back.'

We both breathe hard against each other.

Before

I watched Anna on the second stair down from my front door deliberating about leaving me to the horror of my first weekend without you.

My sister must have been thinking that surely I had friends to call on. *Friends.* Friends are the most important thing to

Anna after her children. Everybody is Anna's friend. She's always hungry for people, devouring their stories, passions, the secrets they unburden to her. Anna never locks her front door at night just in case someone might pass by and need to chat. But this is London, and this is my life. You were my only friend.

And I was lucky to have found you. I hadn't been looking. Anna's always looking. She seems to be the only one in our family who has a sense that there is a world outside the Brenton household.

Dad always blamed Mum for 'what went wrong with Anna'. He disapproved of my mother's wild side: the woman who once got a speeding fine, who could be so cavalier as to leave the house with the washing machine on, but most of all, her latent interest in 'the Arts'. When Mum gave up nursing, she joined a creative writing group which met weekly in Summertown. Dad hadn't approved of his wife reading us Plath, Dickinson and Berryman at night, thought it would invite too much melancholia into our home. Perhaps it did. Anna's imagination became far too sensational for the humdrum world of laboratories, disinfectants and latex gloves. She didn't even contemplate science A levels and, as well as reading books about wily heroines, she wanted to be one.

And now she lives the dream with an errant husband, three children and the messiest home in Oxfordshire. They still have no money but if ever something trickles in from Nick's books or the endless supply of his deceased relatives, they'll blow the whole lot on a harp or a weekend in a London hotel. Meanwhile, the roof's still leaking, the kids run free all over the countryside and Anna sleeps all day only to stay up all night editing Nick's manuscripts.

You adored Anna but you were scathing about Nick's selfish lifestyle, their bohemian existence and non-exclusive relationship. And now, I guess, it will be Nick's turn to sneer at you, or rather, me.

Your mobile phone started ringing. The sound startled me so much I knocked my head against the window. I dived for it as it vibrated out of my hands and across the table. Oh, Marc, for a moment I thought you were back and the torture was over. But why would you call yourself? Panic blocks lateral thinking.

It was my sister.

She was saying your name.

'Anna? It's me. You just called Marc's phone.'

'Oh God, did I? Yes. How stupid of me. Stupid, I–'

'I told you he left *everything* here apart from his keys.'

'Yeah. I meant to call you.'

'But this is *Marc's* number – anyway, what d'you want?'

'I just wanted to say I hope that cake's worth it! Come on, he must be somewhere, we'll find him. Can you let me back in?'

He must be somewhere. He must be somewhere. You know the frantic desperation of losing your keys just as you're about to go out the front door? How your life stops but the rest of the world speeds up – making you twice, three, four times as late. Your future existence rendered down to this one factor. Nothing will ever happen again until those keys are found, and they just aren't there. They've gone. Gone! You search through your bag, coat pockets, your bag, your coat, your bag. You look by the kettle, back pocket, under a hat, in pots. Ha! They're still hanging on the outside of the door. No. Did you change bags? Change coat? Look through another bag and then back to the first bag you looked through. Check pockets again. You stand in the middle of the room. Twirl around. Diving under chairs. Up again. Did you put them in the fridge? Check the fridge. Check the oven while you're at it.

Fingers to your temples, you rerun the last time you saw them. You re-trace your steps. Ask St Anthony to help. You breathe like a dragon. You empty out all the contents of your bag on the floor, spread them out, find a lip balm you lost but didn't know you'd lost. You throw your coat down. Time is passing even faster now; your heart is beating even faster now. You scream inwardly. You shout outwardly. You check down the sides of chairs, tripping over your coat and bin and treading on the contents of both. You start kicking at things. This must be someone else's fault. The keys must be somewhere. They can't have walked off on their own – but what if they have? Try to come up with a backup plan. But with no keys, nothing can start. Check the coat again, by the toilet, check by the kettle, under the sofa, find another lip balm. Hey, St Anthony, patron saint of lost things, think you can come down and help?

I'd lost my husband. Where should I search first?

Friday Night

We're sitting on the floor, you and I, against the wall. It's dark. My head is on your thigh with your hand over it, stroking my hair. I'm coiled around you, not asleep, not awake, it's enough not having to think. Enough to imagine us as two London pigeons keeping each other warm as the world rolls from day to night, week to weekend, winter to spring. We are surrounded by islands of all the stuff I'd thrown around the room.

Earlier today, you must have opened the kitchen window and now the night air has broken in and started scrambling around the back of our necks and hands. You try to stretch without moving me.

'Katherine, I'll make you a tea, huh? Then we'll eat. After, maybe see a movie or stay in. Whatever you like.'

I sit up, rub my arms and legs, bringing them back to life.

'So have you come back after two years and nine months just to entertain me?'

'*Oui, ma cherie*, whatever you like.'

'I'd like some answers.'

'Katherine, all these answers. You know more about me than I do!'

'Yeah, maybe you're right but, Marc, this is what you've done to me.'

You stand up, stretch, and move about picking up the papers, envelopes, the newspaper cuttings and the letters.

'It doesn't help to look for answers now.'

'I want to know why you left me.'

'I'm here now.'

You try to catch me but I push you away.

'But what? Marc, what? You just vanished – what the fuck is "I'm here now?" Is that all? Are you back? Are you just stopping by? And how come you don't have any questions? Eh? Don't *you* want to know things? Like how the restaurant's been doing without you? Are my parents okay? What about your little goddaughter who still asks about you? Have you even wondered how I have been paying the mortgage you left me with? And where are your clothes? Your collection of cookery books? How many kids does Anna have now? Maybe, who did I fuck when you were away? Do you care about any of it or did you just walk out and give none of us a thought?'

You put the kettle on, with your back to me, it's less humiliating to ask, 'And did you ever love me?'

You turn from the cupboard with a box of tea in your hand. You put it down, pour another glass of wine.

'It is what it is.'

'And that is, what exactly?'

My voice cracks with frustration. You taught me to love, and you taught me to hate. I'm not sure which I feel for you right now.

You look older, sadder. When I imagined you coming home, I didn't think that in three years, you would have changed. Aged. It's the crumpled look around your eyes and the way gravity has dragged the skin on your jaw, the grey hairs at your temples, even your hands. Maggie upstairs who has regular contact with the spirit world said that ghosts don't change from the age they die, unless they are children, then they grow up until twenty-one. So you are mortal after all.

'We were married. Remember? You said, in front of me, my family, our friends, you said, "forever".'

'Exactly.'

You drop a tea bag in my cup. Still the same cup I always had my tea in. You remembered.

I don't want to fight but at the same time, I must give you your medicine. It was better when we were quiet, just sitting in silence but now we're up and I'm back in the ring. I'm almost happy with 'exactly' but I have to keep it going for the sake of the person who for the last three years was left with nothing. What do you mean by 'exactly'? Sometimes I didn't always understand you. Sometimes you couldn't express yourself in English and the dictionaries let you down. Somehow, it never really mattered. But I wonder now if it wasn't about language, if it wasn't the words I had confused, it was the person.

I understand that you want to make me food and tea and pour wine and clean around the sink because you feel at home in a kitchen. You look different in a kitchen than you do anywhere else. No one can attack you in a kitchen, you are invincible, able to seduce any member of the public.

'Here.'

You bring me tea and I wonder why you didn't just pour me some wine as you did for yourself. Perhaps I drink more now than I did then. In fact, I know I do.

'You said this morning you had something to ask me?'

'I do.'

'I have so much I want to ask you, Marc, but I'm just so afraid...'

'Of what?'

'That you'll disappoint me.'

'Very probably.'

I take your hands in mine. I'm asking for intimacy. I didn't know until this moment that that is all I've ever wanted, what I thought I had. You let me push back your thumbs, circle your wrists. I loved doing this when we were together. Fitting our fingers into each other, pressing into the warmth, sliding through the spaces, reading the lines, the crosses, valleys and flats, places you've been and will go.

'I know things now, about you, stuff, facts, and dates. I don't know why you kept so much from me – I would have...'

I'm about to say more – there's a lot more that I could say about you – but there's no point hearing it all from me, it has to come from you.

'*Mon amour,*' you say, as if I'm some impossible child, 'will you give me a week?'

'A what?'

'A week. All I ask is for seven days for us to start again, to be together, see what we find. And then, after, you decide.'

'A week? That's all you can come up with? You've been gone nearly three years! A week with you now isn't going to make up for any of it! And – and there's no such thing as "starting again" – you start or you repeat – but not both. You had your chance, Marc, every day you were missing you moved further away from us ever being together like before. You left me! And now – now! – when I've nothing left to give, you want everything.'

'But that's it, not *everything*. Just seven days. Then it's your choice. *Hein*, Katherine? You have one week to tell me.'

'Tell you what?'

'To tell me about you, me, anything. Ask for whatever you need from me. One week. Together. That's all. Seven days, and then, if you want, we'll say goodbye.'

Now your fingers are over mine and you repeat your terms like it's that simple, 'One week.'

Your palms are definitely rougher than they were. You have a cut on your little finger. You are not wearing your wedding ring. Nor am I. But I've a diamond ring on the third finger of my left hand.

You place little kisses on my face like you are decorating the top of a cake with utmost care. It soothes me, returns me to that quiet state. I don't even hear what you're saying now, but the words take effect like the drain of an anaesthetic seeping into my veins… Count backwards from ten… Count backwards from a week… Count backwards from when we met…

Before

The summer I met you, I'd only just qualified as a doctor. I was on holiday before going to live in London to start my in-house training at University College Hospital. And Dave was my boyfriend. My first boyfriend. Ever. Also a medic. We'd been going out since Michaelmas in the fourth year, and by undergraduate standards, we were '*together*-together'. Dave wasn't following me to London but staying on at the Clinical School in Cambridge. This was the beginning of my first grown-

45

up holiday: abroad without my parents, with a boy, paid for with money that I'd earned and staying with people who were my friends – friends who happened to have a château on the Côte d'Azur.

The airport in Nice, eight years ago. Tatyana waving across the Arrivals' Lounge. She streamed towards me like a spot of sunlight while travellers turned to her probably thinking, *Now that's exactly how I want to look on holiday*. She was blonder than when I'd last seen her in London or maybe that was just the contrast of her caramel skin and verdigris eyes. Cigarettes and an oversized box of household matches in one hand, her car keys in the other, she crossed the varnished floors in those Moroccan babouche slippers she'd worn every day at Cambridge whatever the weather. She folded her arms around my neck. Tatyana's hair smelt of swimming pool water, in fact, the girl reeked of holiday. And she was late. But her excuse, made in that low rev of an expensive, powerful engine of a voice, was that she'd been reading on her Lilo all morning and lost all track of time. And that was fine, that was precisely what we'd left England for.

Dave, however, did not think it was fine. He said people like Tatyana always let everyone down and, confident that he knew her character inside out without even having met her, had gone off to find a bus timetable and a hostel.

'So where's the boyfriend?'

I looked around for him.

'Over there.' I flicked my wrist in Dave's direction. It wasn't difficult to pick him out from the hairdos and crisp white shirts. He was in his grey combat trousers, muddied trainers and a Linkin Park T-shirt, fingering leaflets advertising cheap rental cars. He turned to us, nodded, and put the bumph back exactly how he'd found it.

Keeping her eyes on the approaching Dave, Tatyana said,

'He's taller than I expected. Kate, you said he was a *geek*, he's really sexy.'

Dave swaggered over, conscious that we were talking about him.

'Tatyana, hello. David Wheeler.'

'Hello,' said Tatyana, smiling back at my boyfriend. She extended her hand, rested it on his biceps and kissed each of his cheeks in a way I suspected she'd copied from someone she'd admired.

'I'm Tatty. Welcome to the Riviera!'

Dave, not expecting the kisses nor that Tatyana would slide in between us and put an arm around each of our waists, gulped for air.

'Kind of you to fetch us,' boomed Dave, as he waved us towards the glass doors. 'I believe the exit's this way.'

'Oh God, that's my car. Whoops!'

Tatyana pointed to a white Renault 4 parked on the curb surrounded by police.

She wheeled in between the trolleys and on-coming traffic to where three police officers were circling her car. There was a line of waiting drivers behind her, one hooted as he saw us coming.

'*Je suis vraiment désolée,*' she sang, waving her arms, gazing at the uniformed men, her lips pulling back like a wave over those little white teeth. The police put away their ticket books, rested their hands on their guns and motioned her to hurry up. The younger of the three paced by the boot of the car, helping us with our rucksacks, the other two looked on, kicking themselves for not having had the initiative to ingratiate themselves with the blonde in the skimpy top. One came over to Dave and said something that neither of us understood, though the gist was clear. Dave squared up to the policeman, tried to find the words to reply, but nothing came. He tugged at the door and climbed through to the back seat.

Tatyana jumped in and was about to turn on the ignition when we saw the policeman's face in the window. She wound the handle round until his head was almost in the car.

'*Oui?*'

'*Bonnes vacances!*'

'*Merci, c'est trop gentil. Bon après-midi à vous!*'

She winked to me in the wing mirror.

'Should have asked him to come back with us, *n'est-ce pas?*'

Dave was upset at being the recipient of a police chastisement when it wasn't his fault. It would be another mark against my friend I'd have to try to defend, along with her being late. And titled. And a smoker. And hilariously beautiful.

Dave and I had planned a three-week tour around the South of France after our finals and he was not happy when I told him that Tatyana had invited us to stay with her for the first few days. He was outraged that she'd sabotaged what he'd planned to be my introduction to France. As my family usually took the same caravan in south Wales every holiday, he felt it necessary to broaden my cultural experiences. So I was about to decline Tatyana's offer when he changed his mind on the grounds it would save us a few nights' hotel money.

Dave didn't admire Tatyana as I did. The 'Sebastian Flyte Brigade', he called her and her entourage. He couldn't understand why I'd be friends with her, why I'd chosen to do acting with her when I could have been in the Medical Society production of *Whose Life is it Anyway?* with him instead. He'd never spent any time with Tatyana and her friends but despised them on principle. They were public school 'toffs' who'd no right to be taking up university places when much worthier students needed them.

'But, Dave, she got the A-level grades, the university took her on the same merits as you.'

'Even if we agree on the improbable premise that it wasn't nepotism that got her into Cambridge in the first place, she went to one of those selective, exclusive, extremely expensive hot-house schools – she'd have to have been a total moron not to get in – and then all she does is flounce around, drunk, in an all-year tan wearing practically nothing. Hopefully she'll overdose soon and we can all get some peace at night.'

'You know, her life hasn't been all that easy.'

'Really, why is that?'

'For most of her childhood her mother was in rehab.'

'Kate, what happens to working-class alcoholics?'

'What?'

'They die. So don't tell me a three-star Michelin-Guide hospital, overstaffed with private nurses pampering Tory-voting, *Daily-Mail*-reading, fox-hunting dipsomaniacs like your friend's mother is a tragic backstory.'

At this point I reminded Dave that unlike him, I'd also been to a private school. This would shut him up temporarily until he'd argue that my father and mother worked hard to pay for my education as I worked hard to be able to pay them back.

'But Tatyana's mother was a model,' I retorted, turning him apoplectic.

Once inside the hot-plate car, Tatyana wiggled her skirt down so that the tops of her thighs didn't stick to the seat before twisting up her hair in a chignon with an old pencil she'd found in the glove compartment.

My host lit a cigarette, handed it to me. I waved it away.

'David?'

'Cheers,' he said.

I was about to express my surprise because I'd never seen Dave smoke before, but let it go as he took the lighter from Tatyana's fingers.

'There's the Negresco Hotel,' said Tatyana. 'Look, billionaire Russians. Up there, that's where Grace Kelly died.'

Early summer. La Promenade des Anglais. I nudged Dave who was using the sun's glare as an excuse to ignore me, 'That blue!'

'Yup! No one knows why the sky in Provence is this colour. Some say it's the reflection from the Alps, or the salt, others think it's the algae. Cool, *hein*?'

I agreed, unable to match Tatyana's French inflection, while trying to catch Dave's eye. He held a view on palm trees and blue skies. Palm trees, he'd said, looked far too much like pineapples, and blue skies only reminded you they wouldn't stay like that for long.

As we headed towards Cannes, Tatyana pointed out spots of local interest though her commentary was vague, she was better on the subject of herself. She curled the car around a number of treacherous corners on steep hills until we reached a plateau where there were no other houses in sight. A quarter of an hour later, she took a turning through two stone pillars.

I gasped when I saw Tatyana's family home, or rather, one of them. Knowing it was called a *château* I'd been expecting a grey, crenulated building erupting from the earth like a decayed molar, with maybe a moat, Beefeater or two, but this house was beyond all my poetic imaginings.

Le Château de la Gravière stood at the end of a three-minute drive lined with cypress trees and flanked by acres of overgrown grass, a lake, olive groves and two old tennis courts. It was grand, but welcoming and unpretentious. With the sun dropping to the west of its ochre walls, it blazed. Through the vines and wisteria were rows of bottle-green shutters equally placed into the warm stone. Right in the middle of the building were large, open double doors leading into the main hall.

'Cool,' said Dave, as Tatyana swerved up to a line of parked cars.

'Let's get everything off and jump in!'

By the time I'd closed the boot and passed Dave his rucksack, Tatyana was already naked and walking through the castle doors.

Late Friday Night

I'm lying on the floor, face down, you're pressing your hands down my back, over my buttocks, around the top of my thighs, I move my hips up to you, your fingers flicker around my pubic bone and travel up again. Every time your hands come a little nearer to where I want them to go, you leave me wanting more. You stroke the sides of my breasts. Your touch controls my breathing: all I am is just a response to you. You tease me, you take your time. The telephone rings.

Anthony. I have a few seconds to decide whether I pick up, speak to him or risk both of us listening to his 'Goodnight, sleep well' call.

'Okay?'

You sense the tension under your hands.

'Sure.'

It's the first time since you left that I've not rushed to the phone.

The answer machine clicks on.

My mother's voice.

I listen to her forcing a casual up-tempo message, but her heart's not in it, every few words she's stuttering, trying too hard to deflect her concern, aware that I might not be alone.

'Your leaving tore my family apart.'

Mum closes with, 'Daddy and I love you very much, darling, you come home if you need to, we're here. Bye-bye... Bye...'

There's no change in your expression – no guilt. I wonder if that's what I'm looking for at the end of the week, a simple sorry.

'I'll run you a bath.'

You jump up as if you'd been remiss not to think of it before.

'I'd like lots of bubbles.'

'And me?'

'Yes, lots of you.'

While you're in the bathroom, I find my mobile phone and zip through the missed calls. He's been ringing all evening. It won't be long.

I call over the gush of water, 'Let's light some candles and put them around the tub?'

I can afford to be cheerful right now. That was a near miss.

Before

The entrance opened into a hall furnished with a pool table at one end and a piano at the other, apart from that, just ashtrays filled with cigarette butts and burnt-out roaches, empty wine bottles and a pair of red, crocodile high-heeled shoes on the mantelpiece above the walk-in fireplace. Dave and I followed Tatyana past the front staircase through to the garden which sprawled out in various directions. We took the path leading to the swimming pool.

'Hey, you fuckers!' called Tatyana to her houseguests.

'There you are!' called Max Penrose, a notorious heartbreaker and orator, chair of the university debating team and hot-listed to be prime minister one day.

'Ah, did you miss me?' asked Tatyana, testing the water with her toe.

'No, but you took the only matches.'

'That's what they say, you can't start a fire without Tatty. You all know my cousin Kate, don't you?'

Tatyana often called me her 'cousin' but she was, in fact, a cousin of Nick's, my sister's husband. It was through Anna, whom Tatyana idolised, that we'd become friends.

'Course.' Max waved. 'Good trip?'

'Fine,' I replied. 'And this is Dave.'

'Right,' said Max, distracted by Tatyana immersing herself in the water with a long groan of pleasure.

'David Wheeler. Weren't you on the rowing team for Christ's College? I believe we won against you last year?'

Max looked at Dave, shook his head. 'We lost?'

''Fraid so, you stood in for Mike Batton.'

'God, yes! I remember. You know Neil crossed me off the team after that, twat move.'

'Kate, d'you know everyone else?' asked Tatyana, treading water.

'You know me,' said Chris, rolling the dice over a leather backgammon board. 'I came to see you and Tatty in that play, we had dinner after, remember?'

'Of course,' I said, wilting under the weight of my bag.

'I'm having a little pre-prandial Spritzer, fancy one?'

'Thanks,' I said, unsure what I'd agreed to.

I asked Dave if he wanted anything from the pool bar but he was laughing loudly at something Max was saying while sliding his focus over Tatyana's body.

'Kate! Jump in. Aren't you boiling in that jumper?' asked Tatyana.

I was unable to explain why I just didn't feel up to stripping off and leaping into the water. And as for leaping out again...

It seemed ludicrous that someone who was training to be a doctor should be embarrassed by a friend's unabashed nudity, but I was. I probably knew more about the insides of the human body than the outsides. Over the last five years I'd drawn, dissected, and read about every part of it but I'd no idea what it was like to touch or to be touched, or how a body could shimmer in the fading Provençal light. Tatyana certainly didn't look like the cadavers we'd cut up in the science labs. I tried to picture her spleen, her femur, gallstones, perhaps they were hideous, but what glided under the surface of her pool was nothing less than exquisite.

'Want some?' Chris asked, offering me a joint.

'No thanks,' I said.

I was not beautiful, not like Tatyana or my sister, women who could alter people's moods with a smile. My dress sense, before I met you, had been designed for entirely practical purposes and the idea of adorning myself seemed laughable. I'd always had girlfriends, good friends, but most of them were like me, switched off where boys and fashion were concerned, although there were a few who, for some bizarre reason, handed me the role of agony aunt, which seemed highly ironic seeing as the only advice I could offer was theoretical.

'I'm going to have a last splash of the day. You?' asked Chris.

'I'm fine.'

I wasn't. Despite the setting sun, it was still very hot but although I didn't entirely understand what prevented me from joining the others in the pool, I suspected it was because only three nights before I'd had sex for the first time.

It had become an issue I couldn't dodge. After having

turned twenty-two, I couldn't say I was too young, and being an atheist discredited any moral argument – I had no reasons for wanting to put 'it' off but that I simply didn't want to. Yet Dave had been patient long enough, my sister kept reminding me she'd had two children by my age, so a few nights before our holiday, I stayed over at Dave's parents' house while they visited his granny. The opportunity only pointed in one direction. Dave took me to his bed and tried to relax me as much as possible by running over the names of Coventry's football team players. I hadn't expected it to be so painful. Afterwards he said the first time with anybody was always a bit of a let-down, and I believed him because I hadn't yet met you.

'Fantastic! The doctors are here!'

Out from the house a platinum blonde emerged, all smiles and curves. Behind her a large, older woman followed, carrying a tray of cocktails.

Tatyana called out, 'Françoise! *Mon ange! Merci!*'

'Kate, I'm Georgie – Tatty's told us all about you, how you're so brainy and everyone wants you in their plays and you're really nice too. Made us all sick! That's Josh over there. He's dead – or we think he might be dead.'

It was only then I saw someone lying in the grass wearing a velvet jacket and a pair of cycling shorts.

'Is he unconscious?'

Georgie shrugged, crunching on an ice cube. 'That's why we need a professional opinion.'

'Have you checked his pupils?' asked Dave, his eyes crossing as he studied the tip of the joint he was inhaling.

'No way – there might be maggots and gooey bits.'

We gathered around Josh while Tatyana swam slowly up

and down the pool. Dave took his pulse, pulled on his eyelids, and looked up at us.

'What's he taken?' he asked Georgie.

'A few beers, dope...'

'Two bottles of port, Ketamine,' added Chris.

'Ecstasy.'

'And cocaine.' Max yawned.

'Oh, don't offer me any!' said Georgie, kicking Max.

'Nembutal, vitamin C.'

'We thought it best not to touch him. Was that right?' asked Tatty.

Dave looked up at her. 'He's in a PVS.'

'I know, those frightful shorts,' she laughed.

'Persistent Vegetative State.'

'Oh, so nothing unusual then,' said Georgie, arching her back and lifting her breasts to the last of the sun.

Dave opened Josh's mouth, felt for his tongue, and prised open his eyelids again. 'His pupils are responding to the light – he's dreaming.'

'So he's alive?' Chris asked.

'Mostly,' answered Dave.

'Bloody sod, giving us a scare like that!'

Then Chris and Georgie looked at each other, winked at Dave and three of them lifted Josh by his limbs and carried him over to the pool.

'One. Two. Three!' On three, Josh was hurled into the water.

He woke in the water with a shout, kicking, splashing Tatyana as she passed. 'Oh, Josh! I preferred you dead.'

You always called it 'making love', you're probably the last man left who doesn't say it with some inflection of irony. It isn't your lack of vocabulary, but it's what you do, and that is what we do after my bath, from the bathroom to the bedroom and later, watching TV and eating ice cream.

'Did you sleep with many women when you are away?'

'You're my wife.'

'Is that a yes or a no?'

'You're my wife, I promised I'd always be monogamous.'

'Marc, sorry, but... husbands and wives live together, that's the point. I don't mean to be facetious but... you've broken every agreement, every pact, every idea of what husbands and wives are.'

'Maybe.'

'Do you want to know about me?'

'It doesn't matter to me.'

'You were the second man I've ever had, but my first love, first time... you know, that it was... nice. And now, I've probably lost count how many men – and women – I've been with.'

I study your face as you look at the TV, you don't turn to me when you say, 'Why?'

'Because, because it was just a little bit like being with you.'

'I see.'

'And because I was angry. Raging. Murderously furious. At you. And you weren't there, and they were, so, I fucked them. "Making hate" you'd probably call it. Some men might even have said I raped them.'

This makes you chuckle.

'You couldn't rape anybody, Katherine.'

'That's not the point.'

'What's the point?'

'The point is, when you first loved me I was innocent, I saw the good in everyone. I was stupid enough to believe everything you said. And now I'm a slut, soiled goods. And a rapist to boot.'

'You are what you are, you did those things then, you are a different person now, today, with me.'

'Have you been on some Adult Education Philosophy for Beginners course for the last three years?'

You smile, how can you still have light in your eyes when mine has gone?

'So show me, Katherine, show me what you did with those men, eh? Come on, rape me. Hey, I promise I'll put up a fight, oh! Oh no!'

Before

'It's so beautiful here, isn't it?' I said, tracking the moonlight's reflection in the trees outside our windows.

Dave and I had finally gone to bed after a long dinner and several sessions of Truth or Dare. I could still hear voices downstairs and someone splashing about in the pool.

'Kate, try not to gush so much.'

'Gush?'

'Gush. About the food, the view, the house... people like Tatyana don't know anything else so you've just got to act like you expect it all, rather than some third-world kid at the Queen's garden party.'

I thought about what he'd said, perhaps I had been too impressed by the aromatic herb garden, Françoise's cheese soufflé, the hand-painted ceiling in the dining room and the Renoir sketch in the Gents' loo. Okay, I'd gushed.

'You've just got to know how to treat people like that. Goodnight, darling girl.' He turned over and fell asleep.

SATURDAY

Saturday Morning

This time last night you came back to me. I watch you while you sleep, trying to catch your dreams with the rise and fall of your chest and the flicker of your eyelashes. Now the tide has taken you into a slow-wave sleep and I follow the progress of your dim, distant pulse. I count six grey hairs around your temple. Your lips move just a little, but your face is calm, not a ripple. Between our legs, what was a few hours ago wet is drying into a salty film. Your breath is now almost undetectable and, when I'm satisfied that you won't be woken, I slip out of bed.

I'm perched over the side of the bath, running warm water over myself but it won't clean away the question which has been itching away at me since yesterday.

Tying my bathrobe around me and flexing my feet on the cold wooden floor, I stand in the living room. With the light behind me, I can see the outline of your trousers over the back of the sofa. My heart speeds up as I move over to the pile of your clothes. I pick up your trousers and slide my fingers into your pockets. There is no reason, I tell myself, to feel like a thief. Empty pockets. You had a jacket. I spin around in search of it – I was sure I saw a brown suede jacket. When did I see it? You bought the shopping, with what? You must have a wallet, things, in your jacket. Where are your things?

Now I remember dropping my coat over yours when we came in. I lift mine up, careful not to make a noise. The suede jacket is underneath. I feel the cool hide in my fingers; still holding the heaviness of my coat over my other arm I fumble in the inside pockets.

'You lost something?'

I can only see your silhouette in the doorway.

'Where are your things?'

'My things?'

'So, like, how did you pay for the shopping?'

'There was £20 on the table. You see, the change. And receipt.'

I'd left the money for my cleaner last week and now there are a few coins scattered by the flowers, and yes, there's a receipt.

'Is that why you came back? Because you ran out of money?'

'Don't be stupid.'

'But where are your things?'

'Come to bed. It's cold.'

'But you don't have any clothes, a toothbrush, a passport? Everybody has *things*.'

'Let's sleep.'

'Where are your things? I can't sleep until you tell me.'

'Come on, Katherine.'

'How do I know you'll be here in the morning? Don't you see? I can't trust you, Marc, and the fact you refuse to tell me anything just makes it impossible to even try. I always thought that once I found you, dead or alive, I'd understand – but this is... this is worse.'

'Because you don't understand something?'

You walk over, try to lead me back into the bedroom. I use my weight against you and stay with my hand in your empty jacket pocket.

You take the coat from me like a brave policeman might prise a gun from a madman. You rest it over the back of the chair. You speak slowly, trying to reason with me.

'It's morning already. I'm here. Later, too, I'll be here, with you, I'll be right next to you.'

'Marc, I'm even questioning whether you really are here?'

'I'm here. I'm freezing.'

You walk me back to bed. We both lay side by side absorbing the darkness. The central heating, which is set to come on at 6am, clicks before I hear the rush of the boiler's flame. I nestle into you.

'I thought I saw you once, last year, on the Northern Line. You got off the Tube in Barnet. I followed you. You were walking fast, it was about five in the afternoon, you were wearing a grey coat with a long scarf. There were so many people all coming in the other direction and I had to run to catch you up. Then you crossed the road and a bus came in front of me and I lost you... was it you?'

'No.'

'I went back to the Tube station every day for the next week at the same time to see if you'd come again, but you didn't. So it wasn't you then?'

'No.'

'Definitely?'

'I've never been to Barnet.'

We fit perfectly together. You've never crushed or jabbed me, never been too heavy or light. I've never had to complain of sharp elbows in my ribs, scratchy toenails or limbs giving me a dead leg.

'Why don't you have any things?'

'I only have you.'

Saturday, Midday

I know Maggie's little tap at the door, kept light, not to startle or impose.

'Oh sorry, have I... ?'

'I was already awake.'

'Two things. I've just come back from a trip to Sainsbury's – dashed out early before the hordes descended – I know, I should get them to deliver and this is the last time I'm throwing myself into the fray. I'm going to have to learn how to order it all on the internet like you do – even the most steadfast Luddite needs to have their toilet paper brought direct – but! I'm parked miles away and I noticed your car's just outside, any chance we can change parking spots? Just now while I unload? Sorry to be such a nuisance.'

'Sure.'

'Second point,' Maggie continues talking while I go in search of my car keys. 'There's this TV chef – God, what's his name? – the Italian, with an accent and the hair? Anyway, he does a programme where you buy the ingredients beforehand and then cook it in real time with him giving instructions, I doubled up just in case we could do it together? Thursday night, nine o'clock – are you... ?'

Her mouth stops working when you stand by my side. She tries to recover herself as she hears me say, 'Maggie, this is Marc.'

I look to you to see what she is staring at.

You are like a planet, Marc, a vital force that draws us all around you. Even standing there, in my dressing gown, you have us in your pull. You put an arm around me, covering my shoulder in your hand. Maggie doesn't see *me* anymore, she sees *us*. A couple. That two-headed being that doesn't need a girlfriend to food-plan with.

'I remember the little dog,' you say.

'Walter!' Maggie calls out like a game-show contestant.

'Walter, yes. He's okay?'

'Oh yes, well, we had rather a scare.' She looks at me. 'Kate saved his life a while back but he's on fighting form now. Thanks to her.'

'Good,' you say. 'I'll re-park the car. Just a second.'

You turn back into the flat. I'm left at the door watching Maggie wobble.

'Does he know?'

'Know what?'

Maggie's face twitches and tics in different directions as her neurons run back and forth trying to think exactly what Marc might want to know first. Maggie and I have been close these last two years, but now you have returned, there's a dividing line between us.

'That he's... *missing*?'

I shrug.

'When did he come back?'

'Thursday night.'

'Nice that he remembered Walter. I suppose you won't want the recipe now?'

'The what?'

And then her voice is louder, friendlier and I can tell that you are behind me.

'When you have a moment, Kate, I'd be so grateful if you could just set me up on the Sainsbury's site, get me going, but no hurry...'

'Sure.'

You toss my car keys in your hand up and down and kiss me goodbye with, '*A bientôt ma chérie.*'

Before

I'll take you back to when I first met Maggie and how she gave me my first lead to you.

I was woken at six in the morning by frantic knocking at the door. My first thought was that there was news of you. Even in my sleep, I was prepared for that moment and without opening my eyes, I was sliding the door chain.

In front of me stood a middle-aged woman with mascara streaking down her cheeks. Her face was red and her lips quivered. She was holding a little white dog in her hands.

'Oh no, I've woken you up. I'm so sorry, I'm so sorry... I've been waiting for a good time to speak to you all night and look, I've woken you. I'm Maggie, from upstairs. We've passed each other a few times and,' she stopped to sniff loudly, 'this is Walter.'

I'd seen her before and had certainly heard the dog yapping when his owner was out during the day, often when I'd been trying to sleep off a nightshift.

'Is everything all right?'

'No, not at all.' Her eyes welled with tears. She held the dog up to me. 'I think he's dying.'

The dog did look sick. I took him in my hands. His nose was hot, his stomach convulsing.

'Is he passing blood?'

'It's like strawberry jam. Ruined my carpets. He hasn't eaten for two days, no water either. He must be very dehydrated.'

It took Maggie all her strength to keep enough composure to give me the right information.

'Have you rung the vet?'

'The surgery's closed until eight. I've left messages but no one's got back to me! I'm so sorry to have woken you – I see your post on the landing sometimes, "Dr Brenton". You're a doctor, aren't you?'

'Yes, but for people, not for dogs. Sorry.' She didn't move. 'Do you want to come in?'

Maggie stepped into the flat as I bundled up the quivering dog in a tea towel and handed him back to his owner.

'I thought doctors had to train as vets first?'

'It's the other way around.' I switched on the coffee maker. 'Coffee?'

'Two and half sugars, please.'

'Walter's a Westie, isn't he?' Maggie nodded, her approval sealed.

'My parents had one of these, we called her Star. Walter, you'd have liked Star.'

Maggie chewed her bottom lip.

'Could you just look at Walter, please? You're one of those people who I would completely trust him with. I can tell by your face.'

By that time I was completely awake.

'Well, let's have a look at you, Walter.'

Walter rolled over, paws in the air, surrendering to my general prodding. He yelped a little where he was particularly tender.

'My guess – and it's just a guess – is that he's got the doggy equivalent of gastroenteritis, see, it's enflamed here, that's his colon. Shh, shh, that's it, little one. Can you see that this part is in spasm, that's what's aggravating the lining of his lower intestines, causing the bleeding.'

'Can you give him something?'

'I'm afraid not. Drugs for humans don't quite work on dogs, but he seems to like being massaged, here...'

The dog flattened his ears and let me smooth out his hair.

'I knew you'd have magic fingers. This is the calmest he's been. He's not going to...'

She swallowed hard several times before I answered, 'No, no, he'll be all right. Has he been drinking from ponds or been near bird faeces?'

'Um, I don't think... Yes! Yes! We went for a walk by the Serpentine and he went in chasing the geese.'

'That might be it. The vet will give you something to alleviate the activity and some antibiotics. He should be all right by tonight.'

'I had such a scare. You don't really know how much you love them until the thought of...' Maggie didn't continue.

The sky was ordering itself into a tricolour of red, white and blue outside my window. I had to be at work for 8.30.

'Real coffee! What a treat, thank you.'

'My husband always insisted on real coffee, it's quite a palaver but sort of meditative in—'

'That's him, isn't it?' she asked, looking at a photograph of you. It was one of my favourite photographs of you in Barcelona reading a newspaper outside a café.

'Yes. Marc. My husband.'

'I heard what happened and I see all the posters. There's one I pass every day outside the police station. Funnily enough, I overheard the secretaries at work saying if they found him it'd be hard to give him back!'

We looked at your picture. Maggie screwed up her eyes.

'They were only joking. I hope that doesn't sound insensitive. I'm so sorry for you, really... it must be awful. You've really no idea where he could be?'

'No idea at all.'

Those days, I was scared of my own company, terrified to be alone, but around other people, their inevasible presence choked me until I conjured a vaguely plausible excuse to escape them. My patients were the easiest people to deal with, people who had no right or interest in asking about my private life. As for the rest, all day long people said things about you that they immediately regretted. The worst was dealing with their embarrassment and quasi-spiritual aphorisms such as, 'It's all in

God's plan' or, 'It means he wasn't the one for you'. No one could say anything remotely helpful but at the same time, they couldn't leave it alone. It was difficult to remember a time when a simple question wasn't a brutal attack.

'It's just that he really was – I mean – is, quite a dish. I used to pass him on the stairs. He was always polite and friendly. And smelt so heavenly! Sometimes he'd say hello and stroke Walter. Such a gentleman, I used to think that he was the perfect man – "perfect man", is that an oxymoron? It must be coming up to a year now.'

'Nearly.'

Maggie looked at my desk in the corner of the living room.

'I see you're still busy with the search.'

'The Thames Valley Police are producing a new report about missing people, I'm trying to pass on some of my experiences of how Marc's disappearance was handled.'

'Have they been good, the police?'

'They haven't found him, but yeah, I 'spose.'

'I had a policeman come to my door, asking about you and him. What was he like? When had I last seen him? Did you row? I so wanted to help, so wanted to say something that would make a difference, but all I could tell him was that I'd see you both in the supermarket or on the street, always holding hands, laughing, kissing – Oh please don't think I am a nosey neighbour, it's just that in London you can go days without recognising anyone and well, my degree was in Psychology. I told him that you both seemed so much in love.'

I continued patting the dog while she spoke.

'Everyone living in this building was so shocked and sorry. We talked about starting up a collection for you, give you something to show how concerned we were but we couldn't think what to call it, it's not like a death or a divorce–'

'That's very kind.'

The time on my barely used DVD player blinked 7.35. Would I get away with a shower or would it be a case of grabbing my clothes and rushing out?

'Look, we'll be running. Thank you so much for seeing Walter and being here to chat to.'

'Any time, even at night. I don't sleep much these days so if you see my light on and fancy a nightcap or a natter, just knock.'

I handed the dog back to Maggie at the door.

'Thanks again,' she said, stepping into the corridor to look at me. I could see in her eyes she was having second thoughts about saying something.

'There was something I thought about later. I didn't ring the police because it didn't seem important but maybe...' Maggie hesitated.

'What's that?'

'There was a woman.'

My breath stopped mid-flow.

'It must have been about two weeks before he disappeared, I saw a woman. It's probably nothing, but she was often around the building. Sometimes I saw her looking up at your flat. She was small, very, very elegant. Looked rich. But the most striking thing was her red hair – she reminded me of a mermaid. Does that mean anything to you?'

'No.'

'I didn't connect the two until I remembered her talking to a taxi driver one time and I heard her accent. She was French, definitely. I thought she might be a cousin or friend of Marc's from home. It was just a thought. I hope I haven't made you late.'

You put the car keys down. 'Come back to bed.'

I'm supposed to be at my parents, you're supposed to be missing, but we go back to bed. And maybe because you are back and the story is coming to an end, I am reopening those first memories of us, looking through them, sorting, re-filing, and tossing some of them out forever.

Before

Jets of sunlight flooded the room, waking me up to my first day in Provence, alone. Dave's watch was propped up on the bedside table like a centurion guarding the space he must have crept out from. I waited for him to return with a milky tea for me just like my father brought my mother every morning for the last few decades, but when twenty minutes passed, anxiety got the better of me. I dressed and followed the voices along the stone-paved corridors through to the kitchen and outside terrace where the table was already being laid for breakfast.

Tatyana was arguing with someone in the kitchen while carrying out a fresh pot of coffee. She was so involved in her conversation that she didn't see me. She was wearing only a long white lace robe, her pale hair piled on top of her head, matching her golden feet which danced over the tiles. Close behind her shuffled Dave with a basket of croissants. He was raising his voice at her while chewing on a piece of pain au raisin.

'So explain then how America has less social mobility than anywhere else in the Western world?'

I stood by the kitchen door, watching them coming in and out while they set the table. Dave must have been for a run already, his bare torso shone in the light, his hair stood up around his head like black shredded satin.

Even when I sat down and helped myself to orange juice,

Dave didn't acknowledge me. He was waving his fists at the sky in mock exasperation at something Tatyana had said but I'd not heard.

Max came out on the porch. 'Bit bloody early for Milton bloody Freidman, what?' he said, glaring at the coffee pot as if he expected it to pour itself into his cup.

Tatyana sat cross-legged on her chair, waving a spent match in the air after lighting her first cigarette. She was about to say something but was interrupted by a shriek from one of the overhead bedrooms. It was followed by giggling and the unmistakable sound of a hand slapping against bare buttocks.

We looked up at Georgie and Josh's bedroom window as the spanking session got underway in regular sequences, interspersed by yelps, suppressed laughter and synchronised groaning.

'Close your ears, children, that's my pervy little sister up there,' said Max, cutting a strawberry into four quarters.

'Care for some cake, Marie Antoinette?' Dave asked, waving a brioche at Tatyana who opened her mouth wide and snatched a bite from his fingers.

'Didn't you say something about bacon and eggs?'

'Consider it done, Your Majesty!'

With that, Dave put a hand on my shoulder and left for the kitchen.

Leonie came out reading a leather-bound collection of Christina Rossetti's poetry as the next set of spanks started up again in multiples of three followed by a voice saying sternly 'naughty, naughty girl'. She looked up from her book, 'Is that... ?' Leonie pointed to the room upstairs as we heard Georgie Penrose begging, 'No! no!' before another whack was sent from their window.

Chris looked up at the group with a mischievous grin as Tatyana whispered, 'All of you, behave.'

As breakfast was being cleared, Josh and Georgie emerged refreshed and rosy cheeked declaring that they were ravenous. The rest of the day was spent swaying in hammocks or by the pool, interrupted only by Françoise bringing out trays of things to eat.

For our second day an excursion was planned to some nearby waterfalls. It had been a gorgeous day, we'd swum, picnicked and drunk a lot. As we were leaving, Dave suggested that I drive Chris and Leonie back while he went with Tatyana, Georgie and Josh. The parties were split that way because, he explained, he and I were the most sober.

Our car reached the house first and, as it was Françoise's day off, we started making supper for the others. It had been dark a while when we heard the second car pull up, I watched from the kitchen window as Tatyana and Dave fell out of the car, doubled over laughing, both completely naked.

Still laughing, they burst into the house, covering their bodies with their damp clothes.

'We couldn't bear to put our wet clothes on, so we drove back like this! Can you imagine the looks we got at the *péage!*'

I tried to laugh along with the joke, but I felt my stomach turn. Of course if their clothes had been wet, well, it was very sensible to take them off rather than sit in them and risk getting haemorrhoids.

'Where are Georgie and Josh?'

'Oh, dropped them off in Cannes, they wanted a dinner *à deux*. What's for supper?'

Late that night, I woke in the bedroom, again, alone. It was blackout dark, no moon, no birds. I waited for Dave to return from the bathroom but couldn't hear anything. After dozing for about half an hour, I whispered his name, there was no answer.

And then I worried about him, I don't know why, but he'd been very drunk, maybe he'd decided on a late-night swim or to jump off the roof, or simply got lost in the château, there were still floors we'd never been to. Spending time in A&E departments teaches one to fear the most seemingly harmless activities.

The day's heat was being expunged from the old stone walls, even the floor tiles were body temperature. Dave wasn't in the kitchen, or the hall or the drawing room, but hearing a match being struck led me to the library.

As soon as I saw him, even from the threshold, I knew something was terribly wrong. He sat behind the curtains in his M&S white boxers, one knee to his cheek, the other limbs curled around him, distorted like an abandoned pottery project.

'Shouldn't really smoke in here, most of these books are first editions.'

He didn't move. I touched his clammy shoulder.

'Are you all right?'

He continued staring at a space on the floor, I squatted down, intercepting his view.

'Do you want a glass of water?'

He didn't answer me so I went to the kitchen and brought over some ice and water.

'Dave? Say something.'

I rocked his knees. He didn't even turn to look at me. I stayed by him a little longer and then he took my hand. He brought it to his mouth and kissed it.

'Sorry,' he croaked.

'Sorry for what?'

'Sorry.'

I stayed an hour, too tired to stifle my yawns, then went back to bed.

Dave didn't come down for breakfast and I didn't see him all that morning. There was no sign from him at lunchtime or later that afternoon.

'Have you had a row?' Tatyana asked as we swam lengths together.

'I don't think so...'

'You don't think so?' Tatyana laughed.

'Well, we went to bed, he was himself, then he got up in the middle of the night and wouldn't speak to me...'

'Men,' concluded Tatyana, 'he's probably jealous.'

'Why?'

'Chris – he's absolutely mad about you.'

'We're supposed to be leaving tomorrow, I'm just a bit–'

'Oh don't be silly, stay here – really, we all want you to stay.'

Around the time Françoise brought our afternoon tea someone noticed that Dave had moved himself to an attic room on the top floor. Whenever we looked up, we saw him at the window, watching us.

After the afternoon's volleyball tournament, Chris and Max took the opportunity to go on, what they called, 'a peace mission' and invite him to play, but they returned saying he'd refused to speak to them.

At supper I took him some food, chatted about the day and tried to get him to eat something. He looked at me once, and it was a look of hostility, but he did make a request for whisky and more cigarettes.

No one knew what to make of it.

I slept alone that night, hoping Dave would find his way to our room, but he didn't.

The following morning, the house party carried on as usual. In the afternoon Leonie and I went to the shops to buy Dave his nicotine and alcohol provisions. I returned to him in the evening, he'd barely changed positions since midday.

The nocturnal party games lost their appeal, Dave's invisible presence hung over us. I was the first to go to bed; lying there wondering at what point I should call his parents.

The next day was the day Dave had programmed for us to be leaving for the Pyrenees – we should have been halfway through our tour of the South of France but we hadn't even started it, nor did he look like he was going anywhere. Before breakfast I went up to ask him if he was ready to leave, hoping he'd recover himself now that a new adventure was in store. He was gaunt, with stubble and yellow nicotine-stained fingers. I lost my patience with him, said we had to go whether he liked it or not, Tatyana had more guests coming and he was being rude. All I got back was a guttural, 'Go then.'

Returning to the pool area, I overheard what I understood in French to be Françoise berating Tatyana for not calling a doctor and my host replying, '*Mais, c'est lui le medecin!*'

'Any closer to finding out what Dave's crisis is all about?' asked Tatyana, applying some sun cream to her shoulders.

'No idea at all. Do you think I ought to ring his parents or someone?'

'He'll snap out of it.'

I wondered what form this 'snap' would take.

Dave's dinner tray that night was left untouched. He did, however, find enough energy to snatch a packet of cigarettes out of my hands when I'd come to remove it. A few hours later, Max took him up some wine after saying he was determined to find out what the problem was. He came down scratching his head.

'Well?' we asked.

Max took in a deep breath and announced dramatically, 'He has spoken.'

'And what has he spoken?' they chanted, encouraged by the breakthrough.

'He said he wants to speak to Tatyana, and only Tatty.'

We all looked to Tatyana who arched an eyebrow in surprise.

'I'm game,' she said, getting up from the table.

'Shouldn't I come with you?' offered Chris.

'I think I can manage, but if I scream, don't just open another bottle of Chablis, eh?'

The group clustered around Tatyana as she mounted the stairs, they wished her luck as though she were about to steal a sacred pearl from a minotaur's lair.

Georgie tried to engage me in a backgammon game while we bantered about topics far removed from where our minds kept drifting. All ears were trained on the staircase, waiting to hear Tatyana's light tread returning to us.

Later that evening, while I rocked in the hammock staring up at Dave's light, Tatyana emerged from the house carrying a tumbler of cognac for each of us. She lay next to me, sighed.

'Hey,' she said, swinging her hand out to catch mine.

'So?' I asked.

'Oh, cousin Katie,' Tatyana moaned.

'What? Tell me.'

'Finally, I found out what the matter with Dave is.'

I prepared myself.

'I wish he'd tell you himself, but he won't. He's really confused... really, y'know,' she waved her hand around her head, 'really mixed up. Out there. Bats, basically.'

'What did he say?'

'Oh. Life. Parents. Money. Career. Girls. Love. See, he thinks he's in love.'

I lay back watching the sky swinging above me.

'I think I might love him too,' I whispered.

She brought the glass to her lips, shook her head, put the glass back on the ground.

'But, Katie, he thinks he's in love with *me*.'

'Of course... you, yes.'

'I'm sorry, fuck. Oh God, you're upset.'

'I'm not – I'm just – he really said he loves you?'

'Ever since he saw me come for my interview apparently – four years ago.'

'And where am I in all this?'

'Of course he has feelings for you.'

'I get some feelings do I?'

'Babe, he's a total mess right now. He said he wants me to go up to him, at midnight, and if I don't, he's going to throw himself off that window ledge and impale himself on Daddy's Toscano statue.'

'Kill himself?'

'He's serious.'

'But you won't go, will you?'

'I can't say. I can't say, and least of all to you.' She closed her eyes as if the memory of his words swept over her like a moving piece of music.

'And do you love him?'

'The thing is, David is so passionate, strong, romantic. He said inside of him is this nucleic fusion of emotion and I'm the only person who can dismantle him or he'll explode, you know?'

'No. I've never heard such crap in all my life.'

'But that's it – apparently nobody's ever understood him, not his parents, his teachers or you.'

'Go make your decision. I'm obviously nothing to do with this.'

Tatyana tried to catch up with me as I stomped towards the house.

'But *you* do?' I said, swinging around to her.

'I want to try.'

'Well hurry up and "explode" together!'

I anticipated that she'd run after me, but she didn't.

In the darkness of my room, I shoved my stuff into my rucksack. At midnight, while I was rechecking my passport and ticket home, I heard Tatyana's feet padding their way up to Dave's room.

Next morning, Dave shuffled into 'our' room to collect his stuff. He found me sitting on the bed, waiting for him. He appeared surprised to see me, perhaps he had thought I'd already left the house but more likely, he'd forgotten about me altogether.

He grunted, swung out his arms to scoop up T-shirts and his camera from the floor like an over-medicated orangutan.

'What's happening?'

He picked up a pair of boxer shorts and sniffed at them before ploughing his belongings into what had been his laundry bag.

'We're supposed to be in Carcassonne now, Dave.'

'No one's stopping you.'

Rucksack over one shoulder, he tapped the doorframe, gripped the beam and long-jumped out of our relationship.

Saturday Afternoon

'Do you think about when we first met?'

This is what I ask you when you return from moving the car.

'No.'

'When you were gone, I used to think, one day with you was better than my whole life put together.'

'Why are you crying?'

'Because it's only now that you've returned I can let myself feel what it was like to have lost you.'

I have my husband all Saturday – it's how I think of it, 'I'm having him,' like I've heard men say, 'I had her.' I won't let you go until I've finished with you, that missing man, Marc Venelles. Each touch is for all the times I craved you. One for the team. Your body is there for the taking and in those seconds when the world fades out and I arrive at a place where nothing exists but the sensation of you, I'm not searching anymore.

Then I come back and you are still here. And you listen to me. I lay back on the bed and talk, whatever comes into my head. You say little, prompt me, restart me, but most of all, you listen to me.

'I missed going to the park with you. It's something you can't really do on your own, without a dog, I mean, unless you're schizophrenic or training for a marathon.'

'We'll go to the park if you like.'

'I'm scared.'

'I'm here. Don't be afraid.'

'Oh yes, I've got... *five* days left.'

'It's for you to decide, Katherine.'

'To decide what?"

Before

I thought I was prepared for what I'd find at the NMPs' Helpline offices but arriving at the call centre, seeing the volunteers on the phones, the whiteboards covered in scribbled names, the charts full of random details, updates, faces in photos, it was a different world. That's all I can say, Marc, a different place altogether. You left for somewhere and I ended up there, where I didn't want to be at all.

'Kate? Frances.'

I'd liked her voice when I'd first heard it a few days before, and I was warmed by the smile and the colourful wooden beads jangling on her chest, the plump handshake.

'Thanks for coming in.'

It was kind of her to welcome me like this as, in fact, I'd insisted I see her in person. When Detective Wells gave me her card, I'd projected all my hope in it. Even when she said that really, there was little she could do to help, I couldn't shake the belief that this person might crack the code to you. So I just thought if she actually met me, I wouldn't be just another woman enquiring after a wayward partner.

'There's a room at the back which is quieter.'

She was my guide in that new world: what was strange and terrifying to me was just another day's work for her. Walking behind her, I tried to take in everything I saw, the Post-it notes, dates of sightings, deaths, case numbers.

'You all right, darling?'

'So many...'

'So many. You're right there.'

We stopped and looked around us at the gallery of ruptured lives. She put her hand on my shoulder.

'Sometimes I wonder if there's anyone not missing to someone somewhere if you get my drift. The last two years there've been some high-profile cases, it's brought a lot of people out of the woodwork – literally and metaphorically – we've had to move offices twice, double our staff. Our oldest unsolved case is from 1893.'

She gestured at me to sit down in the 'quieter' room – which wasn't quieter – as she manoeuvred herself round her desk dropping a box of tissues on my lap before settling into a cushioned wicker chair opposite me.

'Did you manage to get some of the stuff I asked for?'

'Yes. This is his wallet: bus pass, credit and current account cards. Here's his passport, his driving licence, cheque book, NHS card–'

'Birth certificate?'

'I don't have that.'

'French ID card?'

'No. And a recent photo of him.'

She fingered the belongings as I laid them out, her eyes resting on your photo, asking questions of that face. She moved the pieces around as if contemplating a puzzle.

'Honey, with what's here, I see two possibilities, okay? He's out there and someone's looking after him, I mean, where's he gonna go, eat, sleep without his chequebook, credit card, passport, you know? The other is less likely. He's switched identities. This takes planning, though – since 9/11 even more so – and to some extent, it's illegal – you can't go around on a false identity – you can only go on the run so long like that these days, but, sweetheart, in both these scenarios, he won't want to be found.'

'Could anyone have taken him, harmed him?'

'Unlikely.'

She nudged the tissue box toward me and placed Marc's things next to each other.

'There's no reason he would have wanted to disappear unless something was wrong.'

'Yes. Yes, something's wrong, Kate, there's no denying it –

he's left you without any warning and he's left his stuff. His details are up on the Missing Persons site, they've done routine checks, you've filed your report. This must be hell for you, I totally appreciate that. But it's a waiting game from here on. We're a few weeks in and... even if you were a blood relative, we couldn't do much more.'

'You'd do the posters–'

'Social network sites are much more effective.'

'What about appeals, TV announcements?'

'If you could get a family member to report him, as I said on the phone, yeah, that. It would also open the links with France. But you say he hasn't any family, like any? And you say you know nothing of his life before he met you...'

She blew over your things, a curled bus pass trembled on the table. 'As I said, sweetie, our charity only provides for blood relatives.'

'Mrs White, I'm desperate. What can I do?'

'If you don't have one already, I recommend you invest in a fast, powerful computer with high-speed connection and then, all I can say is, wait. Wait.'

The telephone rings in octaves up and down the solipsistic cavern we've made for ourselves.

'Take his call.'

The answer machine clicks on but the person rings off. I can't hide my relief that we've been spared the discomfort of someone talking out loud to me with you in the room – more precisely, of Anthony talking to me, in front of my husband.

You move into the kitchen, open the fridge and take out possibilities for a late lunch. My mobile phone leaps into a jolly tune from inside the lining of my pocket. You watch me as I move quickly to pull it out. Despite being muffled, the tune becomes increasingly loud until I hold the phone in my hand. I see Anthony's face on the screen, his name, number. I switch off the phone, Anthony's picture dissolves. I don't feel relief, this respite is temporary.

You stand behind me and say something kind of hilarious.

'Don't let me get in the way of your life.'

The coffee machine splutters.

'I'm getting married.'

Before

I didn't sleep at all that last night in France, having been kept awake by the late-night naked-diving competition with Dave shouting out scores as if he'd been elected in-château MC, followed by the lovemaking session between him and Tatyana, which continued even after Françoise had put out the breakfast. At one point, Chris had stopped off at my room. When I asked him what he was doing tugging at my sheets, he mumbled about looking for the loo.

'I am not a toilet. Go to bed.'

Making sure he did exactly that, I led him onto one of the landings. Returning to my room, I caught sight of Dave coming up the back stairs carrying a cup of herbal tea for Tatyana. He stopped when he saw me. He looked like he wanted to say something but changed his mind.

At breakfast the group made a noticeable fuss of me, particularly Chris who insisted I have the last croissant, refilled my coffee cup after every few mouthfuls. Whatever I said, all eyes turned to me with concern, especially when Dave came down and prepared a tray to take back up for himself and

Tatyana. I wondered if the way I felt was similar to when invalids returned home after an accident. I tried to accept their kindness and not let humility slump into humiliation.

The plan was to go to Aix-en-Provence for a late lunch. I was to drive with Leonie, Josh, Georgie and Chris – Dave and Tatyana had sent a message through Leonie that they would be staying in that day. As we were five in the car, Max would zoom ahead on his bike as the 'advance party'. His job was to book a table for lunch and scout around for drugs which they were fast running out of.

As we left, I discreetly lifted my case into the boot of the car.

Approaching Aix, while I was thinking about how to change my flight, my throat contracting with sadness and flicking a tear off my cheek, I noticed that we were driving through the scene of a serious road accident. It was Leonie who saw Max's body being carried into the ambulance.

'If we can't talk about the past or the future, I guess feeding ducks is one way to spend an afternoon.'

A pair of eiders float around a swirl of goose excrement in front of us.

'Sometimes I really wanted to talk about you, just to tell a story or repeat something you said but I couldn't, it was too awkward and embarrassing for other people – apart from Mimi and Bruno, they used to want to talk about Uncle Marc, I was probably happiest with them. When you left you took my future but also my past. All those memories, just kept to myself, and after a while, I didn't know whether they were real or not.'

Your eyes have taken on the shades of the pond.

'But memories aren't real, are they? Just stories.'

'They're all that's left when the person isn't there, you want to know that once they were...'

'But you can't really remake how it was, only how you see it after, you fit the picture to what you want. That's why, Katherine, I don't like to tell stories about me. It's not important and more than that, I would be lying to you. I don't want to lie to you.'

'Do you think I'm so gullible, such a fool? Do you think I take everything at face value – even you? Especially you? Maybe once, but not now. Not after what you've done to me.'

The cold air grazes my throat and I'm aware of a nearby family looking at me and calling their children away from the pond's edge.

'I live in the same world as you, Marc, I know that most relationships are based on heuristics, probability, and a whole lot of blind trust. That's all I had to go by when I married you, but I took that chance. I got you wrong though, didn't I? And I've paid for it.'

I flop against you and we go back into being us. There's so much that goes on between two people that you can never explain to anyone, even if you did understand it yourself.

The ducks waddle away from us at great speed. You put your arm around me and lead me back to the bench where we'd been sitting. You take a cigarette out and jab it on your thigh. I put out my hand for a cigarette too. You shake your head, disappointed, but light both of them. It's too cold to be sitting in a park, even for two refugees like us.

You ask, 'Shall we?'

Before

Georgie paced outside the main entrance of Aix hospital as Chris and Leonie relayed between us and the A&E doctors who were treating Max. I went in search of refreshments.

Once in the hospital vicinity, I started to feel like myself for the first time that holiday. Although it was more like a business hotel compared to where I'd be working, everything about the A&E part of the hospital was familiar to me: the signs leading to the departments, the porters' slippers, the information blinking on the monitors.

I'd forgotten about the next three years of training ahead of me. Thinking about the salary I'd finally be receiving and the badge with the title 'Dr' on it made me excited for my future, even when I saw the yawning junior doctors walking as fast as they could without running down the corridors. I didn't understand the words that passed between the nurses, but I could probably give a good translation.

I was reminded of Anna saying there was nothing better than walking past a screaming baby when it wasn't yours; it was like that for me, being there and not on duty, not having to deal with it.

I found a drink dispenser by the maternity ward. While I tried to decipher the meaning of *noisette, longue, café crème* and negotiating the amount of money in my purse, I was aware of someone standing beside me.

'Sorry, go ahead,' I said, counting through my coins. And then, realising that I'd spoken in English, I looked up at the man.

'*Pardon. Allez devant moi,*' I muttered.

The man was staring at me. Really, really staring as if he had suddenly stumbled on a creature so rare and so nervous even a blink might frighten it away. I must have seemed that way in those days, to you.

The look in your eyes struck me in the chest. That's when he became 'you'. I couldn't catch my breath for long enough to rationalise what exactly had hit me. You didn't break your stare, but you smiled, and when you smiled at me, I was weightless, giddy. Free. You controlled me from the inside.

I never had any choice.

'What would you like?' you asked.

Your voice was deep, relaxed, as if you were just waking from a daytime sleep by the sea, as if we'd always known each other. It was your voice I loved first, your accent, the reverberation, the safety it promised – I heard something then, Marc, on a sonar level, that showed me the way home.

You were looking at the change in my hand and then into my eyes. When you smiled your blue eyes reflected the sunlight, emitting white sparks of light against your skin – or so it seemed to me.

I brought my fingers up to my face, took a deep breath and laughed at my light-headedness. I grounded my equilibrium by inhaling the familiar scent of disinfected floors and not looking up at the stranger.

'I'm getting three coffees and I can't remember how my friends wanted them... so do go ahead.' I looked up, right into your eyes. '*Merci*,' I added.

'English?' you asked, not moving.

'Yes, I'm here on holiday.'

'I didn't know the hospital was a tourist attraction.'

'Ha, well, no, I'm not visiting the hospital.' I laughed. 'My friend was in a motorbike accident.'

'Oh. He is okay?'

'Yes, he's got a fractured tibia, a few broken ribs and clavicle – the usual.' I noticed you were frowning. 'Sorry, a leg break, and his...' I tapped my collarbone.

'Driving in the heat, it's dangerous.'

You shrugged and I had the urge to rest my head on your

shoulders and just stay there till old age took me off. I looked at the buttons on your denim shirt and back to the machine.

'The collarbone will take him a good few months to recover from, though.'

'I'm sorry?'

'This part,' I said, touching my shoulder and noticing that his eyes were running over my hand. 'It's an uncomfortable break.'

'*Aie*, I imagine.'

'And this is such a wonderful hospital, not like where I work in England, this is just...'

I put my arms out in appreciation of the pristine hallways, floor-to-ceiling windows looking out onto open courtyards enclosed by walls of oleander trees. I'd never really said so much to anyone who I'd not been formally introduced to before.

Anna chats to everyone but I don't. I don't know why I wanted to talk to you; it was the shock of the morning and the longing for an ally after so many days feeling alone with people who were supposed to be my friends.

'You're a doctor?'

I nodded my head.

'But you are so young!'

'I'm still in training, five years down, another eight or so to go.' Lights on the drink machine flashed. 'Sorry, do go ahead.'

When you put your finger up to the screen to punch in the number of your order, you turned to me again.

'What would you like?'

I rubbed the back of my head, spilling change on the ground.

'That's so kind. Actually, a hot chocolate would be reviving.'

'*Hot* chocolate – today?'

You faced the whirring machine, laughing. Your back was wide, strong. As you bent to see the drink being poured, I noticed cigarettes in your pocket. You wore a silver chain around your neck and carried a leather wallet. All these things that belonged to you made me feel secure, like being with relatives, we were all joined together as parts of you.

'Are you from London?' you asked as the flow of drink came to a few last drops.

'Oxford, originally, that's where my parents live, but in September I'll be living in London, yes. Have you been there?'

'Many times.'

Stop right there. Why didn't I stop right there? Instead of picking up these clues that would have solved you, I hobbled around the floor picking up coins.

'One hot chocolate for *mademoiselle*.'

I brought my fingers up to yours and, as they touched, the feel of you charged through me.

You were about to say something when I heard, 'Kate! There you are!' Leonie rushed towards me skidding over the linoleum floor. 'There you are,' she repeated, catching her breath.

'Max's ready to leave now. What do you want to do? We could all squeeze in and go back together, or we could come back for you, or you could...'

Leonie looked up at you and then back to me.

My stay at the château was over but she didn't want to be the one to say it.

'No worries. I'll make my own way. Really. I'll get my suitcase out of the car.'

'Sure?' she asked, relieved I was sparing them a complicated exit. I turned to the Frenchman.

'*Au revoir* – and thanks.'

I wanted to say more but couldn't think of anything else.

'Goodbye. Enjoy the rest of your holiday,' you said.

'Yes, you too.'

Cringe. *You too!* You weren't on holiday. And I'd never even asked what you were doing in the hospital.

Max was levered into the car, his head nestled on Georgie's lap as she perched herself over one of Josh's knees, the other was pressed into the back of Chris' seat, which was set as forward into the car as it could go without crushing him against the dashboard.

'Thank God I was driving pissed or I could've died,' concluded Max. 'Have you seen the drugs they've given me? Chris, have you? This is where we should've been coming to score.'

'Can we please just get something to drink?' Georgie said.

Leonie started the car which began rolling out of the hospital car park. Chris was the only one to call out, '*Bon Voyage*, Kate! Aix is that way.'

They drove off and I shuffled out into the viscid midday air. Yes, I did regret bringing my *Oxford Handbook of Clinical Medicine*, and no, I had no idea what to do next. The only part of that whole holiday I'd enjoyed was the last two hours in the hospital, so I turned around and walked back through the electronic doors.

I sat on a chair at the entrance under an air conditioning vent, watching people as they moved in and out the main doors. I opened my case and brought out the plastic wallet that held my passport, flight information and Tatyana's email giving the directions to the château. I looked at the printout of my ticket marked for Saturday and knew I just wasn't up for sightseeing. I wanted to go home. Collecting all my change together I called the airline about changing my flight. I finally managed to book a seat leaving for Gatwick that night. There was an extra cost of a hundred and fifty pounds. I gave her my card number, trembling at the price of immediate freedom. I had set aside contingency money in case of emergencies and decreed this an emergency.

With the last bit of remaining change, I tapped in my home number. It felt pathetic, at twenty-two years old, to need my mum.

We walk in silence in front of the white stucco houses leading to our home. You stop and tuck me into you like a scarf, when we breathe out, ghosts dance between us.

You say, 'Tell me.'

I press my lips together to stop what I don't want to say coming out.

'Do you want me to go? I can go. Maybe it was a bad idea, staying all this time together, maybe you need a chance to think about it all. Katherine, you say, *hein*?'

'I don't want you to go. But...'

'But what?'

I look everywhere but your questioning eyes. You have asked the question, But what? I'm going to answer it.

'You're here. With me. We're feeding the ducks and going home... so, why do I still miss you?'

We walk up to our building, both carrying bags of clothes and stuff we picked out for you. Now you have *things* – some clothes, a toothbrush, razor and foam, bits and pieces to get you through the week.

When we stop at the door, Tom is coming out. He sees us and looks as if he might scuttle back in again but you move fast to catch the door while it's open. There is a wordless exchange between you, two men holding open that damned heavy door.

'Marc, this is Tom. He lives in flat 1.'

Tom stares at you intently.

You put out your hand towards him, Tom takes it, it's a quaint gesture he's not used to.

'Cold, isn't it?' you offer.

Tom looks up into the sky as if trying to remember the opening lines of a sixth-form play – no one prompts him.

'Have a good one!' he hails, before shooting off down the street.

I want to go after Tom, hug him tight, only I could know just how brave he'd been just then.

Coming home to the flat is such a different experience with you than it is alone. Compared with how my life has been, it's like stepping into someone's 21st birthday party: lights go on, the oven's lit, there's running water and music and we light candles, change out of and into clothes, people bob up and down on the TV screen, the fridge opens and closes, cupboards fill with new stuff. I've been so quiet here. It's been almost a game for me sometimes, to exist without disturbing anything, without leaving a trace. I think, Marc, a part of me wanted to live as though I too had disappeared.

Saturday Evening

We lie on the sofa eating cashew nuts and drinking a bottle of wine you've opened.

You ask me what I'm thinking.

'About work.'

'It's the weekend.'

'No, not like that. I was just thinking that I repair people.'

'The human-body mechanic.'

'That's right, open the bonnet, tinker around, try to fix what's gone wrong but I can't make them how they were before they broke.'

I yawn into your chest.

'Sleepy?'

'Yes. But I don't want to close my eyes in case I open them and you're not here.'

'Lie here, in my arms, I won't go anywhere.'

'Keep talking so I can hear your voice. Did I ever tell you that it was your voice I first fell in love with? Talk to me in French.'

'*Bien sûr, ma petite.*'

You enclose me in your arms and in the vibrations of your voice, I drift anchored to nothing but the rhythm of your speech.

Before

I recognised Frances' voice when she phoned, even though it had been a year since we met at the NMPs' Helpline. She said she wanted to talk, but it had to be in person, so we sat in a corner café after my day's shift.

'Last time I saw you, you told me to join Facebook and wait.'

'Good advice.'

'But not much help.'

'So, how are you getting on with your search?'

'Still searching. Every time a child goes missing and they drain the lakes or take apart some serial killer's basement, I

93

wonder if they'll find Marc's remains. I've been down to the morgue to identify bodies – nothing yet – I've made up posters and I've followed up some sightings, but I haven't found him if that's what you mean, haven't come close.'

'The reason I called is because I've left the NMPH – a difficult decision but it was expanding in size, costs and while that's great, everything got bigger except for the budget, if you know what I mean. My life was drowning in admin: getting in donations, fundraising, meeting targets and making deadlines. Okay, you know the feeling. One day I thought, I used to look for *people* and now I just look for *money*! I remembered a time when I wanted to help, particularly those in the Afro-Caribbean community who are woefully under-represented in the media and police searches. So I decided to set up on my own. A detective agency. Sounds all very raincoats and camera-spy pens but I'm basically tracing people, people like your husband. Do any of these names mean anything to you?'

She showed me a page on a notepad with a list of five men's names: Marc Rocher, Xavier Venelles, Momo El-Jahiz, Xavier Rocher and Marc Venelles.

'Only this name. That's Marc.'

'Oh no, sweetie, they're all the same person.'

She took a sip of her chai latte and let me stare at the five new leads.

'See, Kate, I did what I could for you within the confines of where I was working but there are avenues I'd like to go down in terms of looking for – she tapped the page of names – your hubby. Two points to make: I don't believe someone doesn't have any family or contacts; secondly, I don't believe people change – they can modify their behaviour, sure, but not change. If I had a detailed character profile of him – really detailed, Kate – that would take me beyond just names and numbers. When we look for people, we follow what we call "magnets": places, people, habits that our targets are inevitably drawn to – that's how they come into our range.'

The coffee sours my tongue. Did I want to be guided out of my despair? I was only just getting the hang of it.

'Presuming I still want to know where he is.'

'Presuming that, Doctor, yes. Cards on the table: I rarely get thanked for finding someone. Draw your own conclusions, but the way I see it, and I have seen it – over and over – people very often lose more in the search than they ever gain in the find. If you've walked away from it all, go, girlfriend.'

'So why do you do it?'

'I won't lie – we've all got to make a living and I'm good at it. I just came to say that if you need help, I'm here. I felt bad turning you away that day when you came to our offices. I know how hard it can be when the track goes cold.'

'You've lost someone, haven't you?'

'That's right, honey.'

But she doesn't want to talk about it.

'I think you contacting me was a sign. You know, this'll be my second Christmas without him. Last year I bought his presents, wrapped them up and actually got excited about giving them to him. I'm not going to this year, but it doesn't stop me looking at things in shops and wondering if he'd like them. When do we start?'

'I'm expensive, Kate.'

I looked up and saw Tom standing in front of me, bending down to kiss my mouth.

'Frances, this is Tom, my friend.'

'Tom, Frances. Hi.'

'Hi,' he says, biting into my chocolate fudge cake. 'If you wanna see the film, we better mosey.'

'Oh, what are you two going to see?'

'The new Woody Allen.'

'Well, I better get a wiggle on, I've got your address, Kate, I'll pop that stuff into the post. Enjoy the film.'

We watched Frances merging into the Tottenham Court Road crowd. Tom finished the food on both our plates as I wrapped up for the cold night.

'She seemed nice. Colleague?'

'No. She's a private detective.'

'Cool. What she want?'

'It's "private".'

———

Before

'Darling! You wouldn't believe they've just had to call off Wimbledon because of the rain. Daddy came home especially for the match and now he's off to the garden centre. Don't tell me it's gorgeous where you are! Have you met your friend, the titled one?'

'There's been a change of plan.'

'A what?'

I fed in my last coin which gave me another thirty seconds.

'My money's running out.'

'What on earth are you doing on a payphone?'

'I can't phone abroad on my mobile – look, I'll be back tonight. Can you pick me up from the airport? Gatwick. It's the BA flight, coming in 22.35.'

After four consecutive beeps, she asked, 'Is David with you?'

'I've got to go – can you collect me?'

'Well, of course! But are you all right?'

'Please, tonight. Can you?'

Beeps.

I put the phone down and picture Mum standing in our hall, our dog, Biscuit, lying asleep on the landing, Dad plodding down the aisles of the garden centre with the rain tapping on the glass roof. Gradually the sharpness of my picture dulled and I dragged my case outside where the sun seared my skin. I took a few steps before I felt a hand on my shoulder.

'Let me.'

You took my case in exchange for a chilled bottle of cold water.

I walked beside you, unable to think of anything to say. My cerebrum was hard-boiled and polite conversation went up in smoke. We walked down a small hill together and over a main road. On the other side, we stopped, shared the water.

I looked up at the stranger again, but you didn't look at me, just straight ahead. It gave me a little time to admire you. And I did. *He's so handsome*! I thought, wishing I had some knowledge of how to deal with people like you: desirable, confident, adventurous – people you feel alive with. Then you caught my eye, raised an eyebrow to check I'd seen enough and we continued walking. I wondered if we should be talking, if I were being unappreciative by not asking about the population density of Provence or the annual rainfall in Aix, but then, I thought, you weren't saying anything either.

'This is just so beautiful!' I stopped in front of a sculpted sandstone façade. 'You from here?'

'I'm from all over.'

The dimples on either side of your lips gave the effect of a smile, but twice over.

The town hall's clock shifted into position, 1.45pm. Men were spraying down the cobbled streets to wash away remnants of that morning's market.

We sat on the edge of yet another little fountain, letting the spray hit our backs.

'Your friends left?'

'Yes.'

'You eaten?'

'No, no I haven't.'

'Come, I know a restaurant you would like. Don't worry, my treat.'

I'd followed a strange man into town, surely it wouldn't be right to accept lunch with him? But wherever you were, that's where I wanted to be. I wanted to keep looking at you and hearing your voice, I was already addicted to those moments when the heat made us lose our balance and we brushed our bodies against each other. But wasn't the vertiginous thrill a warning that there would be a deep drop down?

I was a little afraid of you. Always have been. The sensible part of me kept reminding myself that I was being shepherded around a new place by a man whose name I didn't even know: I could imagine how a cross-examination would play out: 'And could you tell the court precisely why you gave this complete stranger your rucksack and followed him down shady streets to have lunch?' – 'Your Honour, he had such beautiful eyes.'

'You know, that's really kind of you but I think I should be–'

'As you like.'

'No, I'd really like to, but–'

I tried to keep the squeak out of my voice and come up with a reasonable argument against having a meal with someone I'd only just met.

'It's not far.'

With that settled, we reached a side street where you led me into a lively restaurant. I watched your hand rest on the door as you pushed it open. Then you turned to me.

'Look, before we go in, tell me your name?'

'Katherine Brenton. Kate.'

'Marc.'

You walked to the middle of the restaurant where you were greeted by the waiters and someone who seemed to be the owner. We were seated and each handed a menu. I looked at mine – the prices rather than the dishes. None of it made any sense and, without asking, you closed my menu.

'I'll decide for you.'

I was to come to that restaurant a few years later, and I was to meet with the owner again, but it was to answer all the questions that I should have asked there and then.

'Would we be doing this if you hadn't left three years ago?'

'Of course, why not?'

I look at you from the furrow of your shoulder.

'Because we'd probably have bought a house – outside the centre of London where we could afford a garden and a few bedrooms – we'd have had to stay inside because of gun crime and teenage vandals, we'd have had a child – probably two – we'd be working, looking after kids, tired a lot of the time, spending afternoons in playgrounds trying to prevent our children from harming themselves or others, not able to afford babysitters, resenting the other person if they seemed to be doing anything but making money or looking after the children. Sally said that every time she looks at Paul all she thinks about are the odd jobs in the house he could be doing – so how could it be like this? I see it all the time, once you have children, you can't just grab a bottle of wine and go to bed for a few hours.'

'So we wouldn't be able to make love in the afternoon, but children, it doesn't have to be terrible, if so, people wouldn't have them. I have an idea.'

'What?'

'Why don't we meet again, like it's the first time?'

'Uh-huh…'

'Get out your sexiest dress, your heels, lipstick – let's go dancing! It's Saturday night!'

'What about The Nadir?'

'Okay. I'm gonna pick you up, at the bar, midnight. You don't know me.'

'You're right there, Marc. I don't know you.'

And we've asked the question, if we met again, as we are now, would we still want to spend the rest of our lives together?

Sally believes that marriages should be on seven-year renewable contracts. She said that as we change so much over the years, why spend most of our life trying to force an ever-angular square peg into a round hole. If it fits, it fits, but checks have to done for quality assurance purposes.

I know more about you than I'm letting on. I didn't play games with you in the beginning, but I am now.

Before

What did I know about you that lunch, in Aix? Nothing! And because you talked honestly, I thought you were being honest. I thought you were telling me all about you: that you'd no family, you lived to cook, you were ambitious. Your life was arranged around the seasons, you loved Eastern food, mimosas in February and jazz. You'd travelled everywhere. You'd trained in London, learnt English from Beatles songs and Spanish from a year working in Granada. Life was for enjoying, you said, and that was a new one for me. I was so impressed. You were unlike anyone I'd ever met. So it didn't occur to me that you were, essentially, telling me nothing by telling me what I wanted to hear.

You seemed fascinated by me: asking questions, clarifying details, cross-checking names like you were cramming for an exam. You couldn't have had any idea what it was like to be me, to come from a family of protestant academics, people whose notion of a racy evening was eating in the living room in front of *Inspector Morse*. It must have taken you seconds to see the young doctor with the short sensible haircut was a gentle girl, studious, and calming for your prismatic brain. That her heart had four distinct chambers: one for family, one for work, one for friends and another – vacant for you.

When the lunch ended and you lit a cigarette, you asked if I'd like to go to a secret cove in the Calanques. I had to say no, I was heading home. I told you about my changed flight. You were quiet, and then said it was a shame, you had so much you wanted to show me. Neither of us hid our disappointment. You asked, 'Tell me, if you hadn't changed your flight, would you have come with me now?'

I didn't hesitate. 'Yes.'

You put your hand over mine.

We spent the rest of the afternoon together – you wanted to buy me my first macarons – until it was time for me to leave for Marseille airport. You wanted to come all the way with me but I insisted that I wanted to remember you in Aix, that afternoon, the day we had.

The coach station was just a large road with bus stops along it. We'd arrived late and the bus headed for the airport was already filling up.

'I'll keep the coach here, buy your ticket there.'

I bought my ticket at the office, all the while, watching you from the windows.

'I don't want to go now,' I said, as the coach driver flicked his cigarette to the ground.

You stroked my cheek and held my face in one hand while the other circled my waist.

'Thank you for lunch, the coffees, macarons, the ice cream, the insider's tour. *Everything*. I loved today.'

I struggled with the sadness that it was soon going to be over and I might never see you again. I added, meaning every word, 'Because of today, this has been the best holiday ever.'

As the last of the passengers climbed on, you asked, 'Would you like me to kiss you?'

I wanted more than anything to have you kiss me, to touch you and have our friendship confirmed, to know that you wanted me and wanted to move into something private, romantic, memorable. I wanted it more than the embarrassment of answering, 'Yes. I would like you to kiss me.'

You looked into my face as a couple of breathless British women flagged down the driver and lumbered onto the bus.

I was still waiting for my kiss. You moved your fingers over my lips, brought your mouth to my ear and whispered, 'No, Katherine. You are not ready for me to kiss you. I will come for you when it is the right time. *Et tu seras ma femme.*'

I knew enough French to translate *femme* as meaning either woman or wife. I didn't understand what had happened. The coach's engine started up. I could see the driver looking into his rear-view mirror, preparing to pull out.

I stepped onto the bus, found my seat but when I looked out for you, you'd gone.

The coach began rolling onto the motorway away from the bus station, Aix and you. I strained my neck round to see you once more, to reassure myself it was all real, my modern-day highwayman, the man who nearly made me beg for his kiss and who decided at the last minute, that no, I wasn't quite ready.

But the coach and the plane, my family and my work,

friends and new routines were like quicksand, swallowing up those hours and the moment you robbed me of.

Before

'Don't look now... not now... no... Now look!! Who's the brunette right behind you? Tall, thin, all in black...'

'My sister, Kate,' whispered Anna.

'Good God! I thought you had a *little* sister.'

'She is a *little* sister. Only twenty-eight. A *doctor*.'

'Hmm, certainly all grown up now.'

I'm thinking back to October 2007, the evening of my brother-in-law's book launch, five months after you'd gone. The cast of Anna's and Nick's lives were placed like an assorted mix of deluxe chocolates around two hired rooms in the Royal Geographical Society building. The major roles were obviously parents from both sides, hers all the way from their 1930s semi-detached in Oxford, and Nick's, a short taxi ride from Mayfair. And maybe it was the weather or the guest list or genuine interest in Nick's adventures in Vanuatu, but the gathering was sprouting a surprising capacity for fun and daring that they had thought the years had cemented over. You can still enjoy yourself in your forties, they discovered, it just costs more.

Nick's literary bashes acted as plot points for the developmental stages of their lives. His first book had stimulated envy. Straight out of Oxford, Nick was already published and married when most of his peers were searching for rent money and uncomplicated sex. His second arrived with their friends' first weddings and an increase in London's property prices.

After a five-year hiatus, he wrote his third book recounting his year in a Nicaraguan rainforest. This coincided with the second crop of babies and first grey hairs sprouting from the heavier bodies of distracted parents. 'Crap sales figures,' Anna told us over Sunday lunch. His fourth and most successful book was received by fewer friends: business trips, flaky babysitters, fewer people lived in London – by then there'd been deaths, divorces as well as awards, promotions, and extra-marital affairs. And tonight? They'd made it. Anna could tick off names of celebrities among their entourage: editors, politicians, CEOs, faces from TV – not many of the original couples remained, but what many had lost in their personal lives, they had gained professionally. Did their friends really look like the middle-aged people they were becoming? Anna had asked me earlier. I said, no, not at all, some of them looked just as they always had – although it had probably required time with personal trainers, cosmetic intervention and foregoing desserts. Anna had said that this launch marked a renewed interest in travel, philosophy, culture – and *love!* Imagine, all that again. This was, Anna said, the last-chance saloon for anyone who wanted to test just how fucked-up another human being could get us.

'See, Katie,' she said, slurring a little. 'People go on about the mid-life crisis being about getting *old,* but it's not – it's absolutely not – it's suddenly realising you are *young!'*

Talk about the future terrified me. I was taking life on a minute-by-minute contract.

'So does little sister have some hulking surgeon around who'll slice me up with a scalpel if I try to arrange a full examination?'

'It's complicated,' I overheard Anna say.

'I'm all about complicated. Tell.'

'Her husband just upped and left this summer. Not a word.'

'Ouch.'

Bubbling over with champagne, Anna and Gideon didn't realise I could hear every word and feel them studying me from every perspective as if I were a painting they needed to parse out meaning from.

'My baby sister's been through hell – she might need cheering up.'

I was standing in front of one of Nick's photographs, a ruined Persian palace where a tribe of herdsman had built a makeshift village. I wondered if you were amongst the men in headscarves and sticks. You were getting away, interest in finding you was waning; new missing people had knocked you off your spot. The police no longer hid the fact that they thought I was naïve to the point of delusional. Gone were the smirks, the familiarity, even the irritation. They were not returning my calls. They had proper jobs to do, like looking for people who wanted to be found.

'Katie, this is Gideon. He's an art critic. Gideon this is Kate, my sister. Kate's a heart surgeon. I've just got to say hello to...'

'So you mend broken hearts?' asked Gideon. 'Bad joke. What made you specialise in the ol' ticker?'

'When I was little my father showed me a cross section of a heart diagram and I copied it over and over again. It was the only thing I could draw, so I stuck to that.'

'Gosh, I only ever drew pictures of cocks and boys pissing, what do you think that makes me?'

'A piss artist?'

I tried to move on.

'Course,' he continued, 'my heart's never been the same since your sister married Nick. Devastated I was, and the worst is, she's even more beautiful now, the post-birth *babushka* look's given her an earthy, raw sexuality...'

He appraised Anna as she laughed with a group of

girlfriends. 'She's always been the love of my life. So, you're her little sister! Well, I'd never have known that – not that you're not–'

Someone called my name as heads whirled like turbines to follow Tatyana as she crossed the room. Still as mesmerising as she'd been five years ago when I last saw her in the South of France, she clutched me to her, then, turning to Gideon, she said, 'Hi, I'm Tatyana Davenport,' as if that explained everything.

'Tatyana, I'm Gideon Bradshaw. We've actually met a few–'

'I haven't seen Kate for so many years, do you mind?'

And with that she led me away from Gideon, sat me down and took me by the hands.

'Katie, I really hoped you were here. I never go out, I'm virtually a recluse these days. I only just got off the plane from LA a few hours ago but I had to see you. It's so freaky, I even dreamt about you last night.'

Tatyana said all this while keeping one hand on me and lighting a cigarette with the other.

'Anna told me about your husband.'

A security guard came over and said that if she wanted to smoke, she'd have to go outside.

The night had brought in the indifferent winter chill, and I found it so hard to accept that the season was changing without you. Tatyana's voice took me back to that last night in France. There had been a time before you. Hearing her again was like opening a book and seeing notes in the margin, at some point it must have been important but I'd forgotten why.

'From next week I'm going to change my life completely. I'm doing this deep spiritual cleansing course in Sante Fe and my personal guide recommended that I mend as many rifts as I could before I start. Darling Katie, you were one of the first people on my list.'

'I don't have any bad feeling towards you, or Dave.'

'You know he went completely mad – began stalking and threatening me – my family had to get a restraining order against him. It was hideous. But I deserved it because I'd done a terrible thing to you.'

'Don't be silly, it's all forgotten.'

She clasped her arms around my neck. 'Friends again! And now, what about you?'

Even Tatyana, whose life made up a frieze of extraordinary events couldn't top the last year of mine. She listened, her eyes wide with incredulity.

'You know what you need? Ayahuasca. No, really. Come with me to New Mexico. It's a retreat run by shamans who trained at MIT and they've developed this software program that can read your karmic imprint to overwrite your destiny.'

'Sounds very interesting, but my job is all that's keeping me going at the moment.'

'Is there anything I can do, babe?'

'There is. I've got loads of posters and pictures of Marc – when you go to the States, could you post them up for me?'

'Done.'

Tatyana followed me to my car where I gave her as many flyers about you as could fit in her designer handbag.

'And, Katie, something for me?'

'What?'

'Nick's my favourite cousin. I worry so much about him. I can't say any more but... will you keep an eye on him?'

'On Nick?'

'I've got to be at Quaglino's at nine. *Bisous*!'

So it was thanks to Tatyana that your search went transatlantic.

Saturday Night

I arrive at The Nadir before you. The club is run by your friend Johan, but what you don't know is that it's not new to me. One of the first things I did when you disappeared was seek out all your friends, colleagues and the places you went. Because these people knew you, because they missed you too, we've become close. So when Johan sees me, it is not as great a shock as when he will see you.

'Kate! You're coming to the opening of my new club in New York – it's going to be the party of the year – right in the middle of fashion week. Fly over, bring Tom. You look divine – who are you with?'

I grip Johan's arm.

'Marc.'

'Hmm, darling?'

'Marc. He's back.'

Johan waves the voices around him down. They obey.

'Marc? Back?'

'A few days ago. He won't say where he was, won't say anything, really. But he had this idea we try to start again, meet each other like for the first time – so here we are.'

'Hey, doctor lady, don't let him hurt you again.'

'He's never stopped hurting me.'

'Does he know that you know about Yasmeen?'

'He won't talk, so I won't talk. I'm going to get a drink, if you see him–'

'I'm gonna punch him, darling, he's worth breaking a nail over.'

'Don't. Let's just play this one out. Revenge is a dish–'

'–that'll give him horrible food poisoning and, yah, I did just have a manicure.'

Before

I stood on the corner of Exhibition Road watching the taxi take Tatyana away. There, I'd come to the end of my first party without you. This was the part I was dreading. Going home alone. We would have gone to dinner, or maybe walked back through the park. What was I supposed to do with myself now? Turning back to say my goodbyes, I saw Nick huddled in the doorway.

As I passed him I heard him say, 'Listen ... No! I've been trying to see you all day. Why didn't you ... messages? No. I can't get away ... I told you, this bloody book event. Just wait for me. I've got to ... Okay, okay...'

'Have I signed you a copy, Kate?' Nick asked, as I kissed my parents goodbye. 'Here. Might be worth a fortune in a few years, eh?' He took his book off a nearby pile. *To Kate,* he wrote, and then stopped. He didn't know whether or not to write in Marc's name. For the last two years most of my Christmas cards, postcards, presents had all been addressed to Kate and Marc – at which point do they take your name off?

'To Kate – fuck I don't know what to say.' He waited, pen in air. 'When I look at you, all my problems seem so bloody ridiculous.'

'I didn't know you had any problems.'
He wrote:

> *To Kate,*
> *Never any more,*

While I live,
Need I hope to see his face,
As before.
Once his love grown chill,
Mine may strive:
Bitterly we re-embrace,
Single still.
All love, Nick XXX.

'I hope he's not making you pay for it!' Anna giggled over my shoulder.

I read the lines. 'I don't get it.'

Nick shuffled about.

'Browning. I thought–'

And before finishing his sentence, Nick was led away by his agent.

I was left with my sister and felt angry at her. Something bad was happening in her life and she wasn't paying attention – she was the one who deserved these cryptic lines, not me.

'Fucking fab night,' she said, falling into me. Her breath smelt of apples and her hair was in the process of forming itself into animal shapes. I was sad and scared for my sister, but part of me was vindicated. I'd never thought Nick was fair or honest with Anna and now I'd proved myself right, but who was I to judge other people's husbands?

I was seventeen when Anna first brought Nick Davenport to our house for our traditional Sunday-roast lunch. We met this lanky, laconic boy, supercilious yet at the same time bashful, nervy, which I suspected was an affectation to make people even more indulgent to him than they already were. Every time he spoke, which wasn't often, my sister looked at us, beseeching her family to fully appreciate every syllable that came from his beaky mouth. No one had ever managed to impress Anna before, she'd always been the prize.

'Nick's godmother lives in a palace in Sri Lanka that has a hundred white peacocks on the lawn! His parents have a Turner and a first edition *Oliver Twist*. Do you know, he was kidnapped when he was at prep school?'

My parents made the appropriate 'Ooh's and 'Aaah's but Dad's always been highly suspicious of people who don't have jobs, as was the work status with Nick, or indeed anyone connected with him.

'I don't think Mum and Dad liked Nick,' said Anna on the phone that night when she'd got back to her digs. 'Did you?'

'He's very thin.'

'But he's got the most delicious cock: full of poetry, intelligence and–'

'Is that what he's going to write with in his finals?'

'I'm going to marry him.'

And that's what she did. She dropped ideas of a master's and put all her energy into organising a large, social and stylish wedding which was featured in *Tatler* – the first and only edition my parents ever bought. Anna and Nick travelled the world for nearly two years only stopping when she got pregnant, but Nick continued exploring, drug taking and found, to his surprise, that marriage had increased his sex appeal, especially if his lovers knew of Anna's reputation and wanted to score double points.

Fingertips brushed against my arm, I turned to see that friend of Anna's, Gideon.

'We got off to a rather bad start,' he announced.

'A bad end you mean.'

'It's only just gone ten, fancy a drink?'

'Not with you.'

'I'm a prat. Just got overly impressed by being around a beautiful woman who does life-saving surgery. Hey, I'm going to a club that's just opened. The Nadir. Come with?'

'I'm a married woman.'

'I thought he'd walked out on you?'

'Listen, you little freak,' I hissed in Gideon's ear while pinning both his shoulders against a parked van. 'He didn't *walk out*. Something's happened to him... something happened... something...' I whispered, loosening my grip as the power went from my arm muscles.

'Okay, okay, I get it – you all right?'

I fell to my knees, my ribs closing in on me, my skin freezing cold, clammy. My heart so loud I could barely hear the screeching of car brakes. Gideon hooked his arms under my shoulders and dragged me off the road. Gradually the strobe lights against my vision faded and I managed an even line of consecutive breaths.

'And I thought Anna was the mad one. Let's get you a drink,' Gideon said.

For the first twelve weeks after you'd left, I avoided people and chose to stay home in case you returned or got in touch, but when summer was over, I changed my strategy: I was going out to look for you.

I'd heard you talk about this club – you often went out

dancing after work – and I remember you mentioning the owner, Johan. It was a start.

'Want a toot?' asked Gideon.

He took me into the unisex toilets, which were made of glass and mirrors for the ease of snorting drugs. I copied what I'd seen you doing occasionally with your friends and waited to feel what you must have felt sometimes.

You loved dancing; for you it was like other people going to the pub or jogging around the block. Often we'd be sitting in front of the TV and you'd say, 'Let's go dance.' And we did. When I first met you, I wasn't at all used to this idea – I'd always needed a few days' warning and several drinks before hitting the dance floor. I remember confessing to you that I was embarrassed by the way people exhibited their sexuality to music – wriggling and writhing, thrusting their genitals at strangers – you looked at me quizzically: 'But that's the point, *mon coeur*, a person's sexuality, it's for everybody – sex, ah, that's just for one person.'

Back on the dance floor, Gideon shook his body like he was being electrocuted but he still couldn't keep up with me. I was sharing my sexuality with anyone who wanted a piece; see, Marc, what I'd learnt from you?

'Gideon, d'you think Nick's having an affair?' I shouted over the music.

'They have an open marriage, what d'you expect? Anna's madly in love with some married man anyway, she's always got someone hanging about.'

'She never told me that...'

I was worried about Anna, but I was desperate about you – it didn't cross my mind to put the two together.

'Gideon, I want to meet the man who runs the club... Johan? Introduce me.'

'I've never met him – I mean, I don't know–'

'You're a journalist. Find out.'

Forty-five minutes later Gideon returned to where I was sitting on a banquette upstairs talking to someone.

'Kate, all I've found out is that Johan is some Arab-German poof who doesn't talk to anyone unless they're in the *Forbes* 30 *Under* 30. So can't help with that one. Another drink?'

'Gideon, meet Johan.'

Gideon mumbled something and slunk back to the toilets.

'You see, darling, why I don't do interviews? Those people!'

'Tell me something, Johan. *Anything.*'

'If I knew anything, darling, I would. I loved Marc too – really. Sometimes he came here, late, after work, we'd have such a great time – having a good time, it's an art form with some people, and he was a maestro, eh?'

Johan dabbed a tear from each eye.

'Did he need money? Did he take drugs? Were there women?'

'Marc was a professional, worked hard, played hard. One night he DJed for us! Yah. One of the best nights here. He was a crazy guy, but to just disappear... no one could believe it. And that he would leave you! Especially you. He was uxorious! Always talking about his doctor wife. Hand on heart, I never saw him show attention to a particular woman or man. Never. He had every opportunity. He flirted, he teased, yah. Maybe because he could play at lovemaking, he didn't need to go outside for it. He was a romantic, honourable.'

'So where is he?'

Gideon brought me a drink and stationed himself by my feet like a whippet.

'I don't know.'

'Johan, anything... ?'

'Okay, darling, there was something, but...'

'It doesn't matter how silly.'

'The last night I saw him, it must have been April, there was a woman here, red hair, French, I saw them talking – they were arguing. I could tell she was upset. It's not... particularly revealing, yah? But he didn't say goodbye to me that night. And that was the last time. He didn't say goodbye.'

Johan and I held each other before I turned to Gideon and said, 'You can take me home now.'

After that night, I went in pursuit of men who resembled you. It wasn't running away from you, but towards you. I was reinforcing my fidelity, my rage and a loneliness that caused me to pound my head against the bedroom walls for hours. I'd go out after work with the nurses and junior doctors, we'd go clubbing, drop some Ecstasy tabs, then I'd pick the man who looked most like you. And something would happen. It made me feel better and worse at the same time – but it made me feel something. And I needed to be desired, to show you that other people wanted what you didn't. You would have seen me in a club, and you wouldn't have liked what you saw, and that was a way of getting your attention, even if it was only imagined. Very seldom did I see the same man more than three times, and it was always just for sex, and some of them were nice, Marc, some of them thought they were in love, and I hurt them, just to pass on the infection you gave me.

SUNDAY

Sunday Morning

After a stroke, it's not uncommon to lose your memory. Forget how to tie your shoelaces, what a toothbrush is for, your home address and how to get into an orange. And then you meet your family: someone you apparently married, children that claim you, friends who assume your trust. They ask questions, and another person answers back. Over the days, the weeks, you get to know each other again, tentatively, politely, biting one's tongue and leaving the room before outbursts. Strangers become part of one's intimate life: and sometimes a love develops, and sometimes it doesn't. But whatever passes between you, it isn't what it was before.

I have my memory – it's all I have left. We are not what we were.

It's Sunday and neither of us opens our eyes to see what we have dragged into our bed. Even in your sleep, your hand circles my buttocks as though shining up a piece of furniture – or is it to check if I have scales?

And last night you wanted a new love to develop, but I am not what I was before. Did you think I would be packed up in ice, stored away, my life suspended while you dallied and dithered about coming home to me? No, I took what was left and sprouted a different thing, a new Kate who you are only just beginning to meet.

'On your own?'

I refrained from giving you a sarcastic one-liner and answered, 'Yes.'

'Can I buy you a drink?'

'Vodka and tonic, please.'

You leant in front of me with a fifty-pound note. I wondered where you'd got it from – but let the game go on.

'Do you like Techtronic music?' you asked.

'Not until I take one of these.'

We shared an Ecstasy tab, searched for something to say worth the strain of shouting over the music.

A warm hand on my back.

'Is this man bothering you?' Johan kissed me on the lips.

'Johan, do you remember Marc?'

You clasped one another, punching each other's arms.

'Not seen you lately, Marc? Where've you been?'

'All over. This is my wife, Katherine.'

'I know your wife. I've been looking after her for the last three years. There are ten people on the permanent guest list – and one of them is Kate. She comes here... a lot, yah? She's coming to my opening in New York in two weeks – the new club – it's going to be crazy. January Jones, Brad Pitt, Madonna... Everybody.' And with that, Johan was needed downstairs.

You frowned, genuinely surprised, 'You come here?'

'Weekends, if I'm not working. Follow me.'

I walked into the toilets where there was a crowd, some of who knew me. I snorted a few lines of cocaine with them, laughed a little with a Brazilian ladyboy I sometimes dance with. You stood behind me, watching. You didn't join in. When I finished, I pushed you into a toilet cubicle. With your back to me, I lifted your shirt, moved my breasts against your back, unbuckled your belt, your jeans. I turned you to me, kissed down from your navel, licking the salt off your skin. Dropping to my knees, I curled my tongue around your balls, slid your cock in and out of my mouth. From my pocket, I took out a black surgical latex tube. You caught my wrist with your hand.

'Katherine, what are you doing?'

'This is what I do with people I first meet,' I snarled at you. Someone banged on the door. You pulled up your trousers, shaking your head at me.

'You think you can shock me? You think I'll be impressed with this?'

You flicked the cannula in my fingers.

'I just wanted you to see–'

'I've seen enough.'

'But we haven't even started.'

'Katherine, all I see is that you've confused pleasure with happiness. Let's go.'

We walked through the West End, hand in hand, fast enough to counter the night's frost, but not too fast that we are tired. We set a good pace, you and me.

Passing the Ritz Hotel, we walked alongside Green Park. Peering through the bars into the darkness between trees, you said if my shoes hurt we could get a cab, but outside was easier where there wasn't any pressure to talk, and walking across London fit our situation, because we too were crossing from what was to what is. Safety in numbers. Couples passed us, and we could have been any of them, and I was relieved about that because grief makes you feel like such a freak, I really had begun to wonder.

'You always talked to me like you were such a brave, worldly man, someone who thought about things and made considered, balanced judgements. And yet you weren't like that at all. The hypocrisy! You were too scared to tell me you wanted to leave. Those first few days, you must have known I would have thought you might be dead or hurt. I can't describe the anguish. The unbearable, violent pain – and all you had to do was text!

That's what I can't forgive – not that you left, but how you did it.'

'Because when I first met you, at the hospital, I thought if I could love this girl, and she could love me, all would be right... and yet... I was living a lie because you didn't know me, so I wanted you to know me, to really experience what I'm capable of.'

'Once I knew that, Marc, it was very unlikely I'd take you back... so what was the point?'

'Suicide was too easy, too kind, so I found a worse punishment for myself – killing the part of my life that I wanted the most: you.'

'But why, why all this suffering?'

'You didn't find out why?'

Because you couldn't break a promise to Yasmeen.

Before

There was the day after, two days after, the first week, month, first birthday and Christmas, New Year and then a year, that day, June 6th, the day you'd left.

That date had been waiting ahead of me like an expectant crowd at the gallows. I'd worked the night before at the hospital and it started with the journey of slow-rolling tears down each side of my temple. Hot, airless, in the little doctor's stay-over room with grey nylon curtains and sticky-lino floor. My hairline was wet and itchy, my eyes stung and my nose was blocked. Is that all I had to show after a year without you?

That day last year I'd had a husband next to me and for some reason, I'd hoped that you'd have been there beside me again. If clocks could go backwards and forwards an hour at the season's change, why not one year?

I showered. With the warm water running over me, it was the best place to cry. I dressed in black, had two strong coffees in the doctors' staffroom, a short spell on the PC to check any emails and hit the wards.

I moved through each second of that day as if flicking through snapshots of that time last year. Each breath, corridor, conversation was like a reconstruction of the day one year before. Every time I had to write down the date I felt the earth turning its full 360 degrees, 365 days and 8,760 hours since you'd been missing. I didn't want it to turn anymore – I wanted to remember that fifty-two weeks before, I'd expected you home. A year ago that day, you were my life because you were in it, not out of it: only one year ago – it was almost close enough to grab hold of and pull through.

I followed in the shoes of my former self, the married self, the one who started so many sentences with, 'Marc and I...' That time last year I'd had lunch at the sandwich bar, a prawn cocktail sandwich, and that's what I had a year later, each mouthful a toll bringing me closer to the inevitable. I'd had a triple-espresso coffee in 2007 and, having been awake all night, needed to do the same – the taste was just as revolting.

The afternoon passed like most and at 5.30pm I finished for the day, but continued for another hour writing up notes and checking up on the patients I didn't see earlier. I'd just collected my things from the stay-over room when Callum came in and dropped his bag on the bed.

'Ah, home sweet home. *Not*.'

'Wasn't too bad last night...' I said lifting my rucksack over.

'That doesn't bode well for me... having said that, with a three-month-old baby at home, I get a better kip here.'

Carpe diem. Hold on to the one-year-after day. It hadn't

been so terrible. Not too bad at all. And was nearly over but for the night ahead, which I planned to spend alone. Sally and my sister had said I should do something to mark that date, but it was my grief, and what they didn't seem to understand is that you were not dead. It wasn't a matter of putting flowers on a grave or lighting candles; it wasn't about letting go but holding on.

I had thought that if it'd been a pleasant enough evening, I might go to Primrose Hill or feed the ducks at the Serpentine like we used to, but that evening was wet, dark and smelt like a dank cellar.

Perhaps I'd reread the emails, Post-it notes, cards that you'd written me over the years; maybe I'd go through your clothes; squirt some of your aftershave on my wrist – the one you saved for special occasions, and the one I used to take out and gasp at as a very, very last resort when I needed the only portal left to you.

The Central Line was down and I had to take three different Tubes home. The people on the train looked just as sick and tired, unhappy, and depressed as I did.

Walking down the Bayswater Road, there was little distinction between the colour of the paving stones and the colour of the sky about to burst open with rain. I walked as fast as I could but my feet hurt and my muscles were stiff from carrying my overnight bag. Anniversary of a disappearance or not, all I wanted to do was whack up the heating, watch a few episodes of *Prison Break* and drink white wine until I passed out. It was, after all, just another day.

Turning into my street I reached in my bag for my keys. I couldn't feel them. I moved my fingers over my wallet, diary, pens, scrunched-up pieces of paper. I opened and checked my washbag. They weren't there. When I heard the first crash of thunder, I was emptying my bag out onto the pavement. I checked my pockets, my briefcase, my bag again. Then I remembered the last time I saw my keys – on the bed when Callum put his things down.

I sat back onto my heels as the first drops of rain drummed on my things.

Maggie had keys to my flat so I pressed her bell, once, twice, again and again. No answer. Again and again. Nothing. I'd just have to wait for her or, if the rain let up a little, I could have trudged back to work and slept. I collapsed against the door, clinging on to my bag as if it were driftwood. The clouds shook out the rain like a box of pins. It scratched my face, my hands. I bundled up and cowered from it but the dam burst in me too. So this was where I'd ended up one year later.

I was aware of a dark shape moving over me, blocking out the streetlights – I looked up, heard human sounds but couldn't catch distinct words over the sound of cars sawing through the puddles.

'... you ... for ... one?'

I thought, this is how I am going to die, battered to death on my doorstep on the anniversary of your disappearance. I pressed myself into the wall hoping my attacker would be quick.

'Are you waiting for someone?' His face levelled with mine, hidden inside a hood. It occurred to me that maybe I was at the wrong house. Maybe I'd been going to the wrong house every day for the last year, and you were at home all the time looking for me.

'Are you waiting for someone?'

'My husband,' I said, looking around for witnesses.

'Okay.' He scratched his nose where the rain tickled and took out a bunch of newly cut keys.

'Wanna wait inside?'

It hurt to unlock my joints and stand up again. He waited with the door ajar, holding my bag. The door banged behind us and the boy turned on the lights.

'That's better.'

I could feel cold, minty droplets snaking into my neck. My shoes squelched as I tried to see if I could move my toes but there was no sensation in my feet.

When he opened the door to his flat, we were both blasted by the heat and heady smell of perfumed candles.

'You live here?'

'Yup.'

I'd forgotten all about the first floor to the building. As long as I'd known it, no one had lived here, at one point there'd been developers working on it and then nothing, even before you left.

'Chuck your stuff down anywhere.'

I was afraid of getting the parquet floor wet so I shivered by the door looking at all that space.

'It's a little bare, I know, I only just moved in y'see. I'm Tom, by the way.'

'Kate.'

'So you live upstairs?' Tom pressed a switch and a galaxy of halogen lights glowed above our heads. 'I thought there was a doctor there... okay, got it. You're the doctor. Cool. We should've met before... not like this. I'm rubbish about all that stuff.'

There was nothing in his flat, just a telephone and an enormous plasma TV with a 1930s club leather armchair placed directly in front of it.

I looked at my new neighbour with his soft skin and Labrador brown eyes. He couldn't have been more than twenty-two.

'When are your parents coming back?'

'Huh?'

'Your parents, are they away or... ?'

Tom laughed. 'My parents live in Wales. Abergavenny. No, they wouldn't come to London for anything... especially me.'

'I thought this flat was empty.'

'It was. I bought this place over two years ago but never had the time to move in. The record company found someone to do it up, one of those minimalist people, so it's a bit... *minimal*. I'd just come back from ordering some furniture and stuff to fill it when I saw you. How long have you lived here, Doc?'

'Since 2005. Record company, are you a musician?'

'Yup.'

'What do you play?'

His turn to laugh.

'I don't, it's all...' He wiggled his fingers. 'Machines. I do clubs, private parties. Mixing, mash kind of stuff.'

'Silly me. Like you imagining that Dr Brenton was an old man with whiskers and a white coat.'

'Busted!' He laughed. 'You know, it's funny cos when I saw this place there was another flat I liked in Shoreditch but my manager insisted I buy this one because there was a doctor living in the building – he thought I'd be safer!'

'Ah, and here you are, looking after me,' I said.

He put his hand on a radiator and beckoned me to stand by it.

'Well, now I know the heating works. Shouldn't need it in June but there you go.'

'Am I keeping you from anything?'

'Not at all. I should offer you something to drink but I haven't had time to do a food shop – stay, I'll just run out and get us something. What's your poison?'

'But it's pouring.'

'It's not a problem, I need my Starbucks fix anyway. Hot chocolate? Skinny latte with caramel? I'll be back in a minute – make yourself at home.'

I started peeling off my steaming clothes, spreading them over the radiator. Would it be taking advantage to go to the bathroom in search of a towel for my hair? I took my shoes off, padded around trying not to drip on the glassy floor in search of the bathroom.

I found his bedroom. It was only a little smaller than the living room and done up in shades of white and beige around a bed the size of my living room. There was hardly any sign that anyone lived there apart from three suitcases at the end of the room. Leading off was a bathroom, which looked like it hadn't been used either – nor had the piles of white springy towels resting on warm radiators. I took one and started soaking up the rain from my hair. I tiptoed to my bag, took out my brush and collection of creams and moisturisers, samples I'd collected from shops and the insides of magazines, a system I'd found to lighten my bag as well as economise.

It was still pouring, the sky looked like it had a giant barcode stamped across it, then, on Tom's balcony, in the rain, was a scrunched-up packet of Marlboro Reds, your lighter and a bottle of Sancerre.

'Only me!' said Tom, lowering his hood and shaking off the rain. 'This is my first night in for... I don't know how long. To tell you the truth, I was getting a little creeped out being here on my own. I'm used to having lots of – what's occurring?'

'Where did these come from?'

'No idea.'

'These?'

'I don't smoke, never have, not very rock 'n' roll, but... they could be anybody's!'

'Who has keys to this flat?'

'Oh, quite a few people, actually. See, I've not been here for–'

'Who has keys to this flat, exactly?'

'My manager, Bill; the decorator, the builders, my PA, Skye, that's her name. Probably her assistant. And a mate of mine from home, and the French chap who lives upstairs. Might be others, too.'

The room spun around me. 'Who upstairs?'

'Listen, I don't like smoking much either, dirty habit. But as long as people do it outside, it's their lungs, though I imagine as a doctor...'

'What Frenchman upstairs?'

'I know it's irresponsible but it's not like there's anything to nick! One advantage of minimalism, eh? Hey, relax! Your drink.'

'The French guy.'

'Yeah. What? Oh him. Well, after I bought the flat I came round one day to meet with the decorator, see. I ran into the man who lives upstairs; we chatted and he suggested taking my keys in case I needed anything delivered or if there was an emergency... nice neighbour, I thought, it's what they do, isn't it?'

'Where is he?'

'Never seen him since. I said, I only arrived today.'

'When did you give him your keys?'

'I don't know, last year some time? What's the matter?'

'He was here... he was here... he was here all the time.'

Since Christmas, if I'm not working, I've spent Sundays with either my family or Anthony's and sometimes, if his brother's family couldn't host lunch, his mother would come to my parents'. We'd probably be on our way there now, if I wasn't all tangled up in bed with you.

You and I used to spend Sundays together, at home. We chose to be together because we wanted that more than spending time with anyone else. Doing nothing, like this, being warm, wrapped up, touching, kissing, saying any rubbish that came into our heads, was my favourite way to spend the weekend. Making plans, changing plans, finding different things that we found pleasurable. On Mondays, when colleagues exchanged their weekend stories, I couldn't think what to say. I'd be so relieved if we'd seen a film or an exhibition – something I could talk about. But usually we hadn't left the flat, the bed even.

You move, get up and return bringing me a glass of water. After a few sips I start talking, it comes out in a croak and I've a splitting headache but I need to talk.

'When I first introduced you as my boyfriend everyone was thrilled. They thought you were great. But when I said we were getting married they were shocked. They said I was making a terrible mistake. No one approved of you, you know. My family didn't think you were "husband material".'

'Remember our wedding?'

Of course I do. We married in July at Anna's old college. It was a simple, beautiful day, and whatever reservations anyone had about you evaporated in the blue sky above the flowers in full multicoloured bloom. It might sound corny or clichéd, but that day, I felt reborn. Every time I looked at you, I fell in love with you, over and over.

'Since you left, I've looked through our wedding photos trying to find a sign that you weren't happy or that you were looking for a getaway car, but both of us looked so sure, in love. Had I missed something? Did you know then?'

'No, I loved our wedding too. It was great, eh?'

My eyes moisten. The expectations, the hope, maybe it's too much for any couple to live up to.

You lift the glass as though toasting the two newlyweds we once were.

'The night before we married, remember I cooked that meal for all your family and guests? Your brothers came into the kitchen and said there was an issue about seating. Richard explained that in the church, the bride's family and friends sit to the left and the groom's on the right, but they couldn't do this because I had "no people". You know your family – they hate to do things differently.'

True, particularly Richard, my older brother.

'I said people could sit where they wanted, it wouldn't be a problem for you. Eddie then said, "Yes, well it may not be a problem for Kate now, but it might be in a few years".'

'You never told me that.'

'I tried that night when I said, "Katherine, I am not like the kind of husband your friends and family want for you," and you said you were marrying me, not them.'

'No, Marc, I said I was prepared for anything as long as we faced it together and then you left me.'

'I believed you were better off without me.'

'What more could I have done to prove to you how much I loved you?'

'Maybe this. Being here now, taking me back, making a life starting from the truth.'

'What happened to for better or worse? Couldn't you have taken my word for it?'

'Eddie was right. All the people who warned you about me

were right. We were so different. I just didn't know how to deal with it all.'

'Tell me, tell me now, what happened that morning you left? Had you planned it or was it some sort of dissociative fugue?'

'A what?'

'You know, where people just wander off, forgetting who or where they are... it happens to some people, did that happen to you?'

'I didn't plan it if that's what you want to know. That morning, I was getting ready for work, after you left, and I was shaving and I stopped. I looked at myself in the mirror and I didn't know this man. Those last few weeks my past was coming back, people, memories... The lie I'd built about who I was, it was all falling apart. I wanted to tell you about me but I didn't want you to see me like that, how I really was. I didn't want to disappoint you. I dressed and I was about to go to work, and I just didn't go. I walked out. I believed I had made a mistake in marrying you.'

'Because you didn't love me?'

'No! No! Katherine, that was always true. I loved you – you're missing the point, *cherie* – it's *why* I left!'

'Of all the reasons I came up with for why you left, it never occurred to me that it was because you "loved" me so much. What do you take me for?'

'Think about it. It would hurt for a while, yes, I'm really sorry about that, but you had family, friends, your work. Eventually you'd get on with your own life, you'd get over me, find someone intelligent, balanced – I knew you would – or else what? No, listen, Katherine–'

You bring your eyes to mine. Your voice is firm and resounds from a part of you I've never heard before. 'Or else what? I could tell you everything I was ashamed of, bad things – horrible! – show you what a shit I was, what a liar, I could bring you into all my mess and the disasters I'd made around others. You are loyal and good, Katherine, and you would have felt obliged to stay, and maybe too proud or too sorry for me to leave – it didn't seem fair. That morning, I believed the best way was to go.'

'Didn't you care what would happen to me?'

'Of course I did. I watched you.'

'I know you stayed at Tom's.'

'Yes, I did. I watched until I knew you would be okay. And then I left to work it all out myself, give you space to make a life away from me.'

'So you were right. I did move on. I did find someone else who's interesting, intelligent, balanced and who loves me and wanted to share his life with me. And I stopped wondering where you were. So now I'm wondering, why the fuck did you come back? I mean, what kind of sadistic pain merchant are you?'

'You're free to decide.'

'Do you think I'm free when you've humiliated me and used me and I let you back so you can do it all again?'

You dip your finger in the water, then trace it around my heart. You lean against me and I feel your body against mine. I answer the question in the only way I can before we fall asleep again in each other's arms.

It's just like Sundays used to be, although this time, I know who I'm lying with.

Before

After France, I spent the rest of that summer working in my father's research lab in Oxford. As my friends returned from their holidays, my sorry romantic tale was circulated. Anna, who'd not gone on holiday because Nick was still in Libya camping out with Berber herdsmen, vented her frustration in a 'hate Dave' campaign. She lay on the dog's tartan blanket in the middle of the garden surrounded by her children, phones, books, and friends, forming a nucleus of gossip and loathing towards Dave who was reportedly back in London and hadn't got in touch with me, 'even to apologise!' shouted Anna down the phone at someone I'd never even met.

'Anna, I'm just not the kind of girl men feel that way about,' I argued, trying to assuage my sister's outrage.

'Bollocks!'

But when I said that about myself, it wasn't entirely to do with Dave. It was the way the Frenchman at the bus station had put his hand on my neck, run his thumb across my mouth and refused the goodbye kiss I'd waited for. '*I will kiss you, Katherine, but not now. You are not ready.*' This I kept to myself.

'Shall I tell you about men?' Anna asked. 'Men are only happy when they are unhappy.' She smacked her Plato's *Symposium* against her thighs. 'Read this – it'll teach you all about love.'

'I was thinking of taking up French actually.'

That August, Oxford was particularly hot and crowded with sweltering tourists and I was ready to leave for London and what my father laughingly called 'the killing season' – the months when Foundation House Officers begin and patient mortality goes up.

But it hadn't been what I'd imagined. Sally, whom I was supposed to be living with, had started seeing Paul, a student she'd met while island-trotting in Greece. He was at LSE and had his own flat where Sally spent most of her time. I was left with Ng, a Chinese student who rarely left his room, and Julie from Dublin who was always out of hers. Apart from a book group, which Anna had introduced me to, I was terribly alone. I worked hard and by the end of that first term, came top in our exams – the upside of wanting to be distracted from the flat's yellowing walls, the carpet worn through to the rubber lining, a half-collapsed seventies sofa that took over the front room like an obstinate drunkard and a kitchen that served no dietary purpose – no oven and only a warm fridge which came alive at night with rounds of explosive crackling. So whenever I had the chance, I went home where Mum fed me, left me to study and returned me to London with a full bag of clean, ironed clothes.

My parents knew what to expect from their child's next decade specialising in medicine, they'd been through it themselves and then with Richard, their eldest. But with me, they worried: they worried that I was too thin and lonely.

There were moments, such as on the coach heading home or wandering around the flat when it was empty, listening to music while washing up or braving the bath, when the little scenarios I scripted during the day turned into full-length two-hander performances between you and I. Marc, since the day we met, you'd taken my mind hostage. My thoughts followed the memories of your voice, the fixed blue stare of your eyes and the longing for your touch. Yet a part of me was relieved we were separated by a sea, that you were confined to my fantasy world as the real you had made me afraid. Sartre had said vertigo was not the fear of falling from a great height, but the fear of jumping. I wasn't afraid of you, I was afraid of me.

The weeks built into months; your image became even stronger in my mind. I hadn't said goodbye at all. I was waiting, and not that patiently.

Saturday, Oxford Street. The January sales. Sally's granny had sent her money for Christmas and she was shopping for a coat.

'Kate, do you want my opinion?'

'No,' I answered, standing in front of a mirror in a shop changing room.

'Tough. I find your entire appearance depressing.'

'Depressing?'

'And frustrating. Depressing and frustrating. There it is,' confessed Sally.

I prepared to defend myself, but in fact, I'd come to the same conclusion myself.

'But I don't look that awful, do I?'

'No, of course you don't look *awful* – you couldn't ever look awful. But you don't make anything of yourself. When we go shopping you spend ages deciding which clothes I should buy and when it comes to you, you just pick out the same navy-blue cardi from John Lewis. You dress like your mother.'

'But my mother buys my clothes!'

'Exactly.'

'Exactly what?'

'You dress like you're in some kind of menopausal camouflage gear – hiding yourself from anyone who might want to fumble with your bra strap.'

And again I was back in France, looking to the empty space where you'd been standing.

After bustling through the shoppers and queuing for ages in a café, we collapsed as soon as two seats were free.

'I hope I didn't upset you. It's a compliment really.'

'Right. And could you just run past me how it's a compliment?'

'I'm saying you're gorgeous, Kate – tall, slim, fantastic legs, cheekbones to die for – most people would kill to look like you but you just cover it all up in this kind of fashion asceticism which, in my opinion, is a waste of a very beautiful, feminine being.'

'Urgh!'

I tried to laugh it off, but the truth hit me. It wasn't just about clothes.

'You're pretty rude but, I guess, I don't look like a *woman*,' I said, infusing the word with as much irony as I could. 'It's because of Anna. It'd always been so important to my sister to be *the beautiful one* – to be adored – I never wanted to compete, I just let her have that glory unchallenged. Everyone in my family has their own particular characteristics: Richard's brilliant, Anna's beautiful, Eddie's quirky and I'm... reliable.'

'If you're happy with that.'

'I'm not. Sally, would you... would you give me one of those makeovers?'

'Topshop. Quick. Before you change your mind.'

That weekend Sally worked on my *look* and I was ready for you and that promised kiss.

Several weeks later, on a Monday morning, Mona took the crash bleeper from me as long, gluey strands of sunlight rolled down the corridor walls, along the skirting boards and through the queue of patient trolleys. It was spring, and I hadn't even noticed.

It was into my seventy-ninth hour of work that week – stupid to count the hours but competing over 'who'd done the most?' was a running game we played. I was winning having seen over sixty patients admitted since the Friday morning and had only managed to lie down in the vacuum-packed on-call room for two hours on Sunday morning before I had to tend to the aftermath of Saturday night's casualties. I wasn't really prepared for my first social conversation of the week.

'The weekends are just the bloody worst, aren't they?' sympathised Mona. 'Having said that, we spent the day in IKEA which wasn't that different from A&E. You look so pale, Kate, why don't you pop out and get us carrot cake for later. There's a lecture at lunchtime, we can scoff it down then. No time for proteins – let's cut straight to the glucose.'

I walked through the building in an etiolated daze, the adrenalin and caffeine were wearing off and my legs weren't moving the way I wanted them to. I nodded to a receptionist who was coming in after the weekend, deliberately avoiding eye contact with the patients queuing up. I stifled a yawn – something I was getting adept at – while picking up speed to get that cake to sneak into our compulsory pre-registration doctors' lecture on *Applying Stomach Drains*. After that, I'd be home until the following Thursday.

Outside the building, I listened to my phone messages. Sally: *the landlord's coming around to fix the broken window.* What broken window? Friends from Cambridge: *planning a reunion in a Soho wine bar on Tuesday night.* My mother: on and on. The voices came across like ever-dimming light waves from remote stars. My mother's message was an excitable ramble which I shut off before she'd even gathered momentum. The star receded a little further.

'Katherine?'

And you were standing in front of me. In the time it took to look at you, all the accumulated tiredness and hunger and need for natural light disappeared. I was wide awake, more awake than I had been in months, well, since the last I saw you.

'Remember, from France?'

'Marc.'

'Marc, yes.'

'How did you... ?'

'Your mother.'

'My mother? Oh.'

You looked so handsome in a soft black suit and black T-shirt with something scrawled in white on it that I couldn't read.

'I called your mother. We talked for a long time, now we are both worried about the long hours you do, your diet and not exercising enough. Interesting jacket, Katherine,' you said, looking at my doctor's coat.

My eyes were stinging and my hair filthy. So much for the makeover, the one time I wanted to stun you with my metamorphosis, there I was, exhausted in my M&S cosy-toes shoes, which I had promised Sally I'd thrown away.

'You were looking for me?'

'Of course. I told you we would see each other again. Remember?'

'Yes. How long have you been in London?'

'About three weeks.'

Your eyes sparkled with amusement. Your arms were crossed over your chest, like you were waiting for something.

'Aren't you happy to see me?'

'Yes, yes I am, of course.' I saw my cohort of junior house doctors congregating at the lift. 'How long you staying for?'

'This is my home now. I was offered a job and wanted a change. I thought, well, I know a good doctor in London, what more do I need? Are you free tonight? Good, so then it's your turn to come to my work – here.'

You gave me a card for the restaurant with your mobile number written on the back. I took it in my unsteady fingers. All sense of there being anything else in the world but you zapped into insignificance.

'It's good to see you again, Doctor. *À ce soir.*'

'Why don't I ever have patients like that?' someone asked as I stepped into the lift.

'He's a friend.'

We pushed ourselves up against the metal sides to make way for a family.

'Why don't I ever have friends like that?' someone else opined. 'And I thought you were all work and no play, Dr Brenton. I see you got his phone number.'

'And a dinner date,' I said, unable to control the spread of my grin.

'Dinner! The luck of it! I'm taking part in a study on pancreatic enzymes for the third year's research project. Digest that!'

Sunday, Midday

The intercom buzzes. My heart jolts into systolic overload while I run through the usual questions following a Saturday night at The Nadir: Who am I? Where am I? And, who's he?

Another buzz.

Most weekends when I wasn't on duty I'd go out, find someone who looked as much like you as possible and take them to my bed. On a good morning, the frogs leapt back into their ponds, but sometimes they flapped around croaking on and on until I returned them to the wild. This morning, you lie next to me, my prince is too hungover to stir.

I roll on tracksuit bottoms and socks, keep on the T-shirt I slept in and move as quickly and quietly as I can down the stairs. I can hear the rain outside like soft gunfire in the distance. The front door requires two hands to open against the wind.

Anthony is already walking to his car. If I leave him a few

seconds longer, he will go. But when he hears the creak of the door, he turns, grinning despite the rain.

'I've been trying to ring you for days! I thought you'd gone home for the weekend – then I saw your car.'

He aims a kiss on my lips but I turn and he catches the tip of my ear. He trips a little on the threshold because I won't let him pass.

'I was just on my way to Rachel and David's. We're all meeting up for brunch, thought you might like to join us.'

It's out of Anthony's way to come via mine to Rachel and David's, he must have taken a long route round just to pass my building even though I had been going to my parents. He must have been thrilled to see my car there, that's why he is smiling.

I stand inside the corridor, my face in the shadows. Anthony waits while drops of rain barge past him to get to the ground. I force myself to leave him in the cold: if I can't even bear to see him shivering, how am I going to say what I have to say?

'I can't come to lunch.'

'Oh shame. Work?'

He puts his hand on my arm as if I'm frail and he's about to lead me across the road – or is to lead me to what I have to say?

'Marc.'

The name means little to Anthony: he isn't from the past, but the future. A future being brutally aborted.

I find a few more words might help.

'Marc, my husband. He's come back.'

Anthony takes a few seconds to understand what I'm saying, and then he does.

'He's here, now?'

Anthony looks up in the direction of my flat and back to my bare shoulders. I nod, refuse to look sorry. Apologising would insult him.

'He's come back.'

'So that's… it then?'

'He's my husband.'

Anthony steps away from me. He is a decisive man, a man whom I have watched after hours of surgery who never tires or angers or loses his equilibrium. Please don't now, I beg him with my eyes.

He doesn't know what to ask first. A relief for me, because I've no idea how to answer anything he might confront me with.

I don't dare speak in case 'sorry' comes out.

I give a Gallic shrug of the shoulders, learned from you.

His eyes search my face but there's nothing to be found.

Anthony turns, paces slowly to his car. He presses the bleeper to open the door, it takes three goes. He holds the door open, looks to me again, just to take a parting snapshot of the girl he recently proposed to. I watch him as though I am a sniper, spying on him from a long way off, unseen. But the bullet's already been fired. It's raining harder. He looks at me again, to check I'm the same person. I'm not.

'Oh, congratulations about the job.'

'Sorry?'

'The Heart Hospital. They want you. You should get the letter tomorrow.'

He bangs the top of the car twice as if spurring on a horseman and carriage. And he is gone.

When I turn back into the corridor, the door shuts and the light behind me slowly closes over your silhouette. You are sitting on the stairs, watching me. I walk past you and into the flat.

'I don't want to talk about it.'

'Okay.'

'God knows there are enough things that you don't want to talk about!'

'I said okay, Katherine. It's okay.'

'How is it okay? Don't you get it? That was the most hurtful, cruel, unkind thing I have ever done. That man – he's a good person, Marc. He trusted me. He wanted to spend his life with me, share everything with me and I just shut the door in his face because you wandered in for the weekend. Oh I forgot, for "seven" days.'

You put the coffee on, lean against the sink, both hands on either side of it.

'You've changed,' you say.

'What did you expect? Of course I've changed!' We face each other. It's a standoff to see who can put a name to the difference between then and now. 'I was thinking the same of you.'

You turn, look out the window, and I wonder if this time you'll stay and face it.

'No, it's just that you have new eyes. And he is a good man, I'm not.'

'And nor am I a good woman,' I say, thinking back to last night.

'No, Katherine, you will always be good.'

'Oh, Marc, you just don't know.'

'I can go anytime and you return to "good man".'

'I know, Marc.'

'You're angry, I understand. What are you doing?'

'Making a cake.'

Before

'What's this?' Anthony asked, walking into the conference room of the Chelsea and Westminster Hospital and stopping in front of a side table laid out with food.

Mr Cole from The Heart Hospital answered, 'The rabbit food. Dr Brenton's responsible for that.'

'Oh, I thought I'd wandered into a petting zoo.'

I looked up from the papers I was arranging.

'I just thought it was ridiculous that we have so many meetings about the health of the heart while we're munching on chocolate Hobnobs and drinking coffee. Surely if we are to advise people about diet, we should take our own advice?'

Mr Cole and Anthony gazed at the selection of crudités and wholemeal breads. 'Carrot, Anthony?'

'Could I have it administered intravenously?'

During the meeting, Anthony made a point of catching my eye every time he bit into the apple slices and when we stopped for coffee, Dr Henderson called me over.

'Kate, someone I wanted you to meet. This is Anthony Blanchett, he worked with your father at Johns Hopkins. Anthony, you were asking about Dr Brenton – this is she, why don't you hand her some oats?'

'Healthy foods for doctors, eh? I think the medical profession is probably a population cross-section you'd never succeed in converting, but good for you for trying. I'm Anthony, worked with your father. We really, really thought a lot of him over there.'

'Good.'

'We've met before, though, haven't we? At Gina Brightman's dinner party, long time ago.'

'Here's a napkin,' I snapped, switching off the PowerPoint projector.

Of course I remembered meeting Anthony at that dinner party. The night before you left. He was the reason my old school friend had rung me out of the blue and invited me. Anthony, a friend of hers, had returned from doctoral training in the States, he'd talked about his mentor, my dad, and it'd come out that I'd been at school with Gina, so Anthony asked to meet me. That's why she threw that little dinner, for us to get together.

Well you're not stupid, Marc, you saw the set up for what it was. That night, that last night, you were in a sulk because you hadn't wanted to go out, we were at the stage in our marriage where we no longer had to feign interest in each other's friends. I'd coerced you into coming out, you thought it was concession enough that you'd agreed, but you weren't going to be civil as well. You were difficult even before she introduced us to the tall, handsome starring light of the medical profession. Anthony hadn't disguised his excitement at meeting me – it was innocent enough – my dad had taken him under his wing, his father had only recently died, and then he'd returned to London and was lonely. He was interested in my work, in me, but I could sense your chilly petulance turn into a long-term freeze over.

You found the people dull. Gina was 'boring' because she'd given up trying to ask you questions and wasn't listening to the answers anyway. And the dinner – a perfectly ordinary meal Gina had spent the day repeating from a trendy recipe book – was, for you, inedible. In the taxi home you ranted about everything that was wrong with the middle classes, with dinner parties, with globalisation, the English, but I picked you up on your subterfuge and, buoyed by Anthony's attentions, accused you of being jealous. Then you'd said it, said what was in our minds that night: that Anthony was the sort of person I should have married. That he was the kind of man I needed. And I didn't deny it. I said something I never meant to say and left the incision open.

That last night.

After the initial meeting – the carrots and my presentation – we worked together with Mr Cole on a paper, often at his house. One night after work, Anthony and I ended up in a small Italian restaurant in Hampstead. At that time, my criteria for men was simply whether or not they looked like you. But he couldn't have been more different: his complexion was fair; his accent very English, his words precise, unadorned with adjectives, let alone imagery. He talked as if he were reading from a textbook and when he asked about things, his questions were set like exam questions, *Examine the restaurant menu and briefly assess your choice of starters in order to evaluate its strengths and weaknesses...* When I answered his questions, he nodded as though we were attending a viva. He made mental notes – remembered everything – and once I think he even laughed.

Halfway through the meal, Anthony asked, 'Have you noticed the other people here?'

I looked around. 'What about them?'

'They're all couples.'

It was true, we sat in a line of couples and I saw a red rose between each one.

'Anthony.' I laughed. 'It's Valentine's night!'

Of course, all day there'd been commotion at the nurses' station with flowers arriving and anonymous cards being sent, giggles and jokes with the patients.

'This is the first time I've ever had a date for Valentine's,' he'd said.

I didn't say it, but it was mine too. Remember? Valentine's night was such a busy time for you at the restaurant so we never made plans for us – not that we'd ever have bowed down to institutionalised romance like that, all it meant was bookings and vast sales of champagne.

A pleasant enough evening. Anthony and I cut and swallowed, made room for the silences that squeezed past us like overweight strangers until relevant chat resumed. Anthony surprised me by ordering a pudding, he didn't seem a tiramisu sort but he scraped his bowl while telling me that since his father had died he'd spent his free weekends looking after his mother who was alone and desolate after nearly forty years of marriage to a man she adored. His brother was married with children so the onus was more on Anthony to care for her. It was a change to talk about our mutual families; with you, the subject had been so taboo.

When our meal ended, Anthony kissed me goodbye. Just the one peck on the cheek.

'Thank you for being my Valentine's date,' he said, adding that he had a Saturday free in two weeks and he wondered if I wanted to visit Kew Gardens. His sister-in-law had bought him a year's pass as a Christmas present and he'd never used it. I must have said yes before going on clubbing that night with Tom. I took too much Ecstasy and was sick into the sleeve of my jacket in the taxi home.

Kew Gardens with Anthony. It was nice, Marc. It was a relief to spend a day in fresh air not being whirled around by my pain. We talked about pollinating agents, angiotensin II receptor blockers and the host family he'd stayed with in the US.

I was there by accident – he'd turned up on my doorstep and I was too embarrassed to say I'd forgotten we'd made a plan. But for that day I wasn't someone who needed to visit a counsellor twice a week, who took sleeping pills at night and whose only respite was having a twenty-two-year-old boy lick between my legs until I passed out.

For those few hours, Anthony lent me a little time in a world without you.

Tom was watching TV when I returned from my outing. He looked me up and down and said, 'You're going to marry him, aren't you?'

I laughed, prizing a joint out his fingers.

'What are you talking about?'

'Your date. Dr Anthony. You're going to marry him.'

'You and Maggie saw it in her crystal ball, did you?'

I drew the smoke into my lungs and closed my eyes as part of my face numbed.

'You get over your husband and I lose you. I'm just a symptom, that's how it goes.'

I looked at Tom's sad face. When I kissed him, my bottom lip tasted of salt, but I didn't know which one of us was crying.

Sunday Afternoon

I'm whisking. The oven's preheating. It's raining.

'Do you love him?'

'You're not French by any chance, are you?'

'How did you guess?'

'Questions like that. The obsession with love! Sally says it's just an overwhelming desire to recreate one's family of origin... a yearning to re-find that face we once looked up to and got stuck on. Wanting to go home. And we dress it up in all this medieval, superstitious, opium for the masses claptrap.'

'Apparently it makes the world go around.'

'Apparently it's free. You should've seen his face, Marc.

That's the price. A husband like Anthony is what a girl wants–'

'*Needs.*'

'Needs! Yes! I need a good, solid, tax-paying, meat 'n' two veg man–'

Your mouth is over my mouth. Your fingers enter me and I lay down over the breakfast bar, wrapping my legs around your back, knocking over a glass of water and loose change. You hold my waist, push into me, going right through me as I move closer to you. When our eyes lock I am all heart, all feeling, all an extension of you as much as you are so much a part of me. And as you are about to come, you cry out, 'Oh, *ma cherie*! Ma Katherine!' You give yourself to me, are helpless to me, and all I know is that if this is love, I love you, and I never loved Anthony.

'So, still need a meat 'n' two veg man?' you ask as I wriggle out from under you.

'I need to get out of here.'

Sunday Evening

'Kate! You're soaked. Come in.'

Sally shouts up the stairs, 'It's Kate! Sorry about the mess. We're trying to get the kids off to bed: we thought if we started earlier it would be less of a rush... in fact, it just prolongs the agony.'

'Hi, gorgeous,' says Paul, bounding down the stairs shaking a baby's bottle.

'Sorry, I didn't call or anything.'

'No, you're just what we need – some sane company! There's a bottle of white already open in the fridge. Welcome to what we call the "suicide hours": children's supper, bath and bed... not necessarily in that order.'

147

'What's all that banging up there?' Paul shouts to the top of the house. 'We planned to take the kids to the zoo and it's been bloody raining all day so they're pretty stir-crazy. And as for us!'

'Paul, you do the bath, let us have a little girly time? Then I'll do the stories, or, Kate, maybe you could?'

'As long as it's not Greek myths again.'

Sally shuffles into the kitchen, grabs the wine, kicks away the children's toys and sits us both down. I can still smell their Sunday lunch.

'Ah, that's better. This weather. You okay?'

'Yeah, I just got a bit restless, thought I'd walk over.'

'You walked?'

'Well it looked like it was stopping when I left–'

'Coming to book group Tuesday?'

'I... I don't know...'

'What?' Sally calls upstairs, leaning right out of the chair to try and hear him better. 'What? I can't hear? It's in the laundry basket – doesn't matter, just take it out. Well, then it's – Oh for God's sake – Kate, just a sec.'

When Sally returns from finding a towel for the baby, I'll be gone.

I'm running. Running in the rain, running in the dark. Running away from now, from today, my best friend, you and me. I'm running to catch up with the time when you came back for me.

When I was the person you wanted me to be.

———

Before

The night of our first date. A manicure, a long time in the bath soaking in Sally's expensive oils, a hair mask followed by a blow-dry like people do on TV, swinging from right to left, curling the brush out in the air. Since the day you left me on standby at the coach station, I'd been growing my hair, trying to become the woman you wanted.

'Now that's what I call a real scrub in, Dr Brenton,' said Sally.

'What do you know about French men?'

'They have long lunches, are obsessed with oral sex and dressing up in women's clothes. Oh, and baguettes, they eat a lot of baguettes.'

'Where d'you learn all that?'

'I had a French exchange once. Hang on a sec...'

Sally rummaged in her room and returned with a necklace.

'Here you go, New Look's finest. I'm going to crash – wake me up when you get back tonight... if you come back!'

'Are you still cross I didn't tell you about him?'

'Livid! Sunday night I answer the phone to this deep, sexy voice asking to speak to "Ka-terrr-rine," and then he says, "Can you tell her Marc rang, Marc from France, last summer." You're a dark horse, you are.'

'I sort of wanted to keep him to myself.'

'The cat's out now. Everyone at the hospital knows and after his call to your mother all of the Southeast of England will be gunning for you tonight.'

'Wish me luck.'

'As if you haven't had enough already, mademoiselle.'

The restaurant was off Knightsbridge. I watched it from across the road trying to calm myself while updating all this new information about you. I braced myself before walking into your world.

'I'm here to see Marc?'

The man spoke fast and in French before returning to me.

'Crystalle will show you.'

I followed her through the restaurant and the swing doors to the kitchen.

You didn't see me at first, and although I knew it was you, it took a while to take in this Marc I was re-meeting, the man pacing that busy, bustling metal room. You moved from one person to the next, pointing, suggesting, taking over, shaking your head. You, in your white chef's jacket, your bass-line voice filling the kitchen, your employees frowning in concentration, twitching in dread of your disapproval. You said something, they laughed. You orchestrated: set the pace, syncopated tasks, inspired. Even I, standing at the door, was under your command. It would never have occurred to me to compare a chef of a restaurant to a surgeon – but your kitchen was also a theatre and you, my date for the night, were its star.

'Katherine! *Là voila!*'

Everyone looked up to see who'd come to see you. You introduced me to your team as they relaxed momentarily from their jobs and smiled, amused that their boss had another life which he was sharing with them. Your good manners, Marc, they have got you everywhere. You waved them goodnight, dumped your white coat in the laundry basket, just like I did at the end of my working day. You brought me to the front of house. I didn't understand what you said to the man, but he shook my hand and said, 'So, this is the reason Marc has come back to London!'

Once on the street, you held me by my shoulders. You kissed both my cheeks, slowly, deliberately. You stroked my arms, pressed me against you. No one had ever held me so long without talking.

'It's my night off but I have to babysit them a little. Anyway, I wanted you to see where I work. You like it?'

'Yes, everyone seemed terribly nice.'

You laughed and repeated what I'd said, '*Terribly nice.*'

I could feel the heat of your muscles under your cotton shirt. You were so alive. The antithesis of all the old, disfigured, decaying bodies I patched up all day long. With your palm against my back, you walked me through to Brompton Road.

'I want to cook for you, Katherine, but where I'm living at the moment... it's not right for you.'

'You should see where I live! Ng, my flatmate, has identified eighteen different types of fungus in our bathroom.'

As we walked, women looked at you. I could see them in their cars, at the traffic lights, feeding on you with their eyes.

'Shall we go for a drink first, then dinner?'

You circled your thumb around the curvature of my shoulders.

'Have you made any friends here in London?'

I sounded like my parents.

'Friends? There's a group of us Frenchies who go out at night but as for the English, most people who come to the restaurant can be a little... they think they are better people because they arrive in a limousine, you know?'

'Most people I meet arrive in an ambulance.'

Walking around London in the spring with you, eating dinner and you taking me back to my flat before midnight because you wanted me to get a good night's sleep – as if I would sleep! – was probably the happiest night of my life. I was in love; you dropped me in it from a great height, you worked me, flattered me, seduced me. You made me feel like the most interesting, beautiful, hilarious person alive. You gave me just enough of yourself to leave me wanting you forever. And when you stood at the door of my flat, you put your arms around me.

'Katherine, are you ready now, ready for me?'

'My hair's grown a bit,' I said, tugging at it.

You turned me to face you. The back of your hand glided across my jawbone, from my ear to my chin, your thumb stroked my bottom lip. I opened my mouth a little, closed my eyes and when I opened them again, I wasn't sure if you weren't laughing at me, just a little.

'Katherine, I was a little cruel, what I said, remember? I wanted to kiss you so much that afternoon. But then, it wasn't the right time. You were on holiday, going home, it was not real. But now, I have come here for me, yes, but also for you. This is real.'

You touched my cheek, stroked my neck with your fingertips. It wasn't the first kiss I'd been given, but it was the first one I gave. This time, kissing you, I didn't feel asphyxiated, concerned about the exchange of microbes, I wasn't counting for it to end so I could catch my breath, wipe my chin and have my face back. Your touch formed me, creating something just for you. Your lips, your tongue claimed me, your hands on my back, clasping my waist – if I could be useful for anything, it had to be for you. I would never have stopped, but you drew back, sealed what had passed between us with your lips on mine, just as we had begun.

'I want to cook for you. Next week come to my restaurant, bring a friend, anyone, but not a boyfriend, I would get jealous. Bonsoir, Katherine.'

Today, Marc, I know where you were going that night, but I couldn't have worked it all out then, I wouldn't have known where to start.

———

'I'm really sorry to disturb you on a Sunday.'

'Oh, don't worry, love, you're only keeping me from cleaning out the cat litter tray. You look like a drowned rat.'

'I feel like one.'

'Fancy a rum and Coke?'

While Frances finds a seat near the fire, I order the drinks and look at the same faces I've seen in every pub, 'Man sitting at the bar', 'Man by the jukebox', 'Bartender rinsing a glass and keeping an eye on the football scores'. I want to ask Frances how everything seems so normal when I'm in such a mess.

She switches off her mobile phone when I put the drinks down on the table. The fire's flames light up the amber swirls in our glasses.

'Cheers.'

'Thanks for coming out tonight, I had to talk to someone. I went round to my best friend's but I just couldn't speak to her... I ran out. I feel like such an idiot.'

'When I was getting divorced, I'd find some total stranger on the bus, tell them my whole life story – every intimate detail – and my mum would ask "How are you?" and I'd bite her head off. It's like that sometimes.'

'I didn't know you were married.'

'Briefly. It wasn't for me. All that, "I'm making a cup of tea, do you want one?", "I was thinking of having a friend over, is that okay?", "I'm gonna do a wee now... " Drove me mad. And the usual – he was on the internet chatting to a woman in Bristol saying that his wife was a paraplegic and he couldn't leave her. I was running the London Marathon and a relationship counsellor at the time!'

Frances lets out her solid, woody laugh.

Our pile of coats, hats and scarves lay next to us under the windows. Outside the wind flaps the rain around like tinsel under the streetlights, and you are out there somewhere, wondering where I am. And I like that.

'How did you know Marc was back?'

'I was watching the Hounslow house, saw him go in.'

'Why were you there?'

'I don't know... I had a morning off... intuition.'

'No, Frances, you wouldn't drive to the other side of London and watch that house unless something–'

'You want my job?' Frances laughs and sips her drink. 'Okay, you're right love. But this needs to be checked out. I was searching the records for missing people in California – for another case, an adoption thing – but a man's just run out on a young woman from San Francisco. He was the chef at her restaurant, so I thought, if it were your Marc and he was on the move, that's where he'd go. And I was right. I'll get more info on the US story next week. So, how's it going with lover boy back?'

'He wants us to have a week together. A week to decide.'

'That's very specific.'

'He wants it to be the way it was in the beginning. God knows so do I, and sometimes it's just like he never left – in bed – and then, it's like he's interrupting my life, my grief even.'

'Yeah, honey, sounds right.'

'He won't answer any questions. Just keeps making me cups of coffee and asking if I've eaten.'

'Hmm, nice.'

'It's irritating, actually. I'm used to helping myself.'

'Oh God, don't get like me!'

'I broke off my engagement with Anthony. Frances, what happens when people came back?'

'Roughly twenty per cent of people return after they've been located, forty per cent make some sort of contact but don't want to return, and the last forty per cent don't want to be found. Grim numbers, sweetie, but you're used to dealing in facts.'

'Where does Marc come into all that?'

'He doesn't. Never did. But this is also about you.'

'I want him to really understand what he did when he left, right from the beginning—'

'And he should. For once. This is a man who never stays around long enough to see what he does to people and you deserve to let him know what you've been through.'

You've tidied the flat and are reading the newspapers. A soup is bubbling on the low burner. The flowers you put in water on Friday are browning at the edges. There's music playing on low and the heating is up high.

You look up when I come in and turn the page, begin reading again. You bide your time before saying, 'Sally rang.'

'Did you talk to her?'

'Of course.'

'I bet she was surprised to hear your voice.'

'At first but we had a good talk.'

It's better not to articulate the sarcastic quips that come to mind. How easy it must be for Sally, always half-fancying you, missing you but then able to have a flirtatious natter after a curious two-and-three-quarter years.

I take off my damp clothes and change into a grey velour tracksuit that I usually reserve for nights in front of the TV on my own. I wring out my socks and add them to the bulge of dirty clothes in the washing machine. I turn the settings dial thinking back to Frances' last words as she ran me back in her car.

We'd stopped outside my flat, I'd thanked her for the lift home.

'Why aren't you telling him what you know? Why are you keeping his secrets? On some level, I think you're acting as an accessory to his actions – it's not like you, Kate, to be passive like this.'

'This is between Marc and I.'

'Okay, I'll butt out–'

'I don't mean it like that, it's just... while he's been gone, I've been living in the past, and for just a little bit longer, now he's back, it's like, I want to pretend. And I've had a change of heart.'

Frances looked up at my kitchen window where the man she'd been hired to follow was adding spices to a broth.

'This time last year we had a ten-year-old girl waiting for a heart transplant. We were running out of time and couldn't find a donor. Then a call came through that there was a heart for her, the heart of a sixty-five-year-old man – we had no other option – so we went ahead with the operation. The heart of a grown man is much bigger than the size of a child's, of course it wouldn't fit in her body so we attached it and laid it outside her chest. Several days later it'd shrunk to about half the size, after a week it was just small enough to be closed in. Now she's running around... The heart reshapes itself to fit the person, to match the experience. That's what's happened to me.'

That was probably going to be the last time I ever saw Frances, and there was something I'd always wanted to ask her. If I didn't then, I never would.

'You never told me who it was that you lost.'

'Oh my days! You want to rummage around my past now?'

'Just wondered.'

'I was a war-time baby, apparently my dad was an American GI, "Bob" my mum thought he was called, but then she said it might have been "Bill". He promised he'd come back for her after the war, marry her and all, but I guess something came up. She spent her life waiting for him. I vowed I'd track him down, put his name on my birth certificate, but I never found him.'

We sat, thinking about 'Bob-Bill' and Frances looked different to me now she was half American.

'Thanks for everything, Frances.'

'Just doing my job.'

'You did so much more.'

Before closing the car door, she tapped the window. It lowered itself down. She asked, 'Shall I pursue the San Francisco connection?'

But she already knew the answer.

Forty degrees. Eco Wash. Start.

You put an arm around me.

'You would rather be out in the rain than with me.'

'I just needed to talk to someone.'

'Him?'

'No, not him. A friend.'

'Sally said you ran out on her.'

'I couldn't cope with Sally, and Paul, explaining everything. I knew what they'd ask and I didn't know how I would answer. Anyway, I'm sure you made her feel better.'

'She was upset. And then four hours you were gone. I was worried – you turned your phone off.'

'Can you hear yourself?'

Sunday Night

You make supper while I soak in a bath you've run for me. I'd spent the last half an hour slamming things around and not speaking to you, then I tired myself out, got in the hot water.

I'm thinking about the girl Frances mentioned, the one looking for you in San Francisco. I hear you moving around the kitchen, and she doesn't.

You poke your head around the door.

'Katherine, a woman rang. Mrs Wheeler? I said you'd call her back.'

'Thanks.'

You spend a few minutes looking at me, the soap bubbles sit around my shoulders like a cloak, crackling in my ears. You close the door, respectfully.

Sunday nights if I'm not at the hospital, I call my mum, and I call Mrs Wheeler. I don't know why, it's a homage to grief, I suppose, and guilt. I know what it's like when you've lost someone and everyone else goes back to their lives and you have no life to return to.

I don't know if you'd be interested but I thought I should tell you what happened to Dave. Your predecessor. I can't say my hands have no blood on them either.

Before

I left Dave in France with Tatyana and I met you. I didn't think about him again until about eighteen months after you left. His mother had tracked me down to say that he'd been living at home and was having some 'difficulties'. She thought it'd be good for him to see old friends again. I had three weeks off to revise for exams and Tom was recording, so, in search of distraction, I went there, to Northampton, to fulfil some obligation to a mother who sounded anxious and afraid for her boy. And I wanted to open links with my past, get in touch with old friends who didn't know you, or us. It was easier to be with people who weren't looking at me and wondering where you were.

I remembered Dave's parents from when they'd come to take him out at college. His mother had been a small, lively woman with dark hair swept back and a face with little features which seemed to have been sketched on rice paper. When I met her again, the rice-paper complexion had been scrunched into a ball. She was hunched over and there was a strained warble in her voice as she led me into their house where I'd expected to see Dave.

'Graham, this is Kate. She's one of David's friends from Cambridge. You were in Jesus College, weren't you? Did you want tea?'

Mr Wheeler was in a large armchair by the fire reading *The Telegraph*. He put it down to look at me, then returned to it while his wife talked from the kitchen.

'Was it ghastly getting out of London? The traffic these days. Well we rarely have reason to go there anymore apart from once a year for the theatre with friends – friends who live in Edgware, do you know it? On the A41? – or to a very special exhibition like the last one at the British Museum, which I do really enjoy and then you make a day of it, but with all the pushing and shoving, the rushing about, people wearing their slippers out and spitting on the roads, the congestion charges, parking, pollution, and the rudeness! It's not what it was. For a start there are no English people anymore, I can't understand a word anyone says. David tells me you're not supposed to say that but it's true, all my friends say it as well, so really it's just not worth the... sugar?'

'No, thank you. Would you like a hand?' I asked, going up to the Aga for warmth.

'So how's your life at the hospital? He's been upstairs in his room. You know he probably won't come down till lunchtime writing, writing, well I told you on the phone. Hard work is it, dear?'

'Yes, it's pretty tough but nothing compared to the House Officer years.'

She's not listening, just busying herself with putting the sugar from one bowl into another.

'Poor thing, you must take care of yourself or you'll get ill and then what will the ill people do?'

The house was making my nose itch.

'And then on your day off you come all this way to see David. So kind of you. He always had such good friends, some even from primary school, we never moved, see? I say, David, why don't you ring up some of your friends? Have a get-together – like a dinner or something, I'd do the food – but he never does, never does. Come in, dear, sit down. I won't call him because he usually doesn't come if we do and that's a bit... I'll send you up if he doesn't make an appearance by the end of your tea–'

'Who?' asked Mr Wheeler.

'David, dear. This is Kate. A friend of his from Cambridge – come all the way from London but I said I'll not call him in case he doesn't come down and then that's awkward, so we'll just... wait.'

The tea was served in bone china cups with non-matching saucers.

'Have you still got lots of friends from Cambridge?'

'A few. My best friend, Sally, and some others.'

'He hasn't any friends now of course. Used to have lots and lots of friends.'

Mr Wheeler put his paper down and stared at me.

'We've met you before, haven't we?'

'Yes, at college, a few times when you came to take Dave out for the day I came too.'

'You came top in your first year's – were made a Scholar, I recall. Doctor now?'

I nodded.

'How are you bearing up with the endless policy changes, hospital league tables, these "Foundation" hospitals–'

'Whatever happened to Robinson's Lemon Barley Water and changing a catheter with a smile?' Mrs Wheeler lamented.

'She was a nurse,' said Mr Wheeler, as if informing me of something quite unbelievable.

The floorboards above us creaked.

'David was explaining to us about how magnetic resonance imaging works last night. I didn't know how much medical treatment depended on computers these days. What would happen if there were a power cut, eh? Finished your tea, love? You'll have so much to talk about not having seen each other since... since...'

Mrs Wheeler knocked on Dave's door and let me in.

Dave was standing in the middle of the room like an oil rig amidst a choppy sea of books, papers, clothes and gambling chips. He'd put on weight which made him look like he'd been padded up for a school play, and he'd also grown a beard from which his eyes looked out, dim and distrustful.

'David, a friend's here to see you.'

It was then I realised he hadn't been aware of this visit; he'd been oblivious to his mother calling all the people he'd once known and inviting them over.

When I took a few paces into his room, he stepped back, slipping a book over something he'd been writing. There were so many papers out, so many pencils over his desk, the floor. I'd forgotten that Dave always wrote in pencil, it had been a joke in college that he copied down all his notes from lectures, learnt them, and then rubbed them all out to reuse the paper the next day. His reasoning was more economical than ecological.

Mrs Wheeler mumbled something about getting the lunch on and disappeared down the stairs, closing the door behind her.

I wasn't sure how to approach him, so I just stood there wondering what that unpleasant smell was.

It was a strangely shaped mock-Tudor room in an odd mock-Tudor house. Dark, airless. There was the single bed against the wall where I'd lost my virginity.

'So she sent you.'

'Who?'

'You know who.'

Dave laughed, his chin bulging under the bristles. I'd been long enough in health care to know which types of medication cause that pallor and pudgy weight gain.

'Your cousin-in-law, Lady Davenport, that's who.'

'No, Dave. I haven't seen Tatty for a long time.'

'Good try. I knew she'd send her spies eventually.'

He looked around his room as if he needed to find something, then turned to me as if surprised I was still there.

'Not exactly one of Tatyana's residences but there you go. Not as draughty though, eh? Small but well insulated. My Dad's in the aluminium double-glazing business, he probably told you.'

'You didn't finish your degree.'

'I went back. Sat in the medical library trying to memorise anatomical diagrams and chemical formulae and then... then I started writing poetry!'

The 'P' of poetry came out with such a splutter that Dave was temporarily lifted off the ground.

'Poetry! Lyrics! Dialogues! Lyrical ballads, pastoral ballads! They just came out... out! Out! I couldn't stop. I started reading them to patients, then aloud in surgery waiting rooms, on the wards in Addenbroke's Hospital and people... were... getting *better*! What do you think happened when they found out – they didn't like that, did they? The medical profession – oh no, have to put a stop to that... tut-tut-tut... can't have people getting better without pharmaceutical companies getting richer, and doctors buying yachts with their fat pensions. You wouldn't believe the lengths they went to shut me up – some wanted me dead. Yes, dead. So what better than claiming me mad and in need of... Surprise! Medication! They're still out there – watching, listening, I know they're there – they're not just drug pushers and thieves, they are murderers. But I'm a poet, Kate, they can't take my words away from me. A poet: someone who heals the soul, not the body.'

He fell into the chair, exhausted by his speech.

'I'm sure you're very good.'

'There's no good or bad about it – you either are or you aren't.'

'I'm sure you are, then.'

'I've already been published. Look.'

Dave thrust a local magazine into my hands. 'Go on. Read it.' He pointed his finger to a poem that was between an advert for a family run hotel and someone selling a 1989 Passat.

I read over the poem. It was a clever piece. Anna had written similar poems for the same sort of publications in her early teens. I found myself looking over the car ad.

'They're listening. You've probably not been in fresh air for months. Let's go, darling girl.'

Dave's parents were sitting in silence in their armchairs when Dave announced, 'We're off out.'

Mrs Wheeler leapt to her feet and started on about scarves and hats and catching our deaths, but Dave pushed me ahead and slammed the door behind us.

The day was intensely cold but intensely bright. At the end of Dave's road, the houses, the streetlights and the parked cars came to an end, after that, it was uninterrupted countryside.

Dave crossed the road away from the line of houses and started running fast while rotating his arms around. I jogged behind him, trying to keep up as he shouted things out that I couldn't hear until he turned to me.

'*Solaris! Avarus animus nullo satiatur lucro!*'

For a while we traipsed fast over thickets and under branches until we relaxed into a regular pace.

'I heard you married.'

'Yes. But...'

'Oh, no buts, don't disappoint me – if you can't make that ridiculous institution work there's no hope for any of us!'

'It's not a matter of it working or not, he disappeared.'

'Disappeared you say?'

'A year and a half ago, he vanished. I'm looking for him but...'

'Can you still love someone when they are no longer there?'

The cold air scoured my throat. Dave didn't wait for an answer before putting his hands on my shoulders and shouting into my face.

'They teach children that we all need water, oxygen and food to survive but throw physics to the dogs! We need love. Fuck cancer and heart disease: loneliness is the greatest killer of them all. And what can you prescribe for that, eh?' He jabbed his index finger into my ribs. 'Nothing. Kate, I thought I was going to die. After six years of medical training, I thought a girl would be my cause of death! But look, I've made it! I'm getting better!'

Dave flung himself towards a clearing and up an earth mound where he shouted down.

'They're a rotten lot, all of them. I'm better than the whole damn bunch of them put together! See, I can say that now. You can tell her I'm fine now. She doesn't have to worry about my calls or my letters. Fly, little spy, fly! Go tell her!' His eyes darted in all directions. 'The Great Gatsby,' he said, jumping down and putting a hot hand on my shoulder. 'She bought it for me in Cannes at the English Bookshop... What?'

I kissed his lips in a number of ways before he opened his mouth. It was me who pulled him down on the little bit of grass, who heard a cuckoo as I put my hand into his jogging trousers. Dave's mouth tasted of copper. His jaw didn't seem to be doing what he wanted it to do – he'd smack his lips together, lick and re-lick them – before coming back to the exercise of kissing me again. I sat up to undo my boots, Dave rolled on his back, wriggling on the grass like a large dog picking up the smells of spring. I took one leg out of my jeans, one side of my pants and rolled Dave onto me. Eventually, we managed to fit our bodies together although he never managed a full erection nor to ejaculate, but we went through the motions regardless.

Afterwards, I lay there, small insects gnawing at my flesh. Dave chatted to himself, gathering ideas for something he wanted to write later that day.

What had I just done? Maybe I'd got back at Dave for hurting me that summer in France, but mostly, I'd completed a circle – as always, it was all about you.

I left after the walk; didn't stay for lunch. Said I had an emergency at the hospital to attend to. Dave's eyes filled with tears when he said my visit had changed everything.

'It's a shame you have to go off so soon, you've done him the world of good,' said his mother. 'He's already upstairs writing an ode to you. Oh, can you hear? That's him on the guitar now.'

As I started the car to drive away from the house, Mr Wheeler leant through my window.

'Stay in the middle lane, stick to fifty-six miles per hour, that way you save on petrol and reduce the risk of accidents. Thanks for coming to see our son, we really appreciate it.'

Dave called many times over the next two weeks, sent me letters, poems, cards, but I didn't take his calls and after reading the first two or three letters, I didn't even bother opening them. The next time I saw his parents was at his funeral. Dave had hung himself. His parents thanked me so much for my visit, and I promised to stay in touch. I kept my word. Sunday nights, I ring Mrs Wheeler or she rings me, we always have the same silly conversation, but it eases my conscience.

While you make supper, I call Sally. She's miffed I didn't confide my big news to her but all cheery after speaking with you.

'He's back! You must be over the moon!'

That's exactly why I didn't want to talk to her. I'm ashamed of not feeling the way people think I should feel – whether they expect rage or delight – my sensor must be defective; I don't function like I should.

'Whatever happened, he's been miserable without you, and you've been so unhappy without him – even with you trying to make the best of it with Anthony. Oh, I so hope this all works itself out – he even mentioned maybe renewing your vows; well I said it, but Marc thought it was a really good idea!'

Didn't you say once, it's not that we are attracted to others as much as how attractive they make us feel about ourselves?

Sally, like most people I knew, adored you.

You found all our points of vanity, made us fall in love with ourselves over and over again every time we saw you. From the moment you met someone new, you seemed to pick up from a conversation started years ago. With some you argued politics, had intense discussions about jazz, food, others you cuddled like a big bear. With Anna it was all double-entendre and innuendo; with Sally you were everything her husband wasn't: sensuous, attentive, romantic, good around the house. And it wasn't just the women. Even the kids you berated at the restaurant every night, they couldn't speak for sadness when, as the days went by, they realised you weren't coming back. My dad's lost for which wine to serve without you advising him. My mother has no one to tell her that her eyes go so well with her dress; my nieces and nephews have no one to climb over after Sunday lunch. You didn't just leave me.

'Kate – it's amazing, isn't?'

'Yes, he's alive.'

'So, where was he?'

'He worked on boats for a while, then settled in America.'

'D'you know why?'

'He needed to sort his head out. Something like that.'

'Right. Well, hey, come for dinner next week? We're free Thursday – or maybe the weekend is better, we could...'

It never bothered me that my best friend was half in love with you. There were so many people who loved you, and I felt big and generous lending you out to the world.

You let me flatter myself into imagining that I was above all those impromptu scenarios – that I had the real Marc your fan club didn't see. You had moods, the 'black attacks' as we called them. No one else was privy to those. Sometimes you hardly spoke for days and at other times you were a little too euphoric, bouncing into the flat having spent your week's wages on an olive oil or handbag for me. I recognised the look in your eyes when your past was pulling you down, and I treated it by keeping you calm, secure, loved. I thought that our relationship was the authentic one, all those other people, they were just the tasters, the *amuse-gueule*, but after you left, who was the biggest sucker of them all?

Sally's invited us for dinner, like nothing ever happened. I'm no longer a fraction but something complete. Doesn't Sally remember those first few months? Like the night she came to pick me up for reading group. It was just another night, Marc, one of almost three years of nights.

Before

Sally had called in the day to remind me it was book group night. I could tell she was hoping I'd forgotten or would bow out. I hadn't, although I'd planned not to go, but when I could tell how quick she was to write me off, I said how much I was looking forward to it – just out of spite.

All day at her surgery the phone rang with members of the book group asking if I was really coming and what was the latest news on Marc – should they mention it? – how was I... really? I'm sure she wanted to scream at them, 'Ask her yourself!' But people didn't ask me, it was easier to get all the information from Sally and have silly, meaningless conversations with me.

Sally didn't know what to say anyway because I didn't tell her much. We were best friends but clothes shopping, having a giggle at a film once in a while or having Sunday lunches together is nothing until it's tested by something like this. And Sally had failed. Every time someone asked her how I was, she came out with a big zero. But I chose to feel let down by her, looked for reasons to unleash my rage. I'm a giving person, Marc, and I wanted to share some of the shit you left me with.

That day had been a particularly bad one. I'd been on-call the night before, a night we actually had theatre tickets booked for – if you hadn't have left, we would have been sitting next to my parents watching a play about a Californian therapist having an affair with her mass-murdering patient. We'd probably have all gone on to dinner somewhere in the West End or to your restaurant. It was something we did every few months. I'd thought we'd enjoyed that. Even weeks after you left, I was still cancelling plans we'd made.

At one point that morning I went to the nurses' station to ask for something and I heard a song on the radio that you used to hum, so I spent lunchtime in the toilets crying. I'd had a stupid disagreement with one of the orderlies, and when I got home there were no messages, no post; just the flat, the way I'd left it two days before. I hadn't slept properly for weeks. I'd not been able to gauge, Marc, how far off-centre I was moving; those days when I thought the blackness would chew me up, and I was disappointed when it didn't.

I was on the floor in the 'recovery position' when I heard the buzzer. I shouldn't have answered it but I thought it might be you. I heard Sally push in the light switch where there was the Missing photo of you. The cheap black-and-white home-printed copy, Sally knew it well because she had one up in her surgery. 'Yer friend found her ol' blue eyes, then?' her receptionist apparently asked every morning.

I'm sure that when Sally climbed up the three flights of stairs to our flat, she fought against a shameful urge to run in the opposite direction. It was like that with me then. I made people feel hopelessly inadequate and trivial, often depressed. Sally didn't want to talk to me about her life, her nanny problems, something her mother-in-law said which niggled and what to cook for Christmas lunch. All her life's preoccupations seemed vastly gratuitous and smug in light of my anguish. Or maybe I just liked to think so.

Your leaving affected the whole building. The air of

something not-quite-right started from the street outside us. Gloom in the trees, the empty basement flat, the first floor had recently been bought but no one had moved in, the For Sale sign rotting by the bins. Inside there was a sinister quietness. The doors of the other flats were shut, locked and bolted; our neighbours barricaded themselves against the frightening, unpredictable world. The corridor smelt of damp and that's when the light outside my door stopped working. I was waiting for you to come home and fix it.

The last time Sally had come to collect me for reading group was a May evening, you were playing a new CD of Italian jazz, and the flat was filled with white flowers you'd bought me on your way home. You were tanned, wearing a white tunic shirt and matching trousers. You had a silver fish around your neck hanging from a silver chain, you were barefoot. Most men would look absolute arses dressed like that, Sally said later, but you were always so comfortable in the way you filled your skin. You offered my friend a glass of wine while she was waiting for me to change out of my work clothes. She said she shouldn't, but after a taste, couldn't resist. You lit a cigarette; she took a drag from it. With you, people couldn't say no, you made everything seem too tempting, such fun. I heard you both from the shower, talking about the kids – our godchildren – about your plans to see Paul's new offices in the city. You never made that meeting, Marc, and Paul thought you were his friend. He thought you might not come home to me, but that you'd certainly keep your date with him. You didn't.

This time Sally was in no hurry to get up the stairs, she lumbered, rallying the strength to say the right thing, still thinking there was a right thing to say. She couldn't even think what it would be like to lose her husband. She once insinuated that it wasn't so bad for me because we didn't have children, but when I asked her to imagine what it was like to know I would never have kids by the man I loved, she realised that you couldn't weigh up one person's loss against another's. She felt guilty. That's one of the reasons there was a rift between me and everybody else. I knew people left me and clung on to their loved ones, relieved that disaster wasn't knocking on their doors. That's what I'd have done. Isn't that how pity works?

But to be fair, Sally had lost you too.

She must have been hoping I wouldn't look so tired, so blatantly miserable when I opened the door.

'I haven't read the book.'

'It doesn't matter. We'd all love to see you.'

'Who'd love to see me?'

I'd recently developed a talent for picking people up on words they used and becoming particularly argumentative about them. I could even find a crushing response to an innocent, 'How are you?'

'I can't face it. Sorry. Again.'

'Come on, it's no big deal.'

'Okay... Where are my keys?'

'In your hand.'

I had seen Sally a bit since you left, but I noticed she always tried to make it when Paul was around. He had a way of calming me, bringing out the rational, dispassionate side of my character. He questioned different methods of finding you as if he were referring to a lost file on a computer or credit card. 'Have you tried his gym club? What about down the sofa? Why don't you make a documentary about yourself? Are you sure you've checked all your pockets? Shallow graves?'

When Sally said, 'Just come as you are', she didn't exactly mean it, or at least she'd anticipated I'd change out of my slippers, but no, I came to the book club exactly as I was.

'Come in, come in – isn't it cold? Lovely to see you, Kate.'

I walked into Jessica's home for the first time since you'd left me. The conversation lulled. I'd got use to that. Eyes shifted; people didn't want to stare. Jessica brought me some mulled wine and an ashtray when I pulled out cigarettes from my bag. It is the last habit one would have ever expected of me but you smoked so, when you left, I took up the habit, to be close to you – I liked to think that somewhere in the world, you and I were lighting cigarettes at the same time. While someone was talking to me about their holiday, Deborah stood behind, leaving her hand on my shoulder for a short time. She didn't need to say anything, but I felt how much she cared.

Many people, from close friends to people I'd never met before, had reached out to me those first six months, shown me great kindness. I don't think I ever thanked them for it. Loss of gratitude was just another symptom of my pain.

We didn't begin discussing the book because we were waiting for Becky to arrive with a new member. Sally noticed my eyes darting around when they mentioned a name I hadn't heard before; Sally knew this would make me nervous.

Bells was a tax lawyer and Becky's friend from law school. She seemed unnecessarily tall and loud, Becky stood behind her, introducing her to the group, and I wondered what she'd said about me when she briefed her friend about us beforehand. We had our polite faces on, talked as if there was an echo and nodded pointedly at astute comments – a new member always provoked a bit of showing off.

Halfway in I had to come clean about not having read the book. Bells piped up with 'Naughty, naughty' which was ignored by the group.

Over Thai food we went from talking about the book to the

lives of the readers.

'I've got some news...' Elspeth flushed. 'I'm having a baby!'

'Becky was saying in the car here,' announced Bells, 'that we should dub this the "breeding group" instead of the "reading group"!'

Then Bells went through the members. 'So you've got two, I've got three, Jessica, one... Sally, two...' She stopped at me. 'And what have you got?'

'No kids for me,' I answered.

'Too bad, too bad... better hurry up and get hitched now or you'll end up with other people's leftovers!'

As Becky leant forward to clutch a handful of Doritos, she sunk her foot over her friend's toes.

Elspeth came to my rescue.

'Kate's married.'

'Right, I remember now Becky saying something about that. Well, I put my foot in it!' said Bells, contemplating my ordeal as she scooped up some guacamole sauce. And into the embarrassed silence, she threw in, 'I'm sure he'll be back when he gets tired of her.'

Driving back I looked out of Sally's car window, and said, 'I shouldn't have gone.'

'Wasn't it good to see everyone?'

'No. But I guess I had to see.'

'See what?'

'See that... I am so disconnected. Unplugged from real life. I'm a freak, a parody. It's only the hospital that keeps me functioning and even that is only on the barest level. If I think about why I'm doing it, even saving people's lives is pointless: they're all going to die anyway.'

Sally increased the pressure on the accelerator and resisted the temptation to pipe up with reasons that I should keep going – she'd already learnt that that really aggravated me.

'Bells won't be invited again.'

'Isn't she my replacement?'

'What are you talking about?'

'It's quite obvious. We were eleven tonight, I wasn't supposed to be there.'

Sally turned into my street.

'What are you doing for Christmas?'

'Working. I'll give someone else the time off. I can't face my family at the moment. Anna's a mess over Nick, she thinks he's having an affair, and Mummy's a nervous wreck about me.'

'Come to us if you want.'

Sally stopped outside my flat, waiting for me to hop out and leave her to her life, but I didn't move.

'So what Bells said: does everyone think Marc's just left me for someone else?'

Sally was tired of fencing off my discomfort. She drew up the hand brake. 'It seems the most obvious explanation.'

'So that's what you think?'

Sally's fingers circled the steering wheel.

'Okay, maybe he met someone, why didn't he tell me? People break-up all the time, it's no big deal, that way there wouldn't be Missing posters of him all over London – there wouldn't be police wasting taxpayers' money looking for him. He would have got half the flat, had work references, friends, I wouldn't be going insane!' I breathed in to give myself the strength to shout: 'Why didn't he talk to me?'

'I don't know.'

'Paul used to meet up with Marc, did he suspect anything?'

'He would have said if–'

'Did he? Did he think Marc was unfaithful? Tell me, Sally, I won't hold it against either of you if you know something.'

'Never. Paul never said anything. We both knew Marc loved you so much, Kate, really loved you.'

'But he's gone! He's gone, Sally! Everyone says how happy we were, how much he loved me, but look at me now! He must have fucking hated me! He must have loathed the very sight of me! He must have wished this hell on me! That's the only explanation!' I slapped the tears around my face. 'And you know what? If he's not dead, I'm going to kill him myself!'

I didn't see Sally for a long time after that evening. I'd lost you, I'd lost her, I'd lost me.

All I'd gained was a search. That night, I didn't go to bed. I sat at my computer screen running through the names of every missing person until the winter light went from dark grey to light grey. I thought I was being thorough, but I must have passed over your name several times, I just didn't know it.

Late Sunday Night

You sleep. I don't. You turn in the bed, flinch into the pillow. Your arm makes a barrier between our heads. Your fingers are curled like a baby's and when you exhale, the hair on your forearm trembles. Where have you been sleeping, my darling?

Before

It was sometime after the second Christmas that you'd been gone, I got a call from Tatyana at three o'clock in the morning. I thought it was a wrong number at first. It was difficult to understand her, her voice was slurred, she was half giggling and blowing smoke into the earpiece. She said she was ringing from Miami.

'It's Tatty! Katie, I've got something to tell you.'

I could hear laughter in the background and the sound of people singing karaoke.

Tatyana said that she'd spent the last year and half travelling around Latin America and every time she woke up in a new place, she'd stick up a poster of your face with an announcement that you were missing and her email address. Then she met some American students on a bus who said that there was a man living rough in Mexico who fitted the poster's description. Although the man's appearance wasn't exactly the same – this one was darker with blond streaks in his hair – they'd remembered the tattoo. This man, the *loco,* had made himself a cabin and spent his time drinking tequila and playing with the village kids. Sometimes, when he got it together and needed money, he'd cook incredible meals for travellers who could afford it.

'It's this gorgeous place by the sea – off the beaten track – like Puerto Escondido used to be in the sixties, y'know? Backpackers go there to sleep in hammocks, sit around campfires and apparently that's where he was! So, I thought I'd visit for Christmas, why not, eh?'

The day Tatyana arrived, the man had just left for California with two sisters. These girls were wealthy Americans and one of them had fallen in love with the drifter.

'I'm going to California now, I'll do what I can... but it's something, isn't it?'

Something.

Why did you leave me so you could be homeless, penniless and spend your time with strangers?

MONDAY

Monday Morning

Before

'Y**ou are looking positively beatific! He's a doctor, isn't he? Which one is he? Don't – let me guess.'**

To get Anna to leave the hospital I had to tell her something to satisfy her curiosity, but everything I said only enflamed it. Anna was in London for the day, ostensibly researching something at the British Library, but in reality, to find out about this Frenchman who'd called my mum asking for my number.

'I've got to meet him. Does he know all about us? About me?'

'We only ever talk about you.'

'Really?'

'No. Maybe a little. He doesn't have any family of his own, so he's interested, sure.'

'Everybody has a family. Kate, sure he's not married?'

'No! And he grew up in a foster home.'

'Oh, Kate, people like that...'

'You don't know anything about people *like that*.'

'Invite him to tea.'

'Why, so you can interrogate him?'

'Of course! Hey, why not bring him to the May Day ball. I'm doing a dinner – you know Eddie's going to be over – let's all get terribly drunk and stay out all night, dance on the bridge at sunrise. Oh please!'

'He's not a *ball* sort of person.'

'Don't be silly, all men love looking like James Bond for a night.'

'I'll ask him and see what my schedule's like, and his, he works nights too.'

'So he is a doctor... or a porter... or a–'

'He's nothing to do with medicine, actually,' I said. 'He's a chef.'

'How delicious. I love him already. Tell me, what's it like to French kiss a French man?'

'You can add that question to your agenda.'

'*Au revoir! Voulez-vous couchez avec moi, ce soir!*'

'Don't go.'

You clamped me in your thighs, your arms, your mouth.

'Work, the pressure, the patients, the routine. It's what kept me sane, Marc, when you were away, I need it now.'

'For what?'

'Perspective.'

'I can pick you up some at the supermarket.'

You squeeze me. The corny jokes I used to giggle at in our first year don't make me laugh anymore.

'When will you be back?'

It's been almost three years since anyone's asked me that.

'Six-ish.'

'I'll be here. Or would you rather I wasn't?'

'I don't know, I don't know,' I say, sweeping the duvet back and heading for the bathroom. I hold on to the towel for support, bite into it, press it to my chest. 'I don't know. I don't know. I don't know what I want for dinner, and I don't know anything about you, and I'm wondering if I know even less about me.'

You come in, put your hand on my shoulder, rock me back and forth as I hang off the towel.

'You really messed me up, Marc, really. First by going, and now by coming back.'

'I want to make it better, now, for you. It's for you to decide if you will let me have that chance, that's all, *ma chérie*.'

'Tell me that you love me, that what you did was wrong.'

'I love you. What I did was wrong.'

'You're only saying that because I asked you to.'

'So don't ask.'

A tremor begins at my feet and builds through me, whatever stood between my anger and you, breaks out of me, and like some flimsy, comical, damsel in distress I slap, kick, hit you. You take the blows, absorb the pain without even blinking or losing your balance. Then you catch my wrists. You hold them up to my face. I get the message. Exhausted, I fall into a heap. Fighting has to be learnt, practised, perfected. Just like leaving somebody.

You go about tidying the bathroom, putting everything back to where it was. All but me.

Dressed, I gulp the coffee that you've made. I open my bag and throw in my phone, my wallet and my keys. I look at you, open the door, walk out.

Tom is standing in front of his door.

'Not now.'

'Kate.'

'What?'

'All right?'

'No.'

'Please... can we just... ?'

'Oh. Your money.'

We turn into his flat. He closes the door behind me. I open my bag and take out my cheque book. Tom stands by my side.

'Don't worry about the money, I just wanted to ask if you were okay.'

'I'm not. I'm not. Marc's come back, Anthony and I are done, I'm going to be offered a job I don't know if I want, I've got back-to-back surgery all day and I can't stop shaking and crying and... Tom, this isn't a good time for a chat.'

I continue writing out the cheque for money I owe Tom.

It's rent. Tom has been my landlord since last year.

I was getting into debt trying to pay the mortgage on my own. I was scared I would lose my job when my private life was cracking me up. I couldn't pay for my car when it needed a service, and I couldn't accept any more money from my parents. When I was refused a third loan, Tom offered to buy my flat. He had the money sitting in an account. He insisted it was a good financial deal for him, maybe he'd buy the next flat up, take over the whole building. He even mentioned we might live together one day.

It was a simple transaction with a cash buyer, an offer I couldn't refuse. After I sold the property, I was solvent again. At least money was something I no longer had to worry about.

'So he's back?'

'So it appears.'

'And you're going to just let him come back? Going to act like nothing happened, like he's–'

I whack my hand across his face.

Unlike you, Tom is knocked off his feet. When he steadies himself, he's stunned. His eyes moisten. He looks at me in horror. When he takes his hand away from his face, there's a red mark on his cheek.

Why couldn't I hurt you? Why doesn't your skin redden and bruise? Why can't you cry?

'Oh God!' I rush to him. 'Tom, I'm so sorry.'

We stand there, crying together, in his large, bright room with the TV screen showing the morning news.

I take an ice cube out of his icemaker and dab it on his cheek.

'Let me look at you.'

'Why can't you love me like you do him?'

'Who says I love him?'

I wipe my hands, tear the cheque out of my book and put it on the table between us.

'Tom, I've got to go. I hope you find someone to give your love to – someone who deserves you.'

'I'll see if Anthony's still available.'

'And don't be cheeky to your elders.'

'I got it wrong, didn't I? I thought I was more to you than just a kid to boss around or a quick shag on your way to picking up your post. You meant a lot to me.'

'I'm really sorry.'

'I'm not accepting sorry. You used me big time. You think cos you're posh and a doctor and some dickhead shat on you that all the world owes you something? Thanks for the rent. We're quits.'

Dr McKendrick is in theatre inserting a mitral valve into my patient, the second procedure I've missed this morning.

'I owe you one,' I say, while he rinses his hands. The anaesthetist behind him rolls her eyes and leaves the room.

'You do.'

He wipes his hands, looks at me and turns. I follow him into his office where he closes the door, but we don't sit.

'Do you remember a baby called Jamie? ICU – one of yours. They came in last night. We couldn't get in touch with you, Kate. Your pager was off, so was your phone. You didn't answer our messages. Then this morning. You've never done this before – don't let it start now.'

'How is he?'

'He isn't.'

He looks at his watch.

'I don't need to tell you what'll happen if you ever do that again.'

His phone rings.

'Get to work.'

Monday, Midday

I've been longing to get out of the hospital, to walk, fast and mindlessly, as far away as possible. The last few hours I worked like an automaton, keeping to the routine, the dosages, the same script with everyone I met, and then, just as my lunch break and my chance to get out arrives, I put on my coat, look up and see Anthony. I'm shocked that his misery is so physical, as if he's been struck down by a tropical virus overnight. He holds on to the door, one arm above and one across, as if the impact of seeing me might hurl him down the corridor.

'Kate?'

The smile isn't there, the cheery 'hello', the sneaky kiss in case anyone's looking. When Anthony gave me his heart, he gave me his heart.

Often on Mondays we'd go swimming together, either at lunch or after work, now the idea of it is out of the question.

'Can we talk?'

'Sure, I say.'

Neither of us are big talkers so I wonder how this is going to work.

We walk out of the hospital side by side but not together. I can't look him in the face. I think I should touch his arm, tell him it will all be all right. But I can't.

I don't know who leads who, but we turn into the street.

'Do you want to eat?'

'No. You?'

'No.'

Anthony hasn't thought this through.

'Let's get a coffee then.'

He doesn't even answer, just follows me into a takeaway place where I order two coffees. I pick up a flapjack in an optimistic effort to jolly up the exchange to follow.

I remember challenging my mother about why she never really asked me how I was getting on without you. Out of everyone I knew, she was the least surprised you'd gone, even acted as though you were always going to leave and I was just being melodramatic about it.

She said, 'I became myself when I had children – from Richard to you – each child filled me with love, purpose, real joy. Of course, it was difficult at times, but I suppose I was one of those women feminists must loathe, because I sincerely believed that everything I'd done in my life was a prelude to motherhood. It was my vocation. And then you all grew up and I was out of a job. In a flash, it was all over. Every minute of every day I miss you children. You've all left home and sometimes you come for lunch or not, or Christmas, or Anna drops her kids off to be somewhere, but I miss you all the time. Getting older is just a process of missing people, missing them more and more as the days go by, like watching a boat go out to sea with all those you love on it, receding into the distance. I even miss Daddy, how we used to be, all those friends from school, my parents, my grandparents. I'm sorry Marc has left you, I really am, but you were always going to lose him at some point or another.'

Anthony and I sip at our coffees on a bench. It's freezing. Already I miss him.

'You must be relieved your husband's back. *Alive.*'

'The last time I went to identify a body that might have been his I was disappointed when it wasn't. I wanted all this finished.'

'So it is finished, isn't it? You got the best-fit result, now you can go back to how you were.'

'Can I?'

'How should I know?'

'Marc's return, it wasn't planned, y'know. I haven't been keeping anything from you.'

'When were you going to tell me?'

'He came back just before the weekend. He's given me till Thursday to make up my mind.'

'Surely he's not in a position to start laying down the law – well, it's none of my business.'

'It was just an idea, I was confused, he came up with the week. Seven days to work something out together.'

'How generous. The fact that you were engaged to someone else didn't come into the equation?'

I look at Anthony from the side. His chin jutting out a little, his nostrils flared in disgust, lips cracked, and his eyes so full of rage and worse, disappointment.

It was a mistake to think we could talk.

We watch the pigeons, a school trip troops past, and office workers clip-clop in search of sandwiches. I wanted to stop any one of them and ask them to take my place next to Anthony on the bench, take my life while they were at it.

'It wasn't you, yesterday, the way you answered the door. I mean, *you*, but different.'

'You just saw something you hadn't seen before.'

'Is your husband different?'

'I can't say I ever knew him.'

'But you still want him? Kate, I have to ask.'

'I loved him when we married, and he was there, and then he wasn't there, but I still loved him and now he's back, does the continuum stop?'

'Love him or not, do you really want a man who walked out on you three years ago?'

In my silence, Anthony has his answer. I want to say that love is unconditional, but surely the ones we love are constrained by more conditions than anyone. I'd never expect fidelity from anyone else, demand they spend most of their free time with me, render up all their secrets, ration their pleasures outside my jurisdiction. We say, 'I love you, I'm yours, you're mine': it's slavery.

This idea only comes to me now but it's probably not the time to share it.

'The Johns Hopkins Hospital offered me a position a few weeks ago but I turned it down because of our... er... our situation, but, now, I might ask if it's still open. I liked America, despite their foreign policy and lack of irony. It'll be hard on my mother, of course, but I don't want to stay here now.'

I imagine Anthony in Maryland wearing brightly-coloured Converse trainers, eating waffles. I suppose he's asking for the last time if this really is the end.

'Sounds like a great opportunity.'

'Hmm? Yes.'

Then I remember my engagement ring, start twisting it off.

'Keep it. Sell it. Send the proceeds to medical research.'

He looks at me like a puppy whose owner is tying a brick around his neck and dropping him down a well.

The talk is over.

We are over.

We stand up, face each other like he's going to shake my hand and ask me to consult his secretary for a follow-up appointment. I'm about to say something – something that might put all this right – but I can't. We exchange goodbyes: hands in pockets, faces giving nothing away. I get the feeling, however, that he is the one being released. Anthony turns, starts walking from me and the puppy's neck is out of its noose.

———

Before

'What are you doing in here?'

'I don't want to sleep on my own, it's boring.'

'How did you get past the nurses?' I laughed.

'I have my way. Come here.'

'If anyone catches you...'

'I'll say I'm very sick and you're making me feel better.'

You kissed my ear while untying my hair.

'*Viens ici, ma belle.*'

We undressed each other as if we were being timed, all the while I shook my head at your audacity but I couldn't stop you, or myself. I pecked your arms with kisses as you unclasped my bra.

'My bleeper's going to go off any minute–'

'So's mine, baby!'

It'd been six weeks since you'd found me and we'd spent all the time we could together, usually in my room because... because... why, Marc? How did you always manage to keep me out of your life? I think you said you didn't want me to see where you lived. I went with anything in those days when our skins were like Velcro and every moment was spent plotting and planning to keep it that way.

'Katherine, I want to show you something.' You took off your shirt. 'Look.'

You turned your arm to my face.

'It's not real!' I said.

'Yes, it's real. I did it last night.'

'But... but... it could get infected.'

'You don't like it?'

'Well, it's not a matter of whether I like it... it's a tattoo... of my name...'

'K-A-T-H-E-R–'

'I can read!'

'I was bored, missing you, maybe I had too much to drink but I wanted you to know how much I love you. Whatever happens to us, Katherine, your name is here, under my skin. No one can change that. Now let me make love to you and then go back to sleep.'

'But...'

'Hey, Katherine, it's not such a big deal. I love you so I put your name on my arm, come here, come here.'

The tattoo was permanent: we would be permanent. Our story concrescent with the details of us. Your huge, giving and undeniable love blew away all my defences. You were in a strange country, without friends, family or any security and you were all limbs in. That's what it said on your arm.

'But what if you split up?' asked Sally while we ladled a curry onto our plates. It was a night we'd put aside to revise together but an episode of *Sex and the City* and beers had taken priority.

'He says he'll just put dates under the names, you know, like birth and death.'

'Or he could just carry on going out with Katherines.'

I looked at my friend, 'It's the most romantic thing anyone's ever done for me... the only romantic thing.'

'That's for sure. I think he'll propose soon. God knows what he'll do for that – write your name in the sky or chop off an arm!'

The commercial break ended and we went back to our programme.

'I can't concentrate on watching this. I feel as if I've been pumped full of helium... I just think of Marc and I float away... I can't stop smiling.'

'That's the serotonin. Watch out, it's the hormones drugging you into thinking it'd be good to throw away your life on a bloke and kids. You'll come down with a bump in a few months – by that time, it'll be too late.'

'Cynical.'

'I'm a doctor.' Sally opened her mouth and tilted down the last of her beer.

'I'm just a love thing!' I said, beaming. 'Everything looks so different these days – from black and white to technicolour! I had no idea how big the world is! With Marc, anything is possible and life is to be enjoyed! Why didn't anybody tell me that? Life is to be enjoyed! Marc says–'

'Are you going to finish those poppadoms?'

Three people died today in front of my eyes, under my hands. And no, they didn't go peacefully. They contorted, clawed at their chests, were thrown from side to side, they fought with all their strength for their next breath, their eyes bulged in agony and their tongues turned blue. And then they lost. It's not called a heart *attack* for nothing. People find that out too late. On two occasions the families couldn't get there in time to say goodbye.

This afternoon Jamie's father and grandmother came by to hear the results of the autopsy report and deal with the administration to release his body. They came from the funeral parlour, still undecided about the colour of the coffin.

I catalogue the losses to the on-duty doctor, watch the night nurses come in and transform themselves from students, mothers, lovers into guardians of the sick.

'Going back to your family, doc?' asks the last patient I check up on.

Too difficult a question to answer.

Before leaving the hospital, I check my emails. There's one from Frances. The message is short and there's a phone number.

I don't let myself stop and think before I start dialling.

The woman answers after the first ring. Of course I hadn't thought what time it would be in San Francisco.

'You're looking for a Xavier Rocher?'

'I was, yes. Who is this?'

I can tell she's attractive by her voice and that she must have been sleeping, fitfully, on the alert for any news to come through.

'His wife. I'm calling to let you know he's not coming back to you, he's come home. To me.'

And now it hits her that the man she was looking for might not be the man she was looking for.

'That's not possible. Who is this?'

'Katherine, like it says on his arm.'

'You're saying Xavier's married?'

'He is married.'

'Why are you calling?'

'To save you the pain and waste of time. The woman he left me for enjoyed knowing I was suffering, going mad looking for him. I'm not like that. You can either believe me or not. It's up to you. But he's here, with me, his wife.'

'You're British.'

'Yes. We live in London.'

'Can I speak with him, please?'

'Save yourself. It's finished.'

When I say that, the phone, the office, the world wobbles around me, tears roll down my hands and into my sleeve.

'Is this some kind of joke?'

Through the glass door I see Dr McKendrick standing outside talking to someone. I have to finish this conversation and get back to work.

'Right, well, thanks for your concern but Xavier called me this morning. He just went out of town. He's coming home at the end of the week. Home to me. You've either got the wrong person or you're a very sick lady.'

Monday Afternoon

You're outside the hospital entrance, standing under the bike shelter reading notices about antenatal programmes and the new – now old – legislation prohibiting smoking in public buildings. It doesn't stop you blowing smoke into the light rain. The fleece top I bought you at the weekend looks all wrong. Everything's all wrong.

Your eyes follow a sparrow as he hops around the puddles. I realise that I put you in a world where you didn't belong, and I see that you tried and almost succeeded in covering up from me that you were suffering, until that morning when you closed the door and walked away.

'You must have been waiting ages.'

'It's okay.'

We don't talk much as we make our way home, I didn't have

the kind of day I want to think about again. And you, well, you just don't want to tell me anything.

'Did you have a nice time with your friend at lunch today?'

'You followed me?'

'I wanted to see you.'

'You spied on me?'

'You spied on me.'

All those shelves of folders, boxes and letters about you, maybe that was intrusive, but you left me no choice.

'I was *looking for you*, Marc. That's not the same.'

'I was gone. That's all you needed to know.'

Time. Do you know, I want to ask you, that I have never had a watch? Before I could tell the time, I knew I'd be working in a profession where they were considered unhygienic. I meter out the days by how many beats the heart makes per minute, how fast blood can travel down a vein, how long a person has left to live. And then I loved you, so I never counted the days or the blood cells left between us. I love you now, as you sit in my car trying to find a radio station you like. I love you now and I have about three days until the 'ping' of our timer goes off and I have to decide about us.

As I step out of my shoes, I open the letter saying that I was successful in my interview. I have been given the job I wanted at The Heart Hospital. There's another letter. The lawyers have confirmed that following a meeting and the signing of relevant documentation, our marriage will be annulled.

'Good news?'

'I suppose so. I got offered the job I wanted,' I answer, slipping the lawyer's letter beneath a pile of papers.

'*Félicitations!*'

'Thank you for doing the kitchen, it hasn't looked like that in–'

'I'm going to cook you something really nice, *ma belle*, and then foot massage and early night for you. Forget about today, I'm here now.'

You wink at me. It should be a heart-warming wink. But it isn't. I'd just read Frances' text message on my phone:

> No mistake. Phone call made to SF this
> morning from your home phone. Best, F.

TUESDAY

Tuesday Morning

'I used to relish the feeling of getting over an illness, like a bud unravelling out of the winter frosts: everything was a little brighter, tastier, more scented. I even thought I looked a little handsomer... dare I say it? I don't know if there's a medical reason, probably that one appreciates life more after being out of it, you want to get back in the game. But these days, the mornings come and I don't really wake up, not really. My timetable's full of pills I need to take and doctor's appointments, what hurts and how much. I've been forced into a career of being ill.'

My patient's purple lips barely move as he catalogues his post-operative existence. I don't normally see adults but this man is part of a research study I'm involved in. I've been used to answering the questions that children ask concerning their experience, and it strikes me how much more terrified, bewildered and attached to life an adult is by comparison.

'Some people feel completely different after a heart transplant, full of life and new beginnings, but others don't. They feel like you described. The body has had a lot to deal with: the heart attack, the operation, adapting to new parts. The heart transplant has maybe given you another ten years, possibly more, Mr Miller. Time with your family, time to do what you've always wanted.'

'I know, I know, I'm not ungrateful, I just... I'm not *myself*. Not the same man. I keep wondering whose heart I've got.'

'You know I can't tell you that.'

'Was it a *bad* man? Was it someone with a wicked heart and I'm going around with it in my chest—'

'Mr Miller, the heart is just a pump. Like a pump on a washing machine or a swimming pool. That's all. In most cases, the only difference between a good and bad heart is how much fat is on it.'

'The other consultant said that my old ticker problems might have started as a result of a flu from thirty years ago.'

He places his hands on his chest as if to keep it safe.

'Possibly. Every illness, meal, cigarette, stint in the gym or creamy cake contributes to our heart's well-being – everything we do from the time we're children catches up with us at some point.'

Mr Miller touches the stitched wound left by my blade ten weeks ago.

'So I'm housing the balance sheet of someone else's life. Don't you think that's the stuff of nightmares?'

'I really wouldn't think about that aspect of it too much. The earliest experiments with heart transplants were done with pigs' hearts and no one took on porcine attributes, anyway, looking at these test results, it was a good heart and–'

'But did it come from a good man?'

Tuesday Afternoon

When I left you this morning you were sleeping, and now you are sitting in front of me, shaking your head at a menu. We're in the restaurant around the corner from my work where the consultants come after management meetings, but today, we're the only people here. It's the first time we've been in a place like this, one that, in the past, you would have deemed an insult to food. We used to go to places that had just opened, were renowned or exclusive, often owned or run by friends of yours. We'd make a night of it, dress up, drinks beforehand, often with friends but sometimes just us. It was more than just an evening out, for you it was an experience – otherwise you liked cheap, authentic, regional food: bagels baked overnight from the East End, or curries from Brick Lane, British fish and chips. But this sort of place you despised: expensive, mediocre, derivative. So I don't know why we are here except that you wanted to spend time with me before I returned to work for the night. But I've a suspicion that this is an exercise in compromise: you are demonstrating to me that you can spend money on food you resent just to be with me.

I'm out of the hospital but my mind is still pacing around the wards. You look shattered, defeated, in that brown suede jacket you came back to me in. You touch my arms with your fingers, it's meant to reassure me, bring me back, but right now, that's asking too much.

'What did you do today?'

I ignore your hands sliding over my forearm.

'I went to the restaurant. They said I could get my job back whenever I want. The guy who replaced me is a "knob" apparently.'

'Really? So they'll take you back, just like that?'

'Why not?'

I don't want to start on the reasons why not.

'They must have had a shock. Seeing you.'

'Maybe.'

We roll our thoughts around, taste them out, see if they're worth carrying on with. Most aren't. I keep asking myself why you'd want your job back when there's a woman in San Francisco who's expecting you to return this weekend. How many lives have you been keeping on the go, how many promises do you plan to break?

'So were they thrilled to see you? Not even a little pissed off, I mean...'

'It's the hospitality trade, eh? We're trained to be nice to people's faces if it's good for business.'

'Still, must be a problem trying to find work at your age without any references. Most chefs of your calibre and experience have their own restaurants by now, maybe working towards a star – but you, you just keep coming in at the same level, don't you find that frustrating?'

'Not really.'

I'm going for the low jabs, punching on behalf of those who you let down and abused, those who've just rolled over and let you scratch their tummies. They've done nothing. Like I've done nothing.

'But you were ambitious, surely you wanted to have recognition and–'

'I make a living cooking food, that's all. It's for other people. I don't need to get myself on TV and write books, cook like a celebrity. That's not what I do.'

'Was the food good in California?'

'Sure,' you shrug, 'they have a lot of fresh fish, seafood... Ready to order?'

When the waiter leaves, you ask me if I kept any of your things. I haven't the energy to keep my guard up, and I've forgotten what we are fighting for, so I tell you, honestly, that I couldn't have thrown away your things. I couldn't really have let you go, but an act of providence did. A broken washing machine did.

Before

I was returning home after three days and nights at the hospital, a lecture, a viva and a forty-five-minute Tube wait in a tunnel outside Tottenham Court Road, and opening the door into my building, I could hear voices upstairs, loud and blaring. At first I thought Tom's TV had been left on. Going up the staircase, I saw my door on the other side of the landing. All my towels and sheets were on the stairs leading into my flat, where a fire fighter saw me and asked if I was Kate Brenton. Good question. I answered, keeping my focus on his black thumbnail that moved up and down the wall like a swollen slug extending from his sleeve. He explained that he was sorry, but they had to force entry. Chantal, the American banker who lives upstairs, came out of my bedroom with your dressing gown in her arms. She stopped, opened her mouth and then a rush of words came out. All I could think is that she looked so much younger in her pastel jogging outfit with the stain of tears at the sides of her face. She kept repeating, 'so much water' and then 'pouring, pouring down...' An arm touched my back, led me to our bedroom.

It was raining outside and inside the flat. The ceiling was a voluminous belly unable to bear the load of water. There was a constant flow running into our drawers, into my clothes, my books. Your suits were piled on my bed, my shoes in a mountain on the carpet. It was already starting to smell. Someone said, 'Cognac in the cupboard.' Chantal's BlackBerry rang. Gerry, her boyfriend, was on my sofa, yawning and saying something about only just getting in from Hong Kong. His downturned mouth and standing-up hair, the fire fighters trying not to gawp at Chantal's little breasts, my computer equipment in the bathtub – I was waiting for a commercial break to interrupt this soap opera that had become my life.

'Don't touch those!' I called out to a woman carrying the box file of recipes you'd collected over the years.

'Sorry, I was trying to–'

'That's my sister, Louise,' said Chantal. 'She's the one who called the fire brigade.'

'Sorry, they were wet and–'

'I'll take those. And the jazz CDs. They're my husband's.'

Louise and Chantal exchanged a look.

'Sure,' said Louise, 'I'll put them down right here. All dry. Right here.'

I walked from one dark grey wall to the next as Chantal kept saying 'sorry' and 'insurance' and 'top priority'. Then more people arrived. Maggie came down burning sage twigs from Northern California and said this was a sign that everything would be all right. But I thought, unless you came back right then and there, nothing would ever be all right.

We all stopped when we heard the bedroom ceiling tear – the crack. The deep, ripping crunch of weight through the wood and plaster. The rumble – there was the inevitable crash as it split, no longer able to hold back the mass of water. We just stared as the contents of Chantal and Gerry's sitting room hung over my bed.

While the others did things to prevent further damage, I stood, distracted at how our bodies made shadow puppets against the remaining walls with the blue light of the fire engines coming in from the windows.

'Kate Brenton... B-R-E-N-T-O-N. Get him over here now to do the report!' shouted Chantal down her phone as she lined up my bras over the window ledge.

Two men in overalls nodded to me.

'We've done all we can.'

The speaker had an uncharacteristically high-pitched voice. I kept my eyes on his colleague's infected thumb.

'We've cut the water, the 'lectrics... it's safe, but... got a friend or money for a hotel?'

Gerry stroked Chantal on the shoulder and padded out of the room waving his hand up in the air, half for goodbye, half in surrender.

The blue swirl of the fire engine's lights moved down the street to the next disaster, doors closed in our building, and I too, shut whatever little there was to close so I couldn't hear Chantal and Gerry arguing – we were almost in one flat now.

I sat on a plank of wood across the sofa, looking at the wreck until the candles and the torches sunk into an umber glow. There was the stench of old water in your books, soggy plaster on your clothes. There was a washing machine turned upside down on my television, there were plants tossed over my files. The Montblanc pen you gave me our first Christmas together was floating on my desk next to my sodden diary. Our home looked like the bottom of a drained ocean and you were nowhere to be found.

<hr />

'I wish I'd been there for you.'

'Me too. All your things.'

'Just *things*, Katherine.'

'Things aren't just things when they're all you've got left of someone.'

You hold my hand, squeeze and let it go, sit back as the waiter comes to take our plates.

'You wouldn't have believed the destruction, it was the like the flat expressing its grief, expelling you from its walls... Anyway, I guess it forced me to have a big clear out – find things I'd probably never have known were there.'

'Want dessert?'

'No. Coffee.'

You order two coffees. I wonder why it is that events only seem to have really happened when I shape them into a story to tell you.

'It's a shame it didn't drown that little shit downstairs.'

'Tom?'

'Yeah, him.'

'What's he ever done to you?'

'I don't like his attitude.'

'Attitude?'

'Every time I walk past his flat, he stands there, staring at me. You know, with this look, you scowl like Tom does. I don't find him funny.'

I don't want to talk about Tom with you, I've given you so much – I want to keep my shame to myself.

'Tomorrow's Wednesday.'

'Katherine, if you need more time–'

'No, Marc, you said a week. I need to pull the plug one way or another. You stay or you go, either way, I can start living.'

You turn the palm of my hand up, gaze at it as if it's a compact mirror.

I only have twenty-five minutes left of my break before I need to return to the hospital for the night. In that time, I try to explain to you the bond between Maggie, Tom and I in our building, the solidarity of the 'singles' against the 'couples', but you're not really listening. Hearing about the people who have gone some way to filling the chasm that you left isn't particularly interesting to you. Every so often, I draw in my breath, hold it until the weight of its force presses so hard against me I have to release it.

I can't identify if it's the sadness of what's gone before, or the sadness of what's to come.

'Can I sleep with you tonight? Remember how we used to, when I'd come into the hospital at night?'

'No, Marc. I need space.'

'Tomorrow?'

'I made plans for tomorrow, Marc. It's not like I knew you were coming back.'

'Plans?'

'Yes. Plans. Family commitments. Nick, actually.'

'Anna's Nick?'

'You kept his secret from me.'

You push my hand away, look around the restaurant as if you'd only just noticed where you were. And then I added, 'And hers.'

'Why would I tell you something that would've hurt you? I'll get the cheque.'

Before

'People never appreciate the destruction water causes,' said the insurance-company surveyor. He snapped off the window frame. 'Well,' he concluded, catching another clump of wall in his hand, 'the ceiling's come down, so the anticipation's over. Let's get the electricity back on again, then you'll need to take up all the carpeting unless you want a mushroom colony in your lounge. Could you just give me a hand lifting this cupboard away from the wall? Cheers.'

He picked up his folder.

'You won't be able to repaint until all the plaster's dried through, course March isn't the best month for that... what's the date today?'

It was 777 days since you left.

After the inspection, I started the process of filling black bags with stuff – a bag for me, a bag for you. Mine was to stay, yours to go.

I wiped a malodorous cloth along the back of the cupboard I'd just moved, and I saw the letter. The envelope was black with dust and damp, curled up like a tarantula.

You never kept anything. That was your creed, use it or lose it: what did you used to say? 'Yesterday's history, tomorrow's a mystery', something naff like that.

But the letter was in my hands. You'd slipped up – time had pulled a fast one on you.

My heart ran faster than my eyes could read. The clearer the message, the more confused I got. The sentences recounted meetings and retraced conversations, pages and pages, all about you.

All in my sister's handwriting.

Tom stood in what used to be called 'the doorway'. He'd only just got back from Ibiza and was still holding his suitcase when he joked: 'Ever had the feeling that the sky's just fallen in on top of you?'

'Yes. My sister was in love with my husband.'

'Huh?'

Tom came to kiss me. I was still staring at the letter.

'I found this... All the time Marc and I were together, she... she says... look... "Kate has no idea how she is stifling you, she just wants a husband ... she doesn't understand you... she hasn't got the capacity to love you like I do..."' I tossed the page down, picked up another. 'Listen, "Please, Marc, just give me one chance to show you how happy I could make you..." What kind of teenage, clichéd rambling is this? "You and I are free spirits, passionate, wild..."' I slammed the pages down and looked at Tom, 'All that time, Anna was in love with Marc.'

'And do you think they did it?'

It took me a moment to understand what Tom was asking. But in short, he'd got to the heart of my torment. Did you two do it? Did you 'make love' with my sister?

'I don't think so. She writes of her pain, that he ignored her, he didn't reply to her letters... apparently he told her he would tell me if she carried on. She says here, "Go and tell my sister. I don't care... tell her and maybe she'll let you go... If she really loves you, she'll set you free... "'

'Yeah, well,' Tom sighed, looking around him, 'looks like Basra in here. Just forget about all that, here, come down for a drink... hey, hey, it's all over.'

But not for me. I thought not knowing who you were was bad enough, but not knowing Anna, and being completely unaware that she relished her betrayal, that she despised me, that probably you both did, was worse.

'Where have I been all my life?'

Tom piled my clothes on top of his case before lifting me off my knees.

Tuesday Evening

We stand outside the hospital, the two of us are laughing at Mona's embarrassment. She'd bumped into us. I'd introduced you and for the first time seen her blush.

'You have good friends, Katherine. They love you.'

'I've put them through it.'

'Thank you for having dinner with me.'

'What will you do now?'

'Go back to the flat. Watch some television. Maybe go out for a drink with the little shit downstairs.'

'I'll be home early tomorrow morning.'

'Come into the bed naked, it's the best way for me to wake up. It might be the last time,' you say, catching my hand.

Before

After two years it might have seemed like I was getting on with my life. I was doing placements at different hospitals around London, and the change was a surprising tonic as well as being exhausting. Spending my days where I didn't have memories of you was a distraction and a relief. When I wasn't working or studying, I relaxed with Tom. It was an easy, recreational, and feelings-free affair between two single people who lived in the same building and enjoyed each other's company. We'd made our own little world together that was, at worst, a digression and at best, a comfort. That's how I wanted to think of it, if ever I thought of it at all.

When I spoke of my husband who'd disappeared, it might have seemed like the trauma was receding. There were even days that went by when I didn't speak about 'him' at all. But I still had bad days, times when I fell apart and wondered if I'd make it back again, and then, somehow, I did. I was impressed to discover that time does actually heal. Whether I was in fact being mended on the outside or just simply that I was exhausted and beaten by the search, I didn't know, but the episodes of grief were arriving at less frequent intervals and when they hit, it wasn't as hard.

But after the flood, after finding Anna's letter, those were some of the blackest times. Just when I thought the anguish was getting better, it became worse, worse even than the first weeks after you left – I lost you, and then her. I was told to take time off work and required to see the counsellor at the hospital. I stayed at Tom's and hardly got out of bed. The counsellor asked if I'd considered suicide, and it surprised me that she thought I'd have the energy to contemplate ending my life.

'Yup, stinks all right,' said the plasterer from his ladder as Chantal passed down a coffee through the ceiling. 'I'd get that husband of yours to take you away for a few days while it dries out.'

'He's away,' I answered, fitting a sheet over my new mattress.

'He'll have a shock when he gets back, eh?'

'I'd have a bigger shock, he left two years ago.'

'Oh,' he said, smearing the plaster across the last section of ceiling. 'What, just, *left* left?'

'That's one way of putting it, yes.'

'Happened to me. I was engaged to a girl, been together seven years and three months. Then, two days before the wedding, I came home and she'd gone. Lock, stock and barrel. I had a complete nervous breakdown. It bankrupted my parents – literally – keeping me, my mortgage, cancelling the wedding. We looked everywhere. It was the same time as that little Maddie McCann went missing but no one was looking out for Tracy. Police said it wasn't a crime to get cold feet about a wedding. They found she'd been on internet chat rooms and started up something with a bloke from New Zealand, that's where she went. She later got in touch with her nan. Said she couldn't explain why she left, just didn't want to spend the rest of her life with me but couldn't face letting everybody down. And that was that. Some people have no manners, no guts.'

Usually I would have defended you but I couldn't. This man had lived through what I had, and he knew what it felt like when someone wants to move on and can't be bothered to hang around long enough to say goodbye.

'I used to be so frightened of seeing her again, I just didn't know how I'd react: thought I'd kill her, or maybe beg her to come back, depending on my mood. Then, about three months ago, there she was on the high street. She'd married the chap from down under and come home to show her mum the baby. We said hello and then went our separate ways. It's a strange old thing, but the heart keeps going. I thought the world of that tart, but now, nah, I wouldn't want her back, she'd aged badly and apparently her new man is pretty quick with his fists. There. All done.'

Frances drew up a timeline and plotted where you'd been. It started when you'd lived beneath me in Tom's flat while it was empty – you must have left when the decorators came in. About a year later you were in Mexico and after that, probably San Francisco. Then it peters out. Frances was still working on the hypothesis that you had someone in England who was hiding you. I wanted to know where you were, of course, and I wanted to know why you went. Only one person could answer that. I was starting to forget things about you, like your laugh, the spectrum of your moods, the exact shade of your eyes.

Finding Anna's letter had confirmed that you had secrets from me, that you could betray me and that while our marriage had been everything in my life, for you, perhaps, it was just background noise.

It was during those 'bad' weeks Frances and I met in Hyde Park. She had something to tell me and was being slow about it.

'See this is where my line of work gets philosophical. I have to ask, what difference does information make? I can see you're pretty fragile right now and what I might tell you... well, I risk either sending you over the edge or helping you turn away from it.'

'Aw, you've got me all excited now.'

It was the first time I'd noticed that summer had broken, there were people scattered all over the park, lying in the sun alone or in groups, some seemed to have carried out most of the contents of their living rooms for the day.

'You look anything but excited!'

'The hospital has put me on to a counsellor. She says I need "closure".'

I mimic the way my therapist uses her fingers to ring-fence this word.

'Closure, yes. Usually comes just after you've absolutely bloody had enough.'

Then Frances told me what she'd uncovered about your life before me.

I walked Frances to Bayswater Tube Station.

'I've got time off work next week, maybe I should go to France, maybe going back is the only way forward. It's better than just staring at the wall,' I said, thinking out loud.

If you took the roof off the hospital and watched from above, the people in the white coats must look like pinball balls, shooting up and down, rolling across and back again over the same routes all day long. But at night, the choreography slows, the corridors lay empty and the pings aren't so frequent or loud, apart from the odd emergency when we gather round pushing and shoving to save a life. We do or we don't, either way, we write up the notes.

I tot up today's tallies.

A few hours into the night shift, the patients' faces are dimly lit by the corridor's fluorescent lighting. There's hardly a sound apart from muffled footsteps on lino floors and the regular bleeps of heart monitors. I already know the beds that will most likely be refilled tomorrow night.

'Barely a ripple tonight,' says the night nurse, flicking past a perfume ad in her magazine.

'I might turn in,' I answer, tapping my bleeper. 'Don't hesitate...'

'Sweet dreams.'

I want to call you, see if you are back in the flat where you said you'd be, but I'm not up to facing what I'd feel if you weren't.

Last night you slept with your arms around me, chaining me to you. You breathed regularly. You have spent your life on the run. You came in search of me, because I had a good heart, and you needed a good heart to tell you that you were forgiven. I could only forgive if I had personal experience of your crime, and so you wait for Judgement Thursday when I'm to tell you if what you did was forgivable.

Walking from ward to ward, I see a coffee machine and I see two people. That's us, eight years ago. So long ago. The two people who didn't make it through.

———

Before

When I saw the main fountain in Aix, the one we stood by that hot day, I was prepared to be torn apart – I'd allowed myself to crack at that point – but as the taxi approached, it was just a fountain. I'd over-prepared myself. My memories couldn't kill me.

The taxi pulled up in a side street and I walked into my hotel carrying my laptop, a file of photos and change of clothes.

I tried to speak French but the way the receptionist looked at me was so derisive, I switched to English to let her stumble around her dimly lit vocabulary. The hotel I found for myself was clean, quiet, and expensive. Alone in the room, I paced from the bathroom to the window, waiting for someone to walk in and ask what I was doing there. I unpacked, claimed my space. I missed you. I talked to you. I missed you more because you didn't answer.

The hospital was as I remembered and I saw myself by the entrance, moments before you came to change everything.

This is where Frances' research brought me. A Frenchman, Xavier Marc Rocher was last seen at this hospital the day we met. He was last spotted where he'd left his girlfriend and their newborn baby.

I passed reception, the long corridor where we waited for Max and then the coffee machine where the two of us first spoke. I kept walking towards the maternity wing.

At the nurses' station I asked about the day when this man was there. The nurse looked at your picture. Another woman joined us. They knew what I was talking about but were suspicious of why I was asking questions, they didn't understand what it was I wanted.

When I said I was a doctor, it confused them more. I added that I was looking for my husband who had disappeared. They relayed what I'd said back and forth and from their head shaking, I wasn't sure if they'd understood too little or too much.

A mother padded over in her hospital gown, looking pale and holding her stomach. She asked something, one nurse went off to help her, the other answered the phone and I was left standing alone in the hospital corridor.

If I went to the coffee machine – maybe I might find you there. I walked, light-headed, my feet unsteady, the ground moving under me. I couldn't find my way back. A porter wheeling a trolley motioned to the lifts. More doors. More corridors.

And then a voice called out, and a nurse rushed up to me. I prepared myself for being told off again. Through the scrabble of words I understood that a nurse who was there that day would be coming in later, she was due for the night shift. I had her name: Magali.

I retraced our steps back to the centre and to the restaurant where we'd had lunch. A waiter moving around inside saw me and gestured that they were closed. I stood there, looking at where we sat the day we met. How could I have known that as you poured me wine, your son was being born?

The waiter came to the door, pointed again at the 'Fermé' sign.

'Could I speak to the owner?'

'Madam, *closéd*,' he stressed, holding the sign up to my face.

'I've come to speak to the owner, the boss–'

A man walked out of the darkness.

'*Le patron*. Is me.'

The waiter moved away and I was in front of the man who'd known you that afternoon. I took out your picture. He glanced and laughed. He looked at me and laughed again. He put a hand on my shoulder and led me into the restaurant. He poured a Limoncello for the two of us.

'Xavier,' he said, shaking his head. 'Is it Yasmeen looking?'

'No, me. He's my husband.'

He dropped his head in his palm and looked at me sideways. He was clearly tired but amused enough to sit with me. He rubbed his eyes.

'Where? Where you married with Xavier?'

'London. But we met here – we came here to this restaurant – I remember you talking together; he knew you.'

'A little. He's a romantic... *ça c'est vrai*.'

'Two years ago he vanished. Gone! Disappeared!'

I flicked my fingers apart like a conjurer over a black hat.

He was laughing again, like he'd told a private joke to himself.

'*Et voilà! C'est* Xavier. Y'know?'

'No. Tell me.'

He poured us another drink and lit a cigar.

'Xavier. I met him first time in very chichi resort, in Théoule-sur-Mer, near Cannes. Xavier arrived, no papers, no friends, no experience... but he was very good. Very good. Speaks English, persons like him, soon I make him *Le Responsable*. Yasmeen *était serveuse* – waiter? – there. Xavier had many, many girls, always, but she... like this...' He made a claw with his hand. 'Like this, eh?'

I nodded and had to ask, 'What was she like?'

'*Les yeux verts viper*. She make beautiful clothes, sold them in market. Girl *intelligente,* good English. When the season was over, he want to go in America, he has plans, rich people want him to make parties there. Big opportunities for him. But Yasmeen many problem. She make baby...' He shook his head, sipped at the drink. '*Et lui? Pouf*! Like you say, "disappeared".'

'Have you seen him?'

'Non. No *au revoir, ciao ciao*... I have friend who see him in Maroc.'

'When?'

'Months ago. He still run from Yasmeen! But you too! So he leave you?'

'Seems like it.'

'You find him, you tell him he always has job with me. He's good man, but problem for too many women!'

I left him still clucking at the thought of such a problem.

After an afternoon sleep and a shower at my hotel, I waded back through the tourists to the hospital. Magali was on duty, she had been prepped for my return and, after finding someone to cover for her, led me outside to where she lit a cigarette and told me about that day.

Magali had been on duty the morning Yasmeen was in labour and suggested her partner take a coffee break. Magali directed the soon-to-be-dad to the drinks' machine. He was a little long and the pregnant girl started screaming for her boyfriend. Magali reassured her that he'd be back soon. But the girl wasn't happy to let him out of her sight. When the baby's head could be seen, someone was sent to find her partner. But he wasn't in the corridor, on the ward or in the hospital. The father had gone. The receptionist said she'd seen him talking to some tourists an hour before.

Magali shook her head and closed her eyes. 'Her screaming... like I never heard. I was saying, "He will come back... look at your baby... " But the girl knew he wasn't coming back.'

'Did she call the police?'

'*Hein?*'

She glanced at her watch.

'I know you're busy, but, if you could just tell me about what happened.'

'It's good I practice my English, my sister lives in Miami so, I try, but, then I must work.'

I nodded. 'So did she call the police?'

'Tse, *non*. She was a young, poor, unmarried Arab girl. The police don't care. I was sad, really sad for her. She left the hospital early, before she was officially discharged. But she had to find this man. She was crazy, she made me afraid for her and for the child. I never did this before or after, but I found her address and visited her. I was worried about the baby, and her, and it was...' Magali shook her hand in the air and covered her mouth. 'Terrible! The way she lived. She was crying, the baby was crying. To stop the noise she put sweets in its mouth. They had nothing and the landlord was asking them to leave... I went back the following week, but they'd left.'

'What did she call the child?'

'No name. She didn't even give the baby a name.'

I showed her your photo.

'Yes. That was him. So, you found him?'

'No, I lost him too.'

That night I called Frances from my hotel. Within the hour she faxed me the details about Yasmeen El Jarri. They hadn't been difficult to find: she's now Yasmeen de Lancey. Even I'd heard of her. She's no longer the nineteen-year-old Moroccan whose family had abandoned her when she was pregnant. No longer the waitress you had a fling with and hoped to dump at some point, the girl you left bearing your child. She's now a successful clothes designer married to a property tycoon.

I left the hotel and bought every fashion magazine in the newsagent's. Returning, I spent the evening cutting out pictures of her. There weren't many – just little photos of her fashion shows, clutching models and stepping out with her husband. The internet threw up a few interviews, but the woman talked about her work, not her private life. There was never any mention of a child. I stared at her face all night – it was an obsessive binge which I justified by telling myself I was looking for a link, a clue, a trapdoor.

In the morning I called her work numbers, tried to get hold of her at home. I left messages for her – she had shops in Paris, London and New York, but she didn't return my calls. Then, just before I left France, I received an email from her. It read: *Leave me alone.*

The plane landed through London fog and as it taxied towards the terminal, a dark stain of dread spread through me.

It was a surprise to see Tom at the airport waiting for me. He was smiling, holding flowers, a gesture that was touching but at the same time wholly impractical.

'Good trip?'

'What are you doing here?'

'Oh, thanks! Well, whenever I come through the arrivals hall, I always look out for someone to be there waiting for me and then I'm always disappointed that there isn't. Silly, isn't it? But there you go. Anyway, I thought I'd come meet you, bring you home. Are you cross?'

'No, no. It's very sweet,' I said, trying to manage my bag, my laptop and the flowers without crushing them.

Yes, silly. But then, I hadn't seen Tom at first because I'd been looking out for you.

One decision I'd come to while away was that I had to end whatever it was I was doing with Tom. Somehow, despite never having started, it was already going too far. As the gardens of Victorian terraced houses zapped by the windows of the Gatwick Express, he chattered animatedly about his week. But there was a high-pitched note ringing out behind everything he said that only I could hear: he'd missed me. He thought he loved me. He imagined some kind of future together. We shared the same home, our apartments had merged, our days and stories had fused, but the intimacy of our lives, which he thought was fate, was only consequential. I'd needed so much; he'd thought I needed him.

When we made love that evening, clinging on to each other as if we were falling through the bed, I didn't finish anything between us. If it wasn't him, it would have been someone else. And I wasn't up to ending anything.

A few days later I met with Frances over a beer in a garden pub after work. She put a file down in front of me. It was labelled 'Xavier Rocher'.

'It makes pretty hard reading,' she warned.

I put the folder away and passed her an envelope filled with cash I'd withdrawn regularly from ATM machines in payment for the info she'd collected.

She filled me in on a few details. Yasmeen had been in London to celebrate the opening of her South Molton Street shop. After the first-night party she'd gone on to Johan's club, The Nadir. She was the girl Tom and Maggie had seen around our flat, and Johan identified her as the red-head you were quarrelling with at his club.

'Do you want to pursue this?' asked Frances. 'There's a chance they could still be in contact, maybe together.'

I thought about Yasmeen's email.

'I have to respect her feelings, after what she's gone through.'

'Yeah. If he could do that to her, to a little baby... but read the file, you'll understand him better. One other thing that's niggling...'

'What?'

'Yasmeen's never mentioned having a baby. There are no pictures, photos... nothing. There's the birth certificate, no records of a death. The child must be somewhere.'

Tuesday Night

I'm standing outside the hospital entrance watching the last of the visitors move quickly into the night air. I'd called Anna a few minutes ago, woken her up and she sounded groggy, breathless with the weight of the baby inside her. We agreed to meet at my flat tomorrow – it will be our first meeting for a very long time. And while I have my phone out, and all is quiet, I ring my home number. You are watching TV, but there's nothing on. You too sound sleepy. You say you miss me. I say I'll be home early tomorrow morning, that I miss you.

I do too. I'm about to ask you to tell me about your child – but my pager goes off and I'm called to an emergency.

Before

Late one night a few weeks ago, I was returning from a missing persons charity event when, as the taxi pulled up outside my house, the driver said it looked like I had company.

There was a man curled up on my doorstep. In the darkness, it could have been you. All that day, I'd had this feeling, this was going to be the day you'd come back to me – but then, I'd had that feeling many times before and I'd been wrong.

'Marc? Marc?' I said, just like I did in my dreams.

'Kate?' croaked a voice from inside the coat.

I tumbled onto the body, pulled the hand away from his mouth.

But it wasn't you, it was my brother-in-law Nick.

It'd been over a year since I'd seen him. After reading Anna's letter to you, I broke all ties with my sister: whenever she rang, I slammed the phone down, refused to answer her emails, texts or open the envelopes with her handwriting on them. A few times she'd arrived at my parents' home demanding that we talk, but I'd leave immediately and gradually, I went home less and less. There was nothing to say. I'd read how she'd willed me to lose you and then you'd gone. Anna always got what she wanted.

'Nothing's happened to the children?'

'No, no, they're fine... fine. This is about me.'

'Here, go in,' I said.

On the stairs to my flat, Tom opened his door and stood glaring at us.

'All right?' he asked.

'Sorry, did we wake you?'

'No, I was up,' he said, staring at Nick. I saw the flickering of the TV against the ceiling inside his flat. He kept his eyes on Nick. He probably imagined that this was Anthony, the man he viewed as his rival.

'Tom, this is Nick, my sister's husband.'

Nick wobbled forwards to shake Tom's hand.

'Pleased to meet you. Terribly sorry to disturb you at this hour.'

'No problem, mate.'

Tom looked at me. 'Night then.'

When I let Nick into the flat he took off his sodden coat and then his shoes.

'You thought I was Marc sitting on your doorstep. God I'm sorry.'

'It's not the first time. I think I see him everywhere these days. It was his birthday a few weeks ago.'

'I do that too... think I see him... I've even approached people–'

'Nick, if Anna's asked you to mediate between us, I won't.'

'No, no, Kate, there's something I want to tell you.'

'Sure everything's all right? The baby, everything?'

'Yes, yes, sure.'

I divided up the last of a bottle of wine between us.

'Do your neighbours often check up on you?'

'Tom? No... well, yes, he's a little protective.'

'I thought he was going to challenge me to a duel.'

Nick's scrawny, yellow fingers grappled for a cigarette. 'Do you mind?'

'I'll have one too,' I answered.

'Really? I didn't know you smoked.'

'Occupational hazard. Nick, it's late. What's this about?'

Nick looked at me. At his wife's little sister. I don't know what the picture he saw was, possibly hints of the woman he'd married fifteen years ago, before the lust turned to domesticity, children, constant lack of money and whatever had brought him to my door. There was a time when Anna was curvaceous, provocative, not always pregnant or breastfeeding or asleep. There was a time he wanted to spend his evenings with her, not cowering in doorways.

'I need help.'

'What help, Nick?'

'Big help. I couldn't think who else to turn to...'

Nick stubbed out his cigarette and looked around the room. He pushed his fingers through his damp hair. His eyes were bloodshot. I watched as his thoughts choked him. He gasped for breath. The words just didn't come. I took in a lungful of smoke, let it out, swallowed the wine.

'I'm a heroin addict.'

I went over and held him as he cried into my neck.

'This'll be our fourth baby... and I still can't stop... help me, Kate... help me.'

'How long has this been going on?'

He sniffed in his tears. 'Since I was seventeen. Only on and off and then for the last five years it's been all the time. I need help, Kate. I don't know where to turn.'

'Does Anna know?'

'No one knows. Well, apart from Marc.'

'Marc?'

'He knew. The first time I met him he took me aside and said I disgusted him. He said I was a "low life-form". True.' Nick smiled a little. 'That's why we never really saw eye to eye. He said he'd been involved in drugs when he was a teenager, been in a gang, did terrible things. He never told you? I always wondered if he'd told you.'

'No,' I whispered. 'Never. There's a lot I didn't know. Do you know why I don't speak to Anna?'

'I suspect that she made a play for Marc?'

'I found a love letter.'

'Kate, I'm partly responsible for that. I had my secret – it was in my interest that Anna had hers.'

'You didn't write the letter.'

'No, but I saw how Marc could distract my wife from focusing on me. I exploited her being besotted with him. I didn't want to be the one who made Anna unhappy, I let Marc be the brute, and when he disappeared, well, he finished the job rather well.'

Having unburdened himself, Nick had become quite voluble.

'Did either of you have anything to do with him leaving?'

'No, no... but there was one thing – I couldn't have told you before without letting on about my problem. About a month before he left, we were at your parents for Sunday lunch. I was going up to the bathroom to have a hit and he followed me. He touched me for a line, said he wanted to see if it was still so terrible.'

'He took drugs? With you? In my parents' house?'

'Yeah. He just snorted some heroin, looked at me and said something like, "I'm going to have to go back into my past and clean up the mess I made. One day, you will have to do the same... every day you fuck up now, is another day you have to fix up later".'

We sat in silence.

'Kate?'

'Hmm?'

'When he left, I was pleased. I was grateful someone else was worse than me. I'm sorry, I knew you were in pain but I was relieved. That's what this demon drug has done to me. Messed up everything, more than you could ever imagine. I'm not me, only a sliver of what could have been. I'm not a man or a father, or a... I don't know, I'm a... low life-form.'

'Stay here tonight. Tomorrow I'll make some calls, get you in somewhere–'

'No, I need to score tonight. I'm hanging out, y'know, withdrawing. It'll be my last night. Can you lend me £50? Or do you have anything here?'

'Nick!'

'I just told you: I'm addicted – I can't go through the night without...'

Nick stood over me as I searched for money in my wallet, then I felt a tug and the bag was ripped from my hands. He was out of the flat before I had time to look up. When I shouted after him, he was already out on the street.

Anna was six weeks away from giving birth and her husband had disappeared. She called me and this time, I picked up. I couldn't leave anyone in a pain I knew too well and offered to go up to Oxford to tell her personally what I knew about Nick. I avoided her questions and ducked under her guesses. I was trying to protect her, needless to say, I'd made her worse. So that's how it felt to be on your side of the lies. To be the person who controls, edits and revises what another person knows. You chose to live that way, I didn't.

The afternoon I was due to go to Anna's, two policemen came to my work.

They sat me down in McKendrick's office and told me they'd found Nick in a chemist in north London trying to use my prescription pad to get drugs. I collected him from the police station and from there, drove to the treatment centre that had agreed to give him a bed.

It was terrible being with him – that car journey, his crying amid frantic bursts of laughter. He asked which hospital he was going to, when I said the name, he tried to jump out of the car, 'That's where all the celebrities go! I can't turn up looking like this!'

Passing the gates, I pulled up the hand brake and we sat in silence, both of us with a sense that these were the last minutes before he signed off on what had been his life up to that moment. What I didn't know was that I was about to take a turn and step into yours.

Nick's counsellor, Ewan, met us at the door and welcomed us as if we were his guests for a weekend party. He was only a little older than us but a lot wiser. After he'd recounted the arc of his own addiction and said that he was twelve years 'clean', the disclosure, as well as the promise of duck-down pillows, reassured Nick. We then went through a form detailing Nick's drug history. He listed every legal and illegal drug I'd ever heard of. He said he'd injected in his neck, his feet, that he'd overdosed several times, that he'd stolen from my parents and even pinched his grandmother's morphine as she lay dying.

Ewan wrote it all down without any reaction, I tried to stay impartial, professional, non-judgemental, even when he described burgling his own house.

'Did you not know about this, Kate?' asked Ewan.

I shook my head. 'None of us knew.'

'Right. And how have you organised payment for the treatment, Nick?'

Nick looked down at his hands. 'Can't I smoke?'

'No, sorry,' replied Ewan.

'I'll pay for him to do this,' I said.

Nick looked at me. 'Kate?'

'I want to. We have to start repairing this family or there'll be nothing left.'

'But–'

'Don't worry, Nick. Please. It's for Mimi, Bruno and Ella.'

I looked back to Ewan. 'His wife, my sister, is just about to have her fourth baby. Do you think he'll be ready by then?'

'That's up to him... Nick, we've got Group starting in five minutes. But first...' Ewan lifted a camera out of a drawer, 'we have a tradition of taking pictures of our clients when they arrive and then we can compare it with how they look when they've completed the programme – a before and after shot. May I?'

Nick contorted his face into a best-effort smile while I was thankful we didn't have the same practice in hospitals. Someone came to collect him for therapy leaving me standing with Ewan in the hall.

'I haven't spoken to my sister for over a year... what do I tell her?'

'The truth. Deceit, denial, cover-ups, lies, these aren't just symptoms of an addict but everyone around them. Breaking that down is the first step to attacking the disease. It doesn't help anyone to protect him. Here, I've got some literature you might like to–'

'Just... I'm trying to understand... Nick's here, with you and a bunch of new friends, clean sheets and cooked meals, ping-pong and shiatsu, while Anna's all alone with no help and three children – pregnant with a fourth – how's that fair?'

'She can call me. We can arrange sessions with a female counsellor. Come into my office and I'll get the contact number.'

In Ewan's office, a juggernaut of fatigue crashed into me. My heart started pounding, fast, my blood turned icy, white lights flashed across my eyes. Breathless, I couldn't even call for help.

'Kate, it's okay, rest your head on your knees, there... breathe in, hold, breathe out...'

I moaned into my trembling knees.

'And what about me?'

'Sorry?'

'What about me? What about me?'

I was shaking, visibly pulsating, either suffocating or too full of air.

Ewan's voice was calm, gentle.

'What about you, Kate?'

I was held hostage by my convulsions. Ewan waited for it to end.

'How can they just smash up lives and then go on?'

Ewan passed me a box of tissues.

'What's happened to my family, to Anna and me? We used to be so close and happy and... normal. These people came into our lives, like viruses, they ate up everything good: look at us, we're just walking husks.'

'Slow down, tell me–'

'My husband left me and I can't find him and this search for him, it's a compulsion, a torture... an addiction. I'm no different from Nick.'

I held my body in with my arms, keeping it together, heard myself yelling, 'What did I do wrong?'

Ewan sat opposite me.

'Kate, do you want to talk about this?'

Yes, I did.

The grief was making a break for it – I'd reached a point where 'help' wasn't enough, I needed to be rescued.

When I finished telling Ewan the story of the last two years of my life, the crying didn't abate, I continued while Ewan listened. I heard the group finishing, voices around the building, supper being prepared enthusiastically downstairs.

'When one person in a family reaches out to find help, often the others follow – recovery is contagious like that. I get the feeling you've been carrying your own pain as well as everyone else's. You're a doctor. You're paid to look after others, be in control, have the answers. But you're also a woman whose husband has suddenly "gone" – I'm not surprised it's hitting you now.'

'But how do I make all this stop?'

'*You* stop. Take it in. Feel it. The anger, the hurt, the confusion – all of it – you need to confront it in order to get to the other side of grief. If not, these self-destructive tendencies, these expressions of loss and rage, they'll overwhelm you like they did this afternoon.'

'I have a counsellor, someone at the hospital, but she's just someone else I vent my anger on. No one seems to really understand.'

He rubbed his forehead until a thought came to the surface.

'We have a patient here, someone who's been through a similar experience. I could ask her if she'd like to talk with you, sometimes it helps just to have someone to identify with. Would you like to meet her?'

I nodded. Ewan went outside, there was the mumble of considerate voices. I could hear Nick starting up a conversation with another guy. He was laughing. Ewan returned with a woman behind him.

I knew at once it was her.

'Kate, this is Yasmeen, she's in her last week here. I thought maybe you two could benefit from having a chat.'

Yasmeen studied me as her bony, brittle legs in their thigh-length boots crossed the carpet. Her eyes glanced down at the crumpled tissues in my lap. I saw a little smile, a smile for her, not for me. She had a gap between her two front teeth and grass green eyes set in layers of dark lashes. Settling her waist-length red hair behind her as if it were a pet, she seemed to be deciding whether to toy with me or just finish me off.

'We know each other. Yasmeen de Lancey.' She put out her hand. It was small, soft, like a child's hand, so different from the hardness in her eyes.

'Oh? Well, I'll leave you both to it.' Ewan turned for the door, gave us another look and left.

Yasmeen sat down. I was taken aback by how attractive she was. Not like the photos I saw of just a pretty face. Her voice, the way she moved, her self-assuredness. I was jealous of her. Jealous because I could see what drew you to her. You had a baby together. She was a part of your past, like me. Maybe I would be like her in the future and I didn't want that, there was nothing nice about her.

'If I believed in coincidence I would say, "Wow, my God, what a coincidence!" But every woman involved with Xavier probably ends up in the nuthouse, eh?'

I picked up a tissue from the floor.

'Still finding it hard, Mrs Doctor woman?'

'Didn't you?'

'Look where I am.'

'Because of Marc, you're here?'

'Partly. Whenever life is difficult, I drop in here, take time out, get straight again.'

She saw Nick's confiscated cigarettes sticking out from my jacket pocket. She took the packet, pulled one out and lit it.

'I thought you weren't allowed–'

She waved the thought away.

'*Ça fait du bien.*' She blew the smoke out of the window. 'You had a private detective watching me.'

'Sorry.'

'My husband hired one too. I had two following me everywhere, can you imagine? Certainly made my life a little more interesting, but still.'

She blew the smoke out in one long line just above my face – you used to do that.

'Do you know where he is?'

'The last I heard he was in Marrakech. He had a friend called Momo – Mohammed – we worked together at one time. Momo was like Xavier's – Marc's – brother. Momo had AIDS. I heard that Marc was there when he died. Then Marc took over his bar and his identity. Well, a con artist like your husband wouldn't miss an opportunity like that.'

She looked at the half-smoked cigarette and extinguished it in her fingers, slid the butt back into the pack and the pack into her boots. She walked around the room like a show horse, all the time looking at me with the greenest eyes.

'I left you alone when you told me to, but I'd always wanted to see you, to talk to you.'

'What's the point? If it was right we met, we would, like this. Anyway, I was in a bad way. That's what brought me here, prescription drugs. From doctors. Ever since Marc left, I needed them. He left me with nothing but pain and a baby. You know what some girls do for work, Dr Brenton, when she has a baby and no money? Men pay a lot to suck on lactating nipples, when your vagina bleeds, they pay extra.'

'I didn't... know that.'

'Marc did. He knew.'

Her eyes were on me, pulling me to her face, but I couldn't look at her. I was ashamed for you, ashamed for me. When you left me, it felt like I had nothing, but in fact, compared to Yasmeen, I was spoilt: a home, family, friends, a career. I wanted to apologise to her for that.

'How is the little boy?'

'He's not so little. But he's resilient, well, he's had to be. I don't want to talk about him now.'

'But where is he?'

'Leave him alone.'

I squeezed at the tissue, willing her to speak more.

'I was always curious about you. A young professional, English. You seemed so... excuse me, but... *boring*. Marc left me for you – left our baby for you – I've hated you. So, why give you anything?'

'You knew where he was? And about me? Why didn't you...?'

'I did.'

For some reason, she stopped being tough and clipped and sat down again. And then, without any prompting, she closed her eyes and told me the story of you and her. As she spoke, she relived it but it was like she was talking of another Yasmeen... and I suppose she was. A Yasmeen who had all the men in love with her except the one she wanted: you. You wouldn't let her seduce you, and then one night, after work as she was putting on her bike helmet, a group of men who'd been at the bar, surrounded her – she thought they'd rape her, kill her even –

and you appeared out of nowhere, intervened and saved her. That's how she broke the code to you – you were bored of being adored, you wanted to be there for someone more vulnerable than you, so she dropped all her defences and let you in. Her worst mistake.

When she fell pregnant, the men in her family threatened to murder her and the two of you moved to Aix-en-Provence where you planned to start a life together. She had no idea, Marc, no idea you were going to leave. It was you who wanted to get married, have the child and live together, she'd never have dared dream as much.

'Maybe you know a little of what it was like, but, Katherine, I had his baby.'

She looked down into her hands.

'Why do you think he left you?'

'He was playing a part and then, he just walked off stage. Because he didn't – *couldn't* – stay in one place and be one person. He was afraid he would fail. Fail at being a better man. He always wanted to be the romantic hero. Like you are in the beginning of a love affair, unproven, untested, this is what he wanted. And, Katherine, your private detective, she must have found out about his mother? What do you expect?'

'What happened when you saw him again?'

I knew what she was going to say, Marc. She took out the cigarettes and lit one. She was taking her time: she was relishing the kill.

'It was after I left here for the first time – two and a half years ago – I thought my life was finally making some sense: I was clean, my husband and I were trying to make our marriage work, I'd just signed a big contract designing clothes. One night we all went out to celebrate, and the place that was chosen for our night out was Marc's restaurant. Can you imagine? I always knew I'd see him again – I even wondered as I got out of the taxi if that would be the night – and when I walked into the restaurant, there he was. He came to greet us. He was shocked, really shocked to see me. I didn't want to talk then, and I wanted him to wait. Sweat a little. So he came to see me, the next day, where I was staying, at Claridge's Hotel.'

She stopped speaking. She wanted me to beg and I had no choice.

'Yasmeen, then what? What did he say?'

'Katherine, we didn't really get into all the talking bit.' She leant in and hissed in my ear, 'We spent the whole time in bed.'

And then she kissed me. Her mouth sucking at my lips, spreading them open and moving her tongue over my tears, the emptiness you left. In all those men I looked for you, the closest I came to finding you was in this woman.

Her jaw gradually closed, her lips pressed over mine, she left them there, hesitantly before a last tender touch, her lips getting tighter and drier. She leaned back, her eyes glassy. She was cold, brittle again.

'Katherine, you haven't been too bright about all this, have you? The secret is to *enjoy* the search – it's all you've got left. I'll give you a tip: 44 Hathaway Street, Hounslow.'

WEDNESDAY

Wednesday, Sunrise

When I come out of three emergency operations and look outside, the violet sky is frayed with strands of gold. It's gone five thirty in the morning. The beeping of the monitors is regular, the nurses whisper in their stations, the delivery trucks and the catering staff will be arriving and soon there'll be bashing and clattering in the kitchens before the general high tide of people come in and out all day long. But for now, the new day lies dormant.

I'm writing up the night's notes. Looking into space, hoping that enough words come to make a sentence, I see a smudge of black moving against the white corridor walls in front of me. A man's silhouette. Against the neon lights, you are just a dark shape, but I know your walk.

You slow down when you see me at the desk, pick the chair up and place it opposite me. You sit, drop your head in your hands. When I go to touch your face, it's wet. You take my fingers and press them to your mouth. I can smell alcohol on your breath. Your hands feel like metal in mine. You look at me and tell me without speaking, that it isn't that you won't talk, but you can't.

A nurse passes, stops, widens her eyes at us. I lift my hand for her to leave us. She mouths, 'Sure?' All too frequently we have psychiatric cases, addicts and drunken men coming in off the streets wanting to fight, steal drugs or sexually harass the nurses, but often just to talk. But this one's my problem.

There was a time your eyes took me everywhere: Alpine skies, Mediterranean coasts, caves of lapis lazuli, but now, they lead only to sadness.

'Where does it hurt?'

You press my palm onto your solar plexus.

'I'm going to lose you,' you say, your voice breaking into octaves of sorrow.

'It's not just a matter clicking a switch off and on.'

'I know, Katherine, I know.'

The file Frances gathered on your childhood was terrible to read. Over the pages I learned that your mother had been only twelve when she had you and would probably now be diagnosed as bipolar, although her mental state is difficult to work out due to her drinking and drug taking. She worked in restaurants, as a dancer, a cleaner, beggar, call girl – she did lots of things, but nothing for long. You both moved around regularly and every time you settled in a home or with a foster family, your mother would reappear and insist on taking you back. She'd promise that she'd changed, learnt from her mistakes. She'd spoil you, indulge you, lure you back into her trust until a new man would appear in her life and you were dropped. Her relationships were always violent, obsessive and all-consuming, in no time she'd revert to drinking, drugs and paying for them by prostituting herself. The little boy she went to so much trouble to win over became a nuisance and someone only good for taking her anger out on. There was no mention of a father.

Either the social services got involved or she'd tire of having a child around, and she'd drop you off somewhere, put you back into care, and you'd not hear a thing until she turned up again, unexpectedly, undoing your world with her plans for a new life. The day of your sixteenth birthday, the file was closed. You disappeared from the system.

We doze in each other's arms before day breaks through the wards. Voices shift up a gear from whispers to normal decibel range. Trolleys rumble along the corridors. The lift doors ping open and closed. Daylight. You stretch your legs, stand up unsteadily and walk away.

Before

The day after I met Yasmeen, I went to watch the house in Hounslow.

From ten in the morning to two in the afternoon I sat in my car waiting for you to come out and explain how you could be connected with possibly the most ordinary house in west London. Two-up two-down, 1930s pebble-dash front, crazy paving, overflowing bins, sprouts of grass fighting for survival beside a half-built fence. No gnomes, no satellite dish, no stickers on the windows. Just a house.

And the feeling that Yasmeen had taken me for a big ride.

When the man two doors down closed his gate and started down the road, I chased after him.

'Excuse me? I live just up the next street, I was sent a package for number forty-four by mistake, but I wasn't sure of the person's name–'

'This one, love? Forty-four? That's... er... Sam. Dunno her last name.'

'Is she married?'

The man tried to connect the logic in my questioning.

'I've seen her kids play in the street, but... don't know 'bout that, dear.'

I sat back in the car. Sam. I was ready to drive away but couldn't find the strength to lift the hand brake. Children.

I wanted to start the car and leave. Who was I looking for anyway? I needed to pee. If you weren't really the man I'd married, what was I doing in your business? What was I doing badgering Sam's neighbours? But I was there, in front of the house: one council-painted blue door away from my last chance to kill off the illusion of you. If I didn't do something now, I'd have to come back after the weekend, after work, however painful the truth, my imagination was torture.

I walked to the house, opened the gate and up the inconsequential path. I pressed the bell on the door, heard it ring inside the house, muffled, irritating. Then the sound of fast, light footsteps in the corridor. A chain slid across the catch and I saw the face of a little boy.

'Yeah?'

'Is Sam in?'

The boy nodded.

'Could I speak to her?'

Without looking away from me he shouted up the stairs. 'Mum! It's her from the social.'

I could hear a door opening from inside the house.

'Mum!'

'Yeah, yeah, I heard you.'

Over his head I saw that the house was modern inside, it was well decorated, not like it seemed from the outside at all. There were children's toys scattered across the landing.

I saw Sam, legs first, cantering down the stairs in pale pink jogging trousers, her lithe, tanned waist punctuated by a diamond in her belly button. Above she wore a tight Lycra pink top that enclosed overly large breasts. Then lots of blonde hair caught at the top of her head by a diamanté clip.

'Decided to have a look at us in person, have you?' she said.

She stood a foot away, hips slanted to one side, her hand, weighed down with bracelets and rings, resting on her midriff. She must have been in her early twenties but she had a worldliness about her that made her seem older. Having children young, I guess, must do that to people.

We looked at each other as I searched for a place to start – I know, most of the day sitting in a car doing nothing, you'd have thought I'd rehearsed what to say, but I hadn't. Her directness, the little boy's eyes staring at me, not having eaten, the adrenaline highs and then the lows, it had all emptied me out.

'I saw you there, in the Megane 'cross the road. What's this about?'

'I just wanted to know if you knew this man.'

Papers and things spilled out from my bag as I grappled inside it. She bobbed her head, her mouth a little open, her eyes on me, daring me to waste her time. I stood up, fought an overwhelming light-headedness, and showed her a picture of you.

The boy immediately started chanting, 'It's Marc. It's Uncle Marc.'

'Nah.'

'Your son seems to think so.'

'Yeah, well, he's got a lot of "uncles".'

Her voice was deep, it had a catch in it like something primal inside her was fighting to come out.

'That's–' the boy started to say.

She put her hand on his shoulder, hard.

'Can I come in, just for a few minutes, just to–'

'No. No you can't. Who are you?'

'My name's Katherine. Katherine Brenton. This is my husband – I'm looking for him.'

'What makes you think he's here?'

'Someone gave me this address.'

'The French bird... Yasmeen, the designer? Her, wasn't it?'

'Yes. She and Marc had a relationship, he abandoned her, he married me, he left–'

'Whatever.' She pressed the door against me.

'Please!'

'No, you "please". Marc comes and goes as he feels. What he does when he's not here, that's his business, got it?'

'I'm worried that he might be in trouble or hurt. I just need to know...'

'Mum, she's going to cry.'

'There's nothing to say.'

'You don't have to let me in but imagine if something happened to someone you loved.'

I looked at the boy, she let go of the door, walked down the corridor leaving me to walk in.

'But I've got to pick the others up from school at four.'

I followed her through to the kitchen. I sat down as a glass of lemonade was put in front of me.

'Is Marc the father of your children?'

She spluttered out the drink she'd just taken a sip from, wiping her mouth, laughing.

'Marc's old enough to be my dad! He might be a lot of things, but he's not a kiddy-fiddler.'

'So you're not... with Marc... like that?'

'Marc's like... like Harvey says, "uncle". To all of us. This is why I don't want to piss him off answering questions to all you people who keep coming round. He's done nothing to us. I'm sorry about your thing – your marriage, whatever – but that's just him, innit?'

'I've been searching for him for over two and half years.'

'Your problem.'

'When's the last time you saw him?'

'Like I said, he pops in and out.'

'When did he last "pop in"?'

'Can't answer that.'

'So what's your connection with him?'

She took the clip out of her hair, let it all rush down her back and shoulders, then she went about twisting it all back up again. A gesture perfected to draw men's eyes to her neckline and those expensive breasts.

'My nan was French. She was his social worker when he was growing up in France. They were really close, she loved him like a son, but the authorities didn't allow her to officially adopt him because his mum was around, but every time his mum did something bad to herself or to him, he was sent back to her. Then when my nan and her husband decided to move to England, to run a B&B, he came over, lived here, got it all running for them and that. As I said, he comes and he goes, that's Marc, that's what he does.'

She leant forward, crossing her arms on the table. On the top of her right biceps were four letters tattooed in blue. She looked at what I was looking at, the name, 'MARC'.

'Oh that. We got legless one night, got them done, mine got bloody infected and all. Still, looks all right... Look, I've gotta run.'

'Can I speak to your grandmother or mother–'

'They passed away. Breast cancer, both of them.'

'I'm sorry.'

'S'not your fault. Listen, Marc's like a fairy godfather to me, well, not the *fairy* part – what I'm saying is, I haven't got any other family, nor has he. He looks out for us. Please, Marc needs a safe place – people he can always trust – I don't want to talk to you. Nothing personal. Harvey!' she called up the stairs. 'We've got to go.'

'I was his wife. Why didn't he tell me about you?'

The little boy was playing upstairs, banging something on the floor.

'He didn't tell you nothing about him growing up?'

'He told me he had no family... no one. And yet he had you. Why didn't he tell me?'

'It's complicated. Because of–'

'Because of what? Who?'

'Harvey! Now!' She took my glass and put it in the sink.

She looked into her garden, as though mentally listing the things she had to do later, a deflection tactic.

'Just one thing, please. Did he ever talk about me?'

She turned to me, roughly calculating how much this information would cost her.

'Sure.'

Harvey was now waiting by the door in a white karate outfit.

'He said you was the best thing that ever happened to him, and that you made him want to be good and better every day he was with you.'

I never missed you so much as that moment when I heard her say those words. That's what you'd said to me the day we married.

'And yet he didn't trust me?'

'Someone has to know you completely before you can trust them, it's obvious really, he didn't want you to know him completely or... I've said too much. Please, you have to go.'

'Thank you.'

'Yeah, well. Sorry I can't help you no more, and... er... I don't mean it like it sounds, but don't came back here again, yeah?'

I helped her over the doorstep with a pushchair and Harvey in tow.

When we got into our cars, she gave me a businesslike wave and drove off, relieved I was out of her life and you were still safely in it.

Wednesday Morning

I drive from the hospital back home, over the edges of a creamy mist swilling out from the parks and gardens and into my nostrils, tasting of tin. I roll the car past my flat, look up at the windows. The blinds are down. I park the car, cut the ignition, drop back into the seat.

A bang on the bonnet and she's in front of me.

Anna. She's shouting at me through the windscreen. All in grey but for her red cheeks. Her blonde hair springs out from the top of her coat which she's unable to close over her pregnant stomach. Her arms flail on either side of her belly. She falls over the car when the loudness of her voice forces her off balance. She rolls around to me, opens the door and shouts again, 'You didn't say he was back!'

I hold my hands over my ears to protect myself from her screeching, but she continues ambushing me with her size, her loudness.

'You didn't say! You didn't say he was back!'

She tugs at the passenger door, throws it open and lands into the seat next to me.

'Just go! Go!'

I start the car again, just to shut her up. Disappointment closes in on me. I'm homesick. I'd so wanted to go upstairs, touch your skin, spend time with you and rest a little before leaving for the day. The last time I saw you was at dawn in the hospital, your tearful eyes, the alcohol on your breath, I don't want that to be the final image of you in my mind today.

I was hoping you'd have talked me out of collecting Nick from his treatment centre or that I'd have had time to flake out on my sister, it was a gratuitous offer of kindness to Nick and Anna to pick him up and drive them both back to Oxford. Now I don't feel at all up to it. And this is the last day before I decide about us; I might not have the chance to come home to you again.

'Drive.'

Her breathing is short and fast. The car moves off. She seals her hands over her eyes, either collecting herself or building up to another outburst.

It takes me a while to reverse out of the space. A bicycle passes by that I didn't see. He swerves, shouts something. I stop and let a car go in front of me.

'I can't believe you didn't say anything!'

'I told Mum. I just assumed she'd—'

'She doesn't tell me anything!'

'I thought we'd talk about it today, on the way to see Nick.'

'I rang the bell, went up and there he was – *Marc*! I'm eight and a half months pregnant! Can you imagine a shock like that? Christ!'

'Sorry. I didn't think. I was working last night and I thought I'd be back first, but...'

'You didn't think! Fuck! Go on, drive!'

At the end of my road, I indicate. I'm about to move off but just before I do, I check the rear-view mirror to see the flat once more, and there you are, closing the door behind you, running up to the car. You open the back seat door and lean forward, kiss my cheek.

'Good morning, beautiful Katherine,' you say, your hand on my shoulder. You stroke my neck. Anna looks away.

I drive in silence, no one daring to detonate the charge of fury crackling around Anna. I catch the odd glimpse of you. Your face is somewhat crumpled and bleary-eyed from lack of sleep, but it only adds to your appeal. You catch me looking at you, wink. There's no medical explanation for how you make my heart spin, send everything inside me flying. I look again; you have a little smile on your face. I cover my mouth like a mischievous child who wants to giggle at being told off. Your eyes dart over to my sister, back to me and we both know what the other is thinking. What was it you used to call that? The connection between you and I, *complicité*? For you, it was the sign we were meant to be together, but when I looked it up in the dictionary, under British law, it's a criminal offence.

Traffic gathers around the motorway junction which I sense that Anna blames me for. She can't upset me anymore, not when I have you there, your fingers lightly pressing into the top of my shoulder. I'd forgotten how much easier life is when you have someone else who is on your side, someone who doesn't really care about anything or anyone else. For a moment, we were there again.

Towards Surrey, the roads clear, you suggest we stop off to have a coffee somewhere. I nod in agreement, but then you add that Anna has something she needs to tell me. She flinches but doesn't contradict you.

There is a pub that serves breakfast. Anna and I sit down, take off our coats and scarves while you bring us coffees. After the first sip, Anna goes through a series of long, even exhalations. The bartender keeps looking over at the pregnant woman, anticipating any medical emergencies that might arise on his premises.

'What do you want to say to us, Anna?'

She looks out of the window. Her renowned pearly skin is white, dry. It's the first time I notice the little fans of even pleats on either side of her eyes. She won't look at either of us. You stir your espresso. Anna writhes on her seat, then looks at me, willing me to understand what she has to say before she has to say it so she doesn't have to explain further. I realise that I have missed my sister very much since we've not been speaking. I can afford to be generous now that you are sitting next to me.

She sips her tea, winces before opening out her hands as an expression of honesty. She looks at you, you nod back to her. It's then I want to freeze you both, walk away from all this, go somewhere far, far away, unrecognisable from anything I've known before. I don't need to get a biopsy done on what's built up between us, if it's bad it'll kill us, if not, we'll go on.

'When you told me about Nick, you asked, how could I not have known I was married to a smack addict? I must have seemed like the stupidest wife in the world... after you, of course.'

'Thanks.'

'You're welcome. The thing is, Nick and I have led very separate lives. Even when... well... I wasn't the person he went to when he needed help – it was you.'

Her eyes fill with tears. You yawn.

I know my sister, and I know when she cries, like now, that it is not because she is sad, but afraid. It's when she knows she's done something wrong and been caught out. I could save her from all this and just say I know, I read what she wrote but all I can do is concentrate on the brown and orange geometric-patterned carpet in the pub and avoid reminding myself this could be our last day. And then she's off.

'They say love is blind, but it's not: *lust* is blind. You want someone so much it hurts, whatever is in the way, you just see how to get past it. There's nothing else you can do. All you think about are ways to get that person, how to wear yourself out of that longing, consume all that makes them *them* until you can get your breath back and see that they're just like everybody else – that's just anaclitic obsession. But love, love sees *everything*. That's why, after being with someone at the other end of desire, they no longer leave an impression, they bore you, they drain you. You just get too close. They aren't really what you wanted, and the same image of yourself looks back at you from their eyes, and you aren't the way you wanted. That's how I felt in my marriage – and then... Marc.'

I wait for her to take in a series of deep breaths and a sip of water.

'Marc's a tease, an ache in the groin, an orgasm that never reaches climax.'

This gets your attention. For the first time in her discourse, you react to Anna's summary of your character by whistling. Anna continues to talk to me, but really, she's talking to you.

'Marc keeps people in a permanent state of lust – that's why no one really looks at him, *really* sees him the way he is.'

You listen to Anna's explanation of your power but she might be explaining Phlogiston theory or clinical trials in skin care. Your elbow rests on the back of your chair and you lean your head close to mine, occasionally nod, all the time half-smiling, awaiting vindication.

'I thought I was in love with him, but I realise now, I just wanted to fuck him. Sorry, he's your husband, but I fancied him. I dressed it up as something else, something to justify and romanticise why I'd put so much at stake for such ignoble reasons – I convinced myself that ours could be the greatest passion of all time – because we make out that love is the ultimate, purest emotion and sex is just something for teenagers and randy old men. But lust is a fatal illness: you're paralysed, obsessed, oblivious to everything else around. It keeps you on the scent, leads you in one direction, makes you run everything else down – all I wanted was one fuck and I nearly lost everything because of it. I lost you.'

And now it's my turn to spin out of the loop. I thought I had my guard up, but Anna looks so small, defeated. Someone walks in the pub, turns to her, the blonde hair does that, or maybe it's because she is crying. The barman pours him a drink, both men make a point of looking away from us.

'I told him before you got married that I loved him. You were never right for each other. Marc should have been with me.'

You sit back. It's out. Anna puts her palms up to her eyes

and cries just like Mimi, her daughter, does. I can't hate her for falling in love with you. I remember our squabbles over toys and books and friends that went from childhood into adolescence – never thinking it would extend to husbands.

'I found one of your letters.'

'I guessed something like that.'

Anna takes out a tissue, dabs her eyelashes.

'You need someone like Daddy, or this Anthony Mum's always going on about. Marc is a free spirit, he's a romantic, he needs to feel, to roam, explore – not be domesticated... not mortgages and roasts with the in-laws. Of course he ran away in the end, what did you expect?'

'I read what you wrote. I couldn't believe you could be so bitter towards me.'

'I said, I was in lust.'

'Marc, why didn't you tell me any of this?'

You shrug. 'Why?'

'Because of what my sister was doing behind my back.'

'That's why, you say. But I kept that one letter just in case I did need to tell you one day.'

I look at her again. 'But Marc didn't reciprocate, did he?'

You look around the café, then wink at me.

'You really want to know?' Anna asks.

'Tell her.'

'At Daddy's 60th, he was drunk, so was I, I begged him to make love to me, I promised that if he gave me what I wanted, I'd leave him alone. We went into your old bedroom, he got me to take all my clothes off, he started me up like I've never known – I've never wanted anyone so much in my life – and then... he... he just walked out. Left me there, like that.'

'So you didn't...'

She snorts. 'Humiliation is more his style.'

'She was being annoying,' you say, finishing your drink.

There's a crack in the cellulite clouds and a liquid blue runs beneath it. The light catches your eyes. You are untouched by all this, you make it happen, but you're not to blame because we are not really talking about you. You're sitting right next to me, but I still don't know where you are.

You look back at me. If Anna wasn't watching us, I'd ask you to hold me, wrap me up, ward off the world. Instead, I ask, 'Is Anna one of the reasons you went away?'

'No, Katherine, I loved you, your family and–'

Anna cuts in. 'It was a fucking relief when he went away. For all of us. And you'd be a bloody idiot if you took him back.'

'Like you taking Nick back?'

'Yes, I suppose, I'm a bloody idiot too.'

'Must be genetic.'

'Don't say that to a pregnant mother of three!'

She hugs her stomach and we laugh – like sisters.

Finding out about Anna had been a shock, and yet, on the other hand, I'd known it all along, somewhere. I wonder if your leaving was a search for integrity, perhaps my search for you was as well and all we find is that we love people who can sometimes hurt and disappoint us very much.

'We done?' you ask.

'I know I am,' says Anna, pulling at my sleeve with a grin.

Before

Driving back from meeting Sam, I couldn't keep up the charade of missing someone who didn't exist. I'd never really known you, Marc, and I'd colluded with your disguise – I loved a mirage, fragments I'd created for myself. Anna loved that same person too, and we'd both been left holding on to nothing.

Instead of going straight home, I parked up and walked over to the hairdresser around the corner from my flat.

'Got a special occasion?' asked the hairdresser, turning the ends of my hair disparagingly in her fingers.

'It's Valentine's Day tomorrow.'

'Gotta man taking you somewhere nice?'

'It's our first-year anniversary.'

'Shall we knock him off his feet, eh?'

As she cut, I thought about that moment at the coach station when you told me I wasn't ready for you. After that I'd grown out my hair. And I kept it long, for the day you came back. The pieces fell in clumps to the ground. Seeing Nick trying to break from his addiction, Yasmeen fighting for her career and marriage, I couldn't keep holding on to something that hadn't been there in the first place. I'd operated on enough hearts to know that you can seal up a valve and channel the flow in a new direction.

'There you go, that'll knock years off you,' said the hairdresser.

As I'd guessed, a year after our first dinner together, Anthony proposed. He went down on one knee, presented me with a ring that looked like something out of a cracker – a small, simple diamond poking out of a gold band, a month's salary. I said 'Yes'. We phoned my parents and his mother who were all delighted. Then you returned, just as I was having some good days again.

Wednesday Afternoon

Nick stands at the door, hopping from one leg to the other, bouncing his holdall against his calf with an uneasy smile. Seeing the car he gives us a happy-camper wave, skips over to Anna and works up something close to a hug. He asks after the children, not listening to her answers. He rubs her bulging stomach. He doesn't seem to know what to do with this family he is meeting again. He tries to read Anna's tear-stained face, tugs his hand free of her grip. He does a double take when he sees you getting out of the car. You hug him – the connection is genuine, fond. He recomposes himself, stumped for ways to address you. He looks at me, I don't know how to present you either, what to say, so we laugh, awkward yet excited. You pat his back, he pats yours. Neither of you ever thought you'd have so much in common as you do today.

'Do you mind staying for a little farewell bash they're putting on for me?'

The wind blows twigs and splatters rain into our faces as we follow Nick into the meeting room, which is already filled with people. Ewan has saved seats for us, and without even trying, he manages to make us feel part of the group. When we sit, I see Anna's lips trembling. Someone offers to bring her a tea. And the ceremony is underway.

Nick got a double First from Oxford and the MacMillan Travel Writers' Prize for his first book. His travel writing won impressive acclaim and on the back of the last he even presented a documentary on TV, but I don't think nearly as much of a fuss was made of these achievements as his graduation from rehab.

We sit in a circle as his peers make speeches about him. They applaud, heckle, whoop and clasp each other tightly. They talk about a Nick I haven't seen. Much of the ritual, the vocabulary and the insiders' jokes pass me by, but Anna, you and I clap when prompted and try to stay celebratory. All the time, what Anna said about you earlier has been churning in my mind so that it's now thick, sickening and stuck into my imagination. I can see it: the two of you at Daddy's 60th birthday. Why my bedroom? How long did it take? Did you enjoy humiliating my sister? Is that what you missed from me? Is that what you went in search of?

Where Nick has found friends and support, a 'family' who love him, the three of us are fast orbiting away from each other. A nurse comes forward with anecdotes of Nick's late-night hot chocolate drinking sessions and the group laugh. Ewan shows us Nick's before and after photos and says that Nick is compassionate, percipient and full of warmth towards others. You drop your hand over mine. Ewan concludes by awarding Nick with a medallion and a book is offered, which the inmates have signed. After more applause, it looks like the session is coming to an end. But it isn't.

Standing behind Ewan is a visitor whom he introduces as someone who's come specially to say goodbye and *Bon courage* to Nick. It's Yasmeen. In her smoky French accent she says that she was touched by his story and his courage. Apparently he helped her. She looks at him with those emerald eyes and wishes him luck in his future, especially looking after his young family, his wife, Anna – she searches the faces for Anna's and gives her a half smile. Then she sees me and she says how lucky he is to have such a sister in-law. And then she sees you. She stumbles over the next few words, embraces Nick and leaves the room.

After the final applause, someone announces that there's tea and biscuits being offered in the lounge, this creates another round of cheers and the party stampedes to the other room. Anna mumbles something about going to be sick.

And now there's only the two of us.

In the last week, you haven't reacted to anything, but this time, it's your turn to be stunned by a ghost.

'I met her when I brought Nick here.'

'She's like Nick, a junkie?'

'She had a lot of problems, but she's putting the past behind her. I heard Yasmeen's story. In fact, I've been to your "safe place" in Hounslow – yes, Marc, I've met Sam. I read your notes, the ones the social workers collected on you. It's not everything, I'm sure, but, hey, I've even spoken to the next girl. The one in San Francisco who thinks you're flying in from a training course in New York tomorrow. I get the feeling this week isn't turning out quite how you planned, is it?'

I'm just about to leave when Yasmeen strides into the room. She stands in front of you, smirking.

'Just don't forget your promise. This time,' she says poking her finger in your chest, 'you do it right.'

THURSDAY

Thursday Morning

There was only the dregs of night left after we'd returned from Oxford, not that we would have slept much anyway. Now, as the sky tips towards morning, draining out the colour, we lie on the bed, neither of us having bothered to undress properly. Like that first morning you came back, a week ago, we do not speak. Anything said would brutalise the first layer of membranes sealing us together. And now the cold splash of reality: our last day.

Chantal and Gerry are having a pre-breakfast row upstairs. My sister is waking with Nick, the first morning of their newly minted lives and in a week or so, Anna will have her fourth baby. Later today, I'll have to either accept or reject the offer of my new post at another hospital. And you are waiting to hear if we will begin living our lives together again.

You stop the alarm before it goes off. You hook me in the crux of your arm, draw my head to your lips and kiss the top of it. I could wake up every morning like this. With you.

'Coffee!'

You jump out of bed – then fall back theatrically. The little show makes me laugh because the tension is just so high we'd do anything to let some relief in. And you're trying to make this easy for me. It's not like you haven't been here before, but I'm just a novice.

I'm thinking of Anna and Nick. We were at their house last night when he returned home. The kids chanted their daddy's name, attacked his bag in search of presents while Anna made hot chocolate for them and kept repeating that Daddy was back. But none of them knew who he was anymore or what family he was returning to. For now they are slowly beginning to remove the bandages, pulling out the stitches, assessing what there is to work with.

I roll up your sleeve to look at my name on your arm. Nothing can take me back to that night, you in that tiny hospital bed, showing me the tattoo you had done, signing me over as the architect of your future.

'I learnt more about you when you were away than when we were married. Surely that's not the right way around, is it? But I now understand why you left me. It was all you'd known.'

'I want to change.'

'I know. But maybe, one shouldn't start at the end–'

'It's not the end, it doesn't have to be...' You mumble into my hair.

'What happened to that coffee?'

––––––––––

When we'd left the treatment centre last night, the first port of call was my parents' home to collect the children. Anna got out of the car first, then Nick. I followed. When my mother saw the fourth person in the back of the car, she said, 'Kate, not him. Not *him*. I don't want him in our house.'

You understood, sat in the car until we returned.

My mother showed remarkable restraint not asking about you as she bundled up the children's things, kissed them goodnight and tried not to stare at Nick who was smoking in the rose garden, flicking ash over the buds. Daddy wasn't there, apparently he 'needed to finish something off in the lab'. My dad will take a long time to absorb the information about Nick, let alone you.

But then as we loaded up the car and arranged the sleepy children wrapped up in their pyjamas, my mother rushed from the house up to the car. She banged on the window where you sat and shouted, 'How could you do this! How could you do this to my girl?'

You stared back at her. She opened the car door and looked at you.

'First you leave her – leave her without a word – then you come back! You are selfish! Selfish and cruel. Don't ever think you can come to our house again. Never! You are... *scum*!'

She slammed the car door and ran back into the house.

Anna held the cowering children as Nick and I stood opened-mouthed. None of us had ever heard my mother raise her voice before and 'scum' was the worst word she could possibly come up with.

Nick popped Bruno on Anna's knee, shoved another child beside her and shoe-horned himself in. I turned the ignition key as the headlights lit up the camellia bush that'd been planted the day I was born. You moved to the front passenger seat with Ellie sitting on your lap. I started to reverse, relieved that I could avoid looking at you. I kissed the top of Ellie's head as she looked out the window then back at you.

'Scum,' she repeated against the window, an oval of steam against the glass.

I rest the side of my face against your back, my arms around you as you pour the coffee. I can hear your heart, deep inside you; your good heart, breaking against mine.

'I need the morning free, sort things out,' I say.

'Sure.'

You escaped on boats, airplanes and strangers' cars, and today I revert to my default settings, 'sorting things out'.

'Where will you be this afternoon?'

'At Sam's. I said I'd look after Hervé this afternoon, she's got something she has to do.'

It's the first time you speak these names out loud. And look, it wasn't that difficult, was it?

'I'll come find you there then, eh?'

'Yes, if that's what you want.'

When I return from the bathroom, you are dressed and about to leave. I kiss your cheek, one side, and then other.

'Bye.'

'*A tout à l'heure.*'

You hold my hand. It's a grip that sometimes I give to patients, an earnest 'I'll take care of everything' clasp. We can never promise that to anyone, but doesn't it feel good to try?

Moving around the empty flat after you'd left, I shift things from one place to another, wipe surfaces, empty the bin. I'm not changing anything, I'm not making a difference – with all the expectation that'd been built around this seventh day, I would have thought I'd have something to do apart from plumping up cushions and brushing my teeth.

I open all the windows. The sun has broken out of winter and is charging over London. Everything's in colour. The tops of the roofs steam, birds swoop by busy on missions, music plays from inside cars. It's all going on regardless.

I have a shower, enjoy how easy and freeing it is to dry my hair now it's short, a few rubs and all done. I scan the line of beauty products on the windowsill. These are my things, and they will be here, when maybe you will not.

You preside over all my thoughts, waiting to find out what you will do with your forever. Meanwhile, I'm going out to cash in on the beautiful day, maybe buy a gossip magazine, which I haven't done for years, take a little walk, separate the night from the day.

It's bright, clear enough to see the studs on the branches where new leaves will sprout. People appear from cracks and crevices, without hats and scarves but colourful jumpers and surprised buoyancy. They are sitting outside cafés in sunglasses, laughing loudly, looking around for more people to join them, trying to reassure themselves that it's not completely insane to be sitting outside at the beginning of March – because, in truth, it's still pretty cold.

You said once that this is when you mark the New Year, in spring, when the cycle of nature resets its clock; not in January, dead of winter, when half the living world disappears in hibernation.

With a few groceries and the magazine that I'll probably never have time to read, I return to the building. There's an open van outside and two removal men lifting Tom's sofa into it.

I move quickly to his flat where an emaciated woman all in purple is standing in his living room with a clipboard talking on three telephones at once.

'Where's Tom?'

'Um. Uh. Um.'

She puts up a hand to stop me talking as she takes instructions from someone on the phone: '*Ciao* for now.'

'Where's Tom?'

'New York.'

'Where are you taking his stuff?'

'New York.'

'New York? For good?'

'Maybe.'

She decides to decorate her answers with more than two words, said clearly for the hard of hearing and slow in understanding – just another annoying thing she has to do as part of her job.

'Tom's moving to New York so this apartment is going on the market.'

'I saw him a few days ago, he didn't say anything.'

One of her phones starts ringing.

Tom's flat is heartless without his television on, his boyish smile and constant chatter. I regret the way everything turned out between us, that I could have been so naïve as to think just taking from someone could be simple.

I'll write Tom an email in the next few days. Obviously, I need to know if he's also going to sell my flat, but more than that, it's important to say goodbye.

I walk up the stairs and into the home we bought together, although probably not that much is left of the original flat we first saw. When the insurance money covered the flood damage, I bought new furniture, put in little halogen lights and replaced the old Victorian sash windows – even the outlook is different – and it's not even our home anymore. Yet we say people never change.

Birds tweet, kids shout across the road, buses hoot, it all sounds clearer through a cloudless sky.

After making a few phone calls to the hospital, it's time.

I know where to find you.

Thursday afternoon

The first time I'd seen the house in Hounslow it had seemed so grotty, banal and nothing to do with you, but now I know this late morning, it's everything to do with you. This is where you have a home. This is where your son lives.

Walking up to the front door, I hear shouts and laughter. A family are in the garden playing football and by the sounds of Sam's cries, I guess she's in goal.

I ring the doorbell, asking myself, *Will they let me in?*

Sam comes to the door after the second ring, she stands in front of me, red and laughing.

'Katherine,' she says, catching her breath. 'Sorry, we were... beautiful day, innit?'

She stands to the side, gesturing for me to pass. They were expecting me.

Through the sliding kitchen doors, I see you lying on top of Harvey, grappling for the ball. He has your laugh. You are curled around each other. When you look up and see me, you stop tussling, let him go. You jump up and walk over to me. I speak first.

'He has your laugh.'

'He's a better striker,' you say.

Harvey runs over, looks up at us. 'I met you before.'

You take my hand and kiss it. 'This is my wife.'

'What? You gotta wife?'

'I do. Katherine, this is Hervé, or Harvey.'

The boy laughs. '*Herrrrrvé!*'

You laugh with him and I see Yasmeen's green eyes in his and your dimples.

Sam jogs up with a little girl in her arms, knocks the ball out of Harvey's hand, he chases after her. You shake your head at them, lead me into the kitchen.

'Tea or there's beer?'

'Actually, beer sounds good.'

I follow you to the kitchen. You don't hesitate over where to find the glasses or the bottle opener, and I realise this is the first time I have ever been invited over to your place.

We stand opposite each other, you with one hand in your pocket, the other holding the bottle of beer up to your chest.

'So this is what you tried so hard to keep from me?'

'I'm not ashamed of Harvey, Yasmeen or Sam or anyone... just myself. I wanted to protect you from the big mess I made of their love, and most of all, your love. I don't think I've succeeded to impress you much this week. I dreamed of showing you how much I love you and need to be with you. I missed you every day I was away and then when I saw what I'd done to you... I wondered if I'd just made you suffer more, been just as selfish – and cruel – like your mother said. I thought being away I'd learnt a lot, but then, maybe nothing.'

'I learnt this week that love is all about mess.'

'Me too. But this time I want to stay in it, be the man to deserve it, to make you happier than we've ever been. If you want that too.'

'I do want that too. It's what I always wanted, but I have to ask, Marc, the woman in San Francisco...'

'She was a friend, also my boss. There's been no one else but you. You are my wife.'

We put our beers down and hold each other tightly.

And you are back.

We break apart when Yasmeen walks through the door carrying a tray of food.

'*Allez tout le monde* – sorry I'm late ! Come on, *à table!* Hervé! Sorry – I couldn't get the iced tea he likes but, this okay?'

Sam and Harvey run into the living room to help her with the food she's carrying. They go through to the garden together. Another little boy a few years younger than Harvey waddles out.

'Brownies!' exclaims Harvey and the boy jumps up to see

them. Yasmeen taps his hand down, says something fast in French. Disgruntled, he pulls up a chair.

Sam shouts over to us, 'Marc, don't forget the salad dressing!'

'It's coming!' you call out as you pull bottles out of the cupboards.

'Because of you I forgot all about the vinaigrette! You go on, *cherie*, I won't be a minute.'

I walk back into the garden while Yasmeen is loading food onto the children's plates.

'Katherine,' she says, kissing both my cheeks. 'Marc said you were coming here today. Sorry for yesterday. I was a bitch to you both but it was a shock, *hein*?'

'I can imagine. I should have warned you, but I didn't know you'd be there.'

'Excuse me, who's the winner of hide-and-seek?' Harvey asks me while loading some quiche into his mouth.

'I don't know, who is the winner of hide-and-seek?'

'The skeleton in the cupboard!'

Yasmeen applauds before filling up my plate.

'Did Nick get back all right?'

'Yes, it was a bit rocky with my parents but he seemed pleased to get home.'

Yasmeen shakes her hands in the air, her bracelets rattle and she has an endearing giggle. 'All these skeletons! But I liked him, and your sister too. We plan to have lunch when I get back. I leave for Paris tonight, Fashion Week's coming up and I have a show to prepare. I just came to say goodbye to Hervé.'

The toddler asks Sam for more juice, and she takes her cup to refill it.

It's just Yasmeen, the kids and I around the table. She kisses the crown of Harvey's head.

'He's a really lovely boy. I bet you're very proud of him,' I say.

'I am, *really* proud. I've done nothing else to be pleased with in my life... but him. He's very happy here, and he loves Marc. It's a little crazy, these *familles recomposés* but it's modern life, eh?'

'Marc and I... I think we're going to try to patch things up.'

I don't think she understands the expression but she knows what I'm saying. I add, 'You probably think I'm really stupid but...'

'I think you're brave, and to be brave you have to be a little stupid. Hervé? *Attends*! Katherine...' She drops her head, breathes in, and says, 'It's probably not important but I wanted to confess something. I lied to you when I said that when I saw Marc again, three years ago, we... had...' she lowers her voice, 'sex... It wasn't true. It wasn't like that. We had a dramatic moment, yes – after all those years, as you can imagine – but, in the end, he made me a promise. He said he would accept Hervé, share him with me and be a father. We brought Hervé here and for some time he visited and did things with him, and then he disappeared again. That's why I was so angry with him and I directed it at you. It was unfair. And I'm sorry.'

I look back at the house, the home where you found refuge all those years ago.

'I really do understand. I'm not proud of things I've done either. I just want you to know, I will do everything I can to make sure Harvey has a good father and... stepmother.'

'I know you will. And when Hervé is with me in Paris, you must both come and visit.'

That's the promise you made to Yasmeen, to take her child, your child, and give her back the life she'd not been able to have while she was looking after him alone and juggling her career. This is where you started working out your repentance, and that night before you left, it was I who threatened to tear down the amends you were trying to make.

The night before you left. That dinner party. We were tired from work, we wanted more than anything to be alone in front of the TV and I made us go out. I didn't have time for your protests, I didn't really listen to you when you said you wanted us to be together that night, that you had something to tell me. I thought if it was important, it could wait – and for that, I waited.

That last night, Anthony was there. I saw you watching us while we talked of hospitals and his connection with my father, and I could tell you didn't like it. Seeing you a little jealous was touching, but what you saw was that your wife chose this sort of night rather than being with you. Of course, you'd only just been with Yasmeen, met your son, made a home for him with Sam who was the only person who knew about your childhood and your secrets, that night you must have despaired ever reconciling those two worlds.

Later in the taxi home, you said something you knew would hurt. You said that that man, Anthony, was the sort of man I should have married. And when I couldn't contradict you, it must have wounded you even deeper.

I sit in the garden with Sam, her children and Yasmeen as Harvey talks about the football game we're going to play later now we almost have a full team. Sam ladles out the salad.

'Marc! Get a wiggle on with that dressing!' Sam shouts. There's no answer from the kitchen. She calls again, 'Marc!'

We look at each other.

'Marc?'

'Maaarc?' calls out Harvey.

Sam gets up and goes into the house. A cloud passes over the sun.

Yasmeen and I put our knives and forks down. The little girl starts to cry. Sam comes out again.

'He's gone.'

The night before you left, I knew ours was a holiday romance, and we were dying, we were terminal, Marc. I married you because I wanted to pretend to myself that we could make it, but we couldn't have done. Not as I was then. Before you left, we were already moving apart, expanding into the void, put simply, our marriage was decomposing. You were suffering in front of me but I overlooked the most obvious symptoms.

Once again, you've slipped out of our lives. It's what you've done before, why would you do otherwise?

Yasmeen lights a cigarette. Sam holds Harvey tight against her. Neither woman can face looking at me.

The food's getting cold. Untouched.

It's often the case that a doctor can try everything in their power to help someone get better, but it's just not enough, the miracle doesn't happen and we just have to let go. I thought I could love you better but I was wrong.

The front door slams.

The kitchen door slides open and you appear, carrying a bottle and a handful of spare change.

'You were out of white wine vinegar and Harvey wanted barbecue Monster Munch, not those and... What? What?' you ask, taking a seat next to me.

I hear people around me laughing and feel your arm around my back.

'Katherine, you thought I'd gone?'

Do you remember the time when I let you watch me operate on someone's heart? I'd seen you in your kitchen working, and you came to watch me do what I do. Halfway through, one of the juniors had to lead you out of theatre. It wasn't like when I watched you make *carbonnade flamande*, it made you sick and faint, it does that to most people. When I came out to find you, having a cigarette outside the hospital, white and tremulous, I apologised for exposing you to something so bloody, so violent and terrifying. It's probably best when we don't know what goes on inside. You looked at me and you said, 'It wasn't the blood, Katherine, it was the smell. People really stink.'

I'd forgotten to warn you: bodies cut open, they reek.

You gave me a choice. Seven days ago you returned. You entered my home, a stranger with his own door key. You came into my bed and gave me a week.

Yasmeen fills our glasses with wine and raises hers.

'*Santé!*'

We drink to 'Health'.

Today, a week after you've returned, we need to turn away, continue to live with whatever diagnosis we have. It's time to close it all up and keep going, for the sake of our recovery, for the sake of the stench inside.

THE END

ACKNOWLEDGEMENTS

Seven Days to Tell You in fact took me seven years to tell you, writing late into the night after work and early morning before the school run. I'd like to thank everyone who encouraged me, above all Deborah Paxford, Alex Adamson, Cecilia García-Peñalosa, Pamela Screve, Jamie and Tanya Ivey; the MA Creative Writing class of 2010 at Manchester Metropolitan University and my tutor Paul Magrs; the Arvon Foundation and Sarah Hall for an unforgettable week in August 2005. Thanks to my first editor, Yvonne Barlow of Hookline Books, who brought this novel to life through their Bookline & Thinker Novel Competition. This second edition is all thanks to Betsy Reavley, and the fantastic team at Bloodhound Books, especially Associate Editor, Abbie Rutherford for her creative and painstaking work and Tara Lyons, Editorial and Production Manager.

Finally, Jon Bryant, my harshest critic, best friend and still the funniest man I've ever met. Never forgetting my children, Bluebell and Edison, whose constant interruption while writing this has always been worthwhile.

ABOUT THE AUTHOR

Ruby Soames was born in London – too late for the sixties, too early for the punk era. She studied Literature and Theology at Bristol University and has an MA in Creative Writing from Manchester Metropolitan University and an MSc in Psychology from the University of Liverpool. Ruby lives in the South of France with her two children, journalist husband and a non-allergic dog. She has written three novels and published short stories and articles. This is her first novel.

For more information about the author, please visit" www.rubysoames.com

A NOTE FROM THE PUBLISHER

Thank you for reading this book. If you enjoyed it please do consider leaving a review on Amazon to help others find it too.

We hate typos. All of our books have been rigorously edited and proofread, but sometimes mistakes do slip through. If you have spotted a typo, please do let us know and we can get it amended within hours.

info@bloodhoundbooks.com

Printed in Great Britain
by Amazon

37334759R00158